# FERAL FATES

BOOK ONE | SHADOWMIST PACK

# E.V. MITCHELL

*USA TODAY BESTSELLING AUTHOR*

# THE ONLY THING MORE DANGEROUS THAN THEIR BOND, IS THE WAR IT WILL IGNITE.

Every unmated female must run.
The males give chase.
Whoever catches you becomes your mate.
No exceptions. No escape.

Kitara Silverbrook was born with the gift of sight, but cursed without the ability to shift. In a world where a wolf's strength defines their worth, she's endured whispers, isolation, and the cruel hands of a pack that sees her as nothing but a vessel for power.

When the brutal Claiming ceremony begins, Kitara's only hope is to run fast enough to avoid being caught by the pack's enforcer—the male who's already marked her for torment.

Torn between prophecy and survival, Kitara must decide if she'll risk her heart on the savage alpha who promises to protect her at any cost.

## EVEN IF THAT COST IS WAR.

# ACKNOWLEDGEMENT OF COUNTRY

I acknowledge the Traditional Custodians of the lands on which I write, the Ngunnawal people, and pay my respect to elders both past and present.

I acknowledge the continued and deep spiritual relationship of the Australian Aboriginal and Torres Strait Islander peoples' to this land, and their unique cultural and spiritual relationships to the land, waters and seas, and their rich contribution to society.

**Always was, always will be.**

*To the book babes who read smut with a straight face in public.*

*This one's for you and your dead-eyed Kindle stare. May your headphones be loud, your trauma spicy, and your wolf men feral.*

*And for Rooks. Bite me.*
*Hard.*

# CONTENT INFORMATION

**Please note the following content information include SPOILERS for this book.**

This book contains mature themes and may not be suitable for all readers. Please proceed with care.

- **Sexual content** – explicit scenes including primal mating, knotting, power imbalances, and possessive behavior. All are consensual.
- **Dubious consent / coercive situations** – including the Claiming Ceremony dynamic and suggested forced mating implications.
- **Violence and gore** – including graphic battle scenes, maulings, executions, and murder.
- **Torture / captivity** – imprisonment, chaining, and use of physical restraint.
- **Breeding / forced pregnancy themes** – including discussions of using the heroine for her womb, eugenics-style motives.
- **Sexual assault threat** – attempted assault (interrupted), coercive language, and systemic

sexual violence implications. No sexual assault on page.

- **Ableism themes** – the heroine is considered "defective" for not being able to shift; themes of societal rejection.
- **Psychological trauma** – including gaslighting, emotional abuse, internalized shame, and childhood neglect.
- **Mentions of mental illness** – including the threat of being driven to a mental break through magical or social means.
- **Death of animals and humans** – multiple characters die, sometimes brutally and without much warning.
- **Power imbalances and toxic pack structures** – including commentary on patriarchal dominance, forced bonding, and mate control.
- **Blood and bodily fluids** – descriptive and frequent, both from violence and consensual sex scenes.
- **General themes of war, survival, and rebellion** – including societal oppression and insurgency.

**More information**

If you have any concerns with the depictions in this story or would like further information before reading, please email Evie@EvieMitchell.com

END SPOILERS

# CHAPTER
# ONE

lood.

It pools beneath my bare feet, dark and warm against ancient stone. I try to step back, but my legs won't obey. The scream builds in my throat. Terror or triumph, I can't tell which.

A massive shadow moves at the edge of my vision. I can't see it, but I know it's fixed its gaze on me with an intensity that should terrify me. Should. But the fear bleeding through me feels wrong, misplaced. As if I'm afraid of the wrong thing entirely.

The shadow speaks, voice rough as granite grinding. "Mine."

I reach toward him, fingers trembling, desperate to touch—

—and he's gone. The blood, the stone, the burning eyes. All of it, gone.

What remains is worse. Silver chains bite into my wrists, cold fire against skin. I'm alone, cut off from everything warm and alive, floating in a void that tastes of metal and despair. A woman's voice echoes from somewhere I can't see.

"It ends here."

I jolt back to consciousness, my heart hammering against my ribs like a caged bird. The rough bark of the ancient oak bites into my spine as I press against it. My hands shake as I press them to my face, feeling the wetness on my cheeks.

Blood and tears.

The visions always leave me like this, hollow and aching, with fragments of futures I can't quite grasp rattling around in my skull like broken glass.

I scramble in my pocket for a handkerchief, pressing it to my bleeding nose.

*Blood and shadow. Silver and chains. And that voice...*

*"Mine."*

The word echoes in my mind, and I shiver.

*Whose voice was that?*

I drag in a shuddering breath, forcing myself to focus on the present. The annual Claiming ceremony will begin soon. I can hear the other females' excited chatter and nervous laughter drifting through the trees.

For them, tonight represents possibility of being chosen by a strong male who'll value and love them.

For me, it represents the inevitable.

Every unmated female must run, and the males will give chase. Whoever catches you becomes your mate—no exceptions, no appeals.

*No escape.*

The wolf within me reaches out, nuzzling me gently with a wave of calm.

*A mate cannot harm you.*

The ceremony exists to ensure the survival and strength of the pack. In our world, a female may hold knowledge, skill, and even influence, but at its core, our society is still ruled by the strength of its males. If you haven't been claimed by the time you come of age, you're required to participate in each Claiming until a mate takes you. Because an unclaimed female is seen as a resource left untapped. And every resource must serve the pack.

I close my eyes, trying to make sense of the vision's fragments. The blood, was it mine? The shadow with burning eyes, friend or enemy? And those silver chains...

A chill runs down my spine. Silver suppresses wolf gifts. If someone bound me with silver chains, I'd lose access to my visions entirely. I'd be truly useless then.

I shake my head, frustrated with myself. Visions aren't prophecy, they're possibilities. Fragments of potential futures that may never come to pass. I've learned not to trust them too completely, especially when they're as chaotic as this one.

A twig snaps behind me.

"Well, well... what do we have here? A little kitten trying to hide from the big bad wolves?"

Our pack's most lethal enforcer towers over me, broad-shouldered and thick with muscle, a wall of violence barely contained by skin. His blond hair is cropped short, neat and orderly, a sharp contrast to the chaos he brings. He uses his bulk like a weapon, cornering, crowding, crushing.

His voice drips mockery, his presence pressing in. Kieran doesn't just enforce pack law, he is the punishment. His steel-gray eyes lock onto mine with predatory focus, and I feel my throat go dry. When he smiles, it's slow and sharp, full of teeth and threats.

"I'm not hiding," I lie, lifting my chin despite my trembling legs.

His laugh is dark velvet. "No? You're certainly acting like it, crouching here in the shadows, ready to scatter at the first sign of danger." He leans down, bringing his face close to mine. "But we both know there's no hiding, don't we, Kitara?"

I can't stop the shiver that runs down my spine.

"The ceremony begins soon," he says, reaching out to brush a fallen leaf from my hair. The casual touch sends cold dread racing along my skin. The wolf within me bristles, but we both know she's unable to protect me.

"I'd recommend finding a better hiding spot than this, kitten. Unless..." His smirk widens. "You want me to catch you."

My stomach turns at his words. For the past few weeks, Kieran has been my constant shadow. He's Alpha Varick's chosen enforcer, tasked with keeping me in line. Every time I left my room, he was there. Every time I was forced to speak to a wolf from another pack, he appeared. He's made it his mission to remind me daily that I belong to the Silvercrest Pack.

To him.

"Alpha Varick has chosen me as your mate," he tells me, crowding me into the tree. "No more games, no more delays." His fingers trace my cheek, and I see the cruel intent in his eyes. "I know how to make you behave, little seer."

*All will be well*, my wolf says once more. *A mate cannot harm you.*

But I know better. I've seen the bruises on claimed females, heard the whispered stories of mates who view their bonds as ownership. A claiming mark doesn't guarantee kindness.

Besides, I'm nothing but a broken wolf with little to offer a pack. I've always known my place. I'm the seer who can't shift.

The vision flickers once more at the edges of my consciousness—*blood, hot and crimson, a dark silhouette, eyes watching from shadows*—I push it away before it can take hold. I can't afford the weakness now, can't risk collapsing in front of Kieran, and each vision has the potential to leave me bleeding and shaking for days.

I meet Kieran's gaze directly, remembering the burning eyes from my vision. "What if you're not meant to catch me?"

His expression darkens. "Who else will want you?" He laughs, but there's an edge to it now. "You'll learn your place soon enough."

Before I can respond, a howl pierces the night—the signal for all females to take their positions. Kieran's eyes flash amber as his wolf stirs just beneath the surface.

"Run well, little Kit," he growls. "But know this—no matter where you hide tonight, I will catch you. I've seen how you move, how you think... and unlike the others, I know exactly what that pretty little head of yours can do. You're mine, kitten. You just don't know it yet."

With those words hanging in the air between us, he melts into the shadows, leaving me trembling against the ancient oak.

If he catches me tonight, I'll never be free.

*Please, Mother Wolf. Help me.*

I close my eyes, seeking calm. Instead, my earliest memory surfaces, my mother's face crumpling in disappointment during my first attempted shift. While other pups exploded into fur and fang with pure joy, I remained stubbornly human. No matter how hard I tried, my wolf stayed locked away, just out of reach.

"Again," my father demanded, his patience wearing thinner each time at my childish attempts. "Focus."

But focusing wasn't the problem. Even as a toddler, I could feel her, my wolf, coiled tight inside me, fierce and wild. I could sense her power, her heartbeat echoing mine. My wolf wasn't silent. She spoke in instincts, howled behind my ribs when danger neared. She simply couldn't shift. Her body—*our* body—wasn't built for the change.

The healers called it a curse. The elders called it a weakness. Until I turned seven.

I breathe out slowly and step forward, feet crunching over dried pine needles. The air is thick with tension. Wolves gather, murmuring, waiting for the moon to rise and the challenge to begin. My stomach flips as I move through them, head high, spine locked tight with practiced calm.

They can smell my fear. Taste my difference.

But they don't know the whole of it. Not yet.

The first time I saw death was in a vision.

It had come to me as I stood watching the pack's hunters prepare for a raid on Redclaw territory. Pups my age had drifted between the hunter's legs as they listened to Alpha Varick outline their plans.

I'd watched them, aching to be included. To feel as connected and whole as they were. Then my world had turned white before snapping into sharp contrast in a time and place unlike our own.

*A shadow at the edge of the woods. A warning on the wind. I screamed for the others to run, but they didn't listen and the trap sprung.*

I woke from my faint, bloody, shaking, screaming warnings until my throat became raw and my tears stopped flowing.

They didn't believe me at first. But when Varick sent scouts ahead, they found exactly what I'd seen—a massacre avoided because of my gift.

In that moment, everything changed. The disgust in my parents' eyes transformed into something far worse—cold calculation.

I was no longer just the girl without a wolf. I was the girl who knew things she shouldn't.

Naked females hurry past, jostling me in their haste. I follow suit, folding each piece of clothing carefully with shaking hands.

*My only hope lies in being caught by a wolf from another pack,* I think, placing my clothes at the base of a tree. But who is powerful enough to stand against Kieran?

The grass is cold under my bare feet as I step forward. The last of the trees part, and the grove opens before me, a perfect circle of ancient oaks with the claiming stone at its center.

Torches flicker around its edges, casting long, swaying shadows across the crowd. The Claiming has drawn alphas and unmated males from four territories. I feel their hungry, assessing stares as I enter.

Naked. Human. Alone.

I've never felt more vulnerable.

They shift with ease, fur rippling, claws unsheathing, muscles snapping into new forms. I remain bare, bound to skin and bone. I cannot transform like them, can't shed this fragile flesh for the armor of fang and fury. My gift has always made me valuable, but safety is not a luxury provided by it.

*You'll see*, my she-wolf whispers.

I scan the grove, heart pounding. Goose bumps rise along my arms despite the heat of the torches. The ground feels too wide. The sky too low. There are too many eyes, and claws, and teeth.

*They're not seeking us to mate*, I tell her. *They want to control our gift.*

She nuzzles me, her presence warm and reassuring. *A mate cannot harm.* She's calm. Certain. She doesn't understand because wolves are simple creatures. Honest, instinctive. When they love, they love wholly. When they choose, they do so without games or cruelty. They know their mates the moment they catch their scent at the Claiming. They enter, expecting to chase down their soul match.

It's an urge that is primitive and wild, anchored in the body and soul.

A wolf can be trusted to find their mate, to value her in body, mind, and soul.

But it's not the wolf I fear. It's the men.

It's the wolves who wear fur but think like men—calculating, manipulative, always seeking to take rather than cherish. It's the human minds inside that want my gift, not my heart.

My she-wolf doesn't understand. And why would she? She's a creature of moonlight and bone-deep devotion.

She believes in mates. I believe in betrayal.

The wind shifts, carrying whispers to my ears.

"My Alpha demands I claim the seer. But she's weak and old," one of them tells a friend, his voice laced with disdain. "Barely worth the effort."

I stiffen, the sting of his words sharper than I expect. At twenty-five, I'm considered long overdue for claiming, my worth already bartered down to scraps. To them, I am a cracked cup, barely useful enough to drink from.

My wolf growls inside me, but I quiet her.

*Now would be a great time to show me what happens next*, I tell her.

She just yawns and curls up, her ears twitching. *All will be well.*

I can't see my own future, or the futures of the people I care about most. My visions don't work that way. They skip over the things closest to me, as if my own story isn't important.

It's why my pack kept their distance. Why I've lived a solitary life. Because if I can't see them, then I become useless.

"She is weak," another wolf agrees, "but her gift is of value. If she bears pups, there's a chance they'll inherit it."

A low hum of approval ripples across the air, terrifying me.

"She wouldn't be a true mate," someone says, their voice calculating. "Too weak to take the mating we crave. She'd be a breeding opportunity, a runty fuck before seeking your satisfaction elsewhere."

"My Alpha promised me a second mate upon her death. But only after I've had her push out a pup or two."

My stomach turns, a bitter taste flooding my mouth. They don't see me as a person—just a vessel. A means to an end.

I turn my head to study the packs, considering what I know of them through word, deed, and vision.

The Moonclaw Pack's alpha, Xavier Drake, stands with his enforcers, their silver-tipped hair marking them even in human form. Their territory borders ours to the east, and they've long coveted our river access. I've been forced to spy on them countless times and know the hunger in Xavier's eyes when he looks at me isn't just for my body—it's for the strategic advantage my gift would bring.

The Red River Pack clusters near them, their Alpha Female, Selena Peachut, watching the unmated women with calculating eyes. Her pack is known for its female leadership and fierce independence. In another life, I might have sought refuge with them, but they're pragmatic to a fault. They wouldn't offer their protection without demanding a high payment.

The Grayback Pack holds the high ground near the ceremonial stone, fitting for a pack that rules the northern mountains. Their alpha, Darius Vale, is known for breeding some of the largest, most physically powerful wolves in the territories. His pack's trademark gray fur and massive size make them easy to spot among the gathered wolves. I've heard he's particularly interested in my gift—the Grayback Pack has a history of producing berserker wolves, and a seer's ability to predict their violent episodes would be invaluable.

*Grayback*, I decide, turning away from the gathered packs. *If I must be claimed, let it be from the Grayback clan. They have little interest in politics and despite their berserker ways, seem to treat their females well.*

I turn away when a new scent cuts through the air, dancing across my nostrils. It's like earth and smoke, like rain on stone, sharp enough to steal my breath.

My wolf stirs, ears pricking. Her nostrils flare, then her hope catches in my chest.

*Mate.*

The word isn't thought. It's *known.* Bone-deep. A truth that hums through me like a string pulled tight.

I whirl, searching for him among the crowd. But the wind shifts, taking the scent with it before I can find its source.

A howl sounds, low and commanding.

Grand Alpha Thaddeus steps forward, his white ceremonial cloak pooling around his feet like mist. His voice is calm and cold, designed to carry. "We gather tonight for the Claiming. Let us begin."

The words send a jolt through me. *Too soon. Too fast.*

He lifts a hand, and the packs begin shifting, growls rippling through the grove as the unmated males tense, their hunger rising.

*No. Not yet.*

The bond in my chest hums, my wolf straining.

*They're here,* she tells me. *Find them.*

Grand Alpha Thaddeus gestures with his hand. "I call on the alphas of the four packs represented here to—"

A growl, deep and violent, tears through the clearing like thunder cracking stone. Wolves stumble back. Darkness moves at the edge of the firelight, and the hair on the back of my neck rises.

And then I see him.

Ryker Ashmere, alpha of the Shadowmist Pack, emerges from the trees like a nightmare given form. Towering and scarred, his bare chest displays a map of violence survived— claw marks, bite wounds, and the distinctive silvery lines of wounds that should have killed any normal wolf. One eye burns amber gold, the other a blood crimson that seems to glow in the firelight.

Unlike the other alphas who affect a civilized appearance, he embraces his savage nature. His black hair falls wild to his shoulders, threaded with gray at the temples. Each step is calculated and lethal, like a predator perpetually on the edge of violence. The shadows themselves seem to cling to him, writhing around his feet like living things.

Whispers erupt around me.

"The Shadowmist wolves weren't supposed to be here..."

"They haven't participated in a Claiming ceremony in decades..."

"He's even more terrifying than the stories..."

I've heard those stories since childhood, how as a pup not much older than myself he slaughtered his way through three rival packs in a single night, how he drinks the blood of his enemies, how even silver wounds can't stop him.

*Not him*, I think, instinctively stepping back. *Anyone would be better than him.*

His gaze sweeps the grove, and for one heart-stopping moment, locks onto mine. Recognition flickers as his nostrils flare. A cold wave washes over me, not a vision but something equally powerful—a certainty that my fate has just been sealed.

I look away, forcing myself to focus on the ceremony. My own pack, the Silvercrest, stands closest to the stone, though our position feels shaky. We've always controlled the least land, but that was before my gift showed up. Now Alpha Varick plays a dangerous game, having used my power to raise our pack's standing. Tonight, he stands to lose me entirely, if Kieran or another of the unmated enforcers fail.

Grand Alpha Thaddeus stands on the claiming stone, power rolling off him in waves that make the torchlight flicker. His white hair catches the moonlight like fresh snow, the scars across his face silver in the darkness. Ancient magic clings to him like a cloak, a reminder that he is more than just a political leader, he is the voice of the Moon Goddess herself.

"*All* who would compete, step forward." His voice shakes the ground itself. "Present your offerings for the right to hunt tonight."

As ruler of all the territories, the Grand Alpha's word is

law. He keeps peace between the packs, settles disputes over land, and makes sure our oldest traditions are followed. Every alpha must bow to him or risk losing their pack's standing.

Or worse, their life.

This is why the alphas approach one by one, each knowing that their offerings aren't just for the hunt, but for Thaddeus's favor.

Xavier of Moonclaw steps forward first. "We offer thirty percent shares in our southern tech company and exclusive hunting rights to the river valley for three years, Grand Alpha," he says smoothly. "And request six of our sons be allowed to run."

Thaddeus's smile doesn't reach his eyes. "Accepted."

Selena follows, her red hair—a symbol of the Red River wolves—catches the firelight. "Five million in cash and twenty percent of our diamond mining profits for the next five years to the Grand Pack," she states confidently. "For five of our hunters to participate."

"Accepted."

Darius Vale's massive form towers over the others as the Grayback alpha speaks. "Four of our trained security teams at your disposal for special assignments, Grand Alpha, along with our new mountain resort's penthouse suite for your personal use." His voice rumbles like distant thunder. "We ask the right to run four of our strongest."

"Accepted."

When Alpha Varick steps forward, tension crackles through the grove. His steps are slower, shoulders tight. The weight of eyes and whispers trails him like smoke. Before he can speak, Thaddeus raises a hand.

"Make your offer generous, Alpha Varick." His tone is icy. Controlled. Deadly. "You've committed a grave offense, hiding a seer from the packs."

Varick had kept me hidden for years. He would have

continued to do so, if not for the Grand Pack's enforcers catching my scent when they'd come to summon the unmated females to the Claiming. After that, hiding wasn't an option.

I watch Varick duck his head. He's tall, broad through the shoulders, with graying hair tied neatly at the nape of his neck. His clothes are rich, showing a wolf who rules with pride and confidence—or he did. Tonight there's a crack noticeable in the way his jaw is clenched tight, and his eyes flick nervously to the crowd, then to Thaddeus.

Strength and confidence mean little when the Grand Alpha's judgment has already turned against you.

I shrink back, trying to stay hidden within the crowd, but it's too late. Thaddeus's gaze sweeps the grove and locks onto me. His nostrils flare as he confirms my scent, and a smile touches his lips.

"Bring forth the seer," he commands.

The crowd parts like water, leaving me exposed. Bare feet, bare skin, bare soul. I stand frozen as all eyes turn to me.

"So this is her?" Thaddeus's voice carries across the silent grove. "A seer who cannot shift. Step forward, girl."

My legs move without my permission, carrying me toward the claiming stone. I feel the weight of a hundred stares burning into my skin.

I stop at the base of the stone, looking up at Thaddeus. This close, I can see the cruel intelligence in his pale eyes.

"Your name?" he asks.

"Kitara," I whisper, then clear my throat and speak louder. "Kitara Silverbrook."

He circles me slowly, like a wolf inspecting prey. "Show us your gift, seer."

Fear claws at my throat. "I-it doesn't work like that."

"Try," he says, and it's not a request.

I close my eyes, reaching for the currents of possibility that sometimes wash through me. Nothing comes. Only darkness.

"I'm sorry, I—"

His hand shoots out, gripping my chin with bruising force. "Look at me."

Our eyes meet, and the world falls away. My body goes rigid, my head snapping back. The familiar burning starts behind my eyes, spreading through my skull like wildfire. Someone gasps, maybe me, maybe the crowd. When I speak again, it's not my voice that comes out, but it's a feminine voice far older and deeper, as though the Moon Goddess herself speaks through me.

*"The crown will fall, the throne will shatter. You shall kneel, throat bared to the prince with eyes that pierce truths. Some howl in rage, others in triumph, but all will bow to the new order when darkness claims what was promised."*

Blood trickles from my nose, metallic on my tongue. The ground sways beneath me as the vision releases its grip. The grove has gone deadly silent, every wolf frozen in shock.

Thaddeus's face has gone pale. "What does it mean?" he hisses, his hand now trembling against my skin.

I blink, confused. "I... I don't know. That's not how a vision works."

Murmurs ripple through the crowd. A prophecy spoken aloud cannot be taken back. The Moon Goddess has declared a truth that will come to pass, no matter what any wolf might do to prevent it.

"Who?" Thaddeus demands, his voice cutting through the ringing in my ears.

I shake my head, trying to clear it. "I didn't see any one wolf. Just... shadows. Fragments."

Thaddeus studies me, suspicion in his eyes before tossing me away. "You must run tonight, but know this—our business is not yet complete." He turns, dismissing me in the same movement as he approaches Varick. "Now. Your offering?"

Varick ducks his head. "I offer my vote on the Alpha

Council to the Grand Alpha's appointed heir and double tithings for two years. In exchange we ask to run four wolves."

A low murmur ripples through the gathering.

Varick's offering is no small thing. Giving up his Council seat and promising double tithings will cripple the pack for years. It's a sacrifice born of desperation, not honor.

Thaddeus smiles, slow and sharp. "I accept, but in punishment for concealing the seer, you may run only one wolf."

A muscle in Varick's jaw twitches but he nods, accepting his punishment.

The wind brings me the scent of the wolf meant for me, and once again, the bond in my chest tugs—harder this time—a reminder that somewhere among the gathered is my mate.

*May they be strong and kind.*

My wolf nuzzles me, reassuring me that they will be everything we've hoped for.

Thaddeus turns to the Shadowmist alpha. "And what do the Shadowmist wolves offer?"

Ryker's laugh is as dark and humorless. "We offer nothing. Our debt has already been paid in the blood we've shed in your great war, old wolf. We will run five wolves, one for each of the lives given by my pack."

The air crackles with tension. No one speaks to the Grand Alpha this way. But Thaddeus merely nods, though his eyes narrow dangerously.

"The old debt is honored... one final time."

Mara, an unmated female, shifts beside me, her golden wolf already rippling beneath her skin. "Ready to run, little prophet?" Her smile is cruel. "Or should I say, ready to stumble?"

My fingers tremble as I stand naked among the other females, watching as they shift into their wolf forms. I might not be able to change, but I refuse to show fear. "I can still run."

"Not fast enough," she laughs, then throws back her head as her wolf bursts forth.

The first howl comes—the signal to take positions. I move to the edge of the grove with the others, my bare feet already aching against the rough ground. Behind us, I hear the males gathering, their energy wild and hungry.

I risk one glance back. Kieran stands at the front of the Silvercrest hunters, his eyes locked on me with possessive intent. The Moonclaw wolves flank him, their silver-tipped fur catching the moonlight. Grayback's massive gray wolves pace behind them, nearly twice the size of normal wolves. The Red River Pack spreads out strategically, clearly planning to control the chase paths.

Only the Shadowmist wolves remain in the darkness. I catch glimpses of scarred black fur, of eyes that seem to glow in the shadows. And before them stands their alpha, his gaze locked on me.

My pulse spikes.

"Don't look at him," Kieran calls across the grove. "You're mine, little seer."

A cold jolt zips down my spine. I whirl toward the chase trails, yanking my focus forward.

Adrenaline floods my system, fire licking beneath my skin. My limbs vibrate, tense and twitching, caught between fight and flight. The scent of moss and loam hits me. Every nerve is alight, screaming *run, run, run.*

The second howl pierces the night.

Time to choose my path. I know these woods, have memorized every bend, every hidden dip, every trick root that might snap an ankle.

But knowing a maze doesn't mean you'll outrun the monster inside it.

And Kieran knows them too.

My only chance is to do the unexpected. Something no one would predict.

As the moon crests the horizon, bathing the grove in light, a third howl splits the night.

The Claiming has begun.

I run.

CHAPTER

# TWO

I sprint into the darkness as she-wolves bound past me on all sides, streaks of fur and muscle slicing through the trees like wind incarnate. Their paws make barely a sound on the forest floor, while every branch I snap underfoot sounds like a gunshot in the quiet.

My breath comes in sharp, ragged gasps. My legs pump hard, but I'm clumsy and slower, my human form no match for the speed and elegance of the pack.

Branches whip at my bare skin, biting welts into my thighs and arms. My feet slip on damp leaves, stumble on roots. I'm loud. Exposed.

The forest feels alive, an endless, suffocating mass of trees and shadows closing in around me with every frantic, thudding step.

But unlike the others, who charge forward along the main paths, I veer sharply left.

Toward the one place no shifter in wolf form would willingly go.

The Dead Zone.

Years ago, silver miners had poisoned this section of forest, scarring the land beyond repair. The ground itself is

19

toxic to wolves, burning their paws on contact and seeping into their bloodstream. But to my human feet? It's just earth. Dangerous, yes, but not immediately deadly. Prolonged exposure to silver will still hurt me in this form—headaches, nausea, tissue damage if I stay too long—but in wolf form? The effect is instant.

Which makes this the one place in this cursed forest where I'll have a slight advantage. If I can make it.

The change in the air is almost imperceptible at first, thicker, tinged with the metallic tang of old blood and decay. Even the trees seem twisted, gnarled branches reaching out like skeletal fingers, their leaves wilted and blackened from the lingering poison.

Behind me, I hear Kieran's howl of frustration as he realizes my path. His growl reverberates through the forest, filled with fury and desperation. He can't follow me through the Dead Zone in wolf form—none of them can. Not without risking silver poisoning.

I've bought myself minutes at most. But minutes might be enough to—

A weight slams into me from the side, and everything shatters.

I hit the ground hard, the poisoned earth knocking the breath from my lungs. Dirt grits between my teeth, dead leaves choking my mouth and nose. The world tilts, blurred and spinning. My thoughts scatter like startled birds, instinct taking over.

Panic surges hot, sharp, suffocating.

I roll, coughing, scratching, fighting blindly. But it's no use.

Kieran's massive wolf form pins me down, a wall of fur and weight and cruel inevitability. His claws dig into the ground on either side of my head, the earth trembling with his rage. His breath is hot against my neck—too close, too real—as his body shifts, bones cracking, fur retreating. Human again. Still just as monstrous.

My mind is blank. Not empty, but flooded. Drowning in terror. "Got you, kitten," he growls, his voice rough with triumph. His teeth graze my throat, sharp and possessive. "Time to—"

A savage roar shatters the night.

A massive black form crashes into Kieran, ripping him away from me with brutal force. I scramble backward, heart pounding as I watch on in horror. The largest wolf I've ever seen looms over Kieran, his thick black fur bristling, muscles rippling beneath his pelt. His size dwarfs Kieran, his sheer presence making the air feel heavier, charged with danger.

Kieran shifts back to his wolf form, trying to circle behind the black wolf, but the creature is death itself. It spins with impossible speed to catch Kieran's lunging form. His massive jaws clamp onto Kieran's throat, powerful paws pinning the smaller wolf as he begins to crush his windpipe. There's no mercy in his mismatched eyes—no hesitation. Just cold, methodical killing.

I'm frozen, horror rooting me in place as Kieran's struggles grow weaker. His wolf form writhes beneath the black wolf's relentless grip, his paws scraping at the earth, trying to shift back to human form. But the pressure on his throat is too great, the grip too tight. The sound of grinding bones fills the forest, sharp and final.

I should run. Every human instinct screams at me to flee while these monsters fight, but my wolf...

She doesn't move. She watches in stillness, ears forward, tail low in submission, recognizing and honoring the power snapping through the clearing.

A russet blur launches from the shadows—one of the Red River enforcers, fur bristling, eyes wild with rage as it lunges at the black wolf. But it's over before it begins. The massive wolf releases Kieran's mangled throat only to catch the new attacker mid-leap. His jaw snaps shut with terrifying force, crushing the russet wolf's spine. The sickening crack echoes through the trees like a gunshot, followed by the thud of a limp body hitting the ground.

Two more wolves charge from the darkness—Moonclaw enforcers, their silver-tipped fur gleaming under the moonlight. They move in perfect tandem, trained killers. But it makes no difference. The black wolf moves like a living shadow, fluid and devastating. He catches the first enforcer by the throat, using its momentum to snap its neck with brutal ease, while his back claws rake deep into the second, disemboweling it in a spray of blood and guts.

The forest floor is slick with gore, fallen leaves soaked black under the cold moonlight. Four wolves lie broken and bleeding, and still the black wolf stands, his breathing barely labored. He shows no sign of exertion, and no remorse.

Then he turns to me.

Those mismatched eyes fix on me, glowing with predatory focus. Blood drips from his muzzle, staining his already dark fur even blacker.

Before my mind can scream, before my legs can obey, my wolf knows. His scent hits us like a tidal wave—earth and rain and wild storms.

The same scent I caught in the grove. It coils around me, seeping into my lungs, my skin, my bones.

I scramble backward until my spine hits a tree, halting my escape, but it's already too late.

He stalks forward, impossibly graceful despite his massive size. A jagged silver scar slashes across his right eye, and the tip of his left ear is missing—testaments to battles fought and won. More scars pepper his body, hidden beneath thick fur but visible as pale lines where no hair grows.

*Ryker Ashmere.*

*Run,* my mind screams. But my body and my wolf refuse to move. I can only watch as he approaches, power rolling off him in waves. This close, I can see that his fur isn't purely black. There are strands of silver shot through it, like moonlight caught in darkness.

I've seen wolves shift before, but never like this—never with such fluid, predatory grace. It's as if the shadows themselves reach up to help him change. Bones crack and reform, fur recedes into skin, claws retract into fingers. But where most shifts are violent, painful things, his is almost beautiful in its lethal precision. One moment he is wolf, the next he is man, with barely a sound to mark the transformation.

Even in his human skin, he moves like a predator, all coiled muscle and lethal grace. Blood still stains his mouth and chest. The savage violence lingers in his mismatched eyes, tempered only by the dangerous, dark amusement that curls his bloodstained lips into a grin.

"Mine," he growls, voice rough and raw, as though it's been dragged from the depths of the earth. He reaches for me with blood-stained hands. His touch is startlingly gentle despite the violence I just witnessed. "Say it, little seer," he rumbles. "Say you're mine."

"I—" I gasp, but his teeth are already at my neck, sharp and demanding.

"Mine," he snarls again, and then he bites down, marking me as his mate with a claim that will never fade.

Pain lances through me, sharp and blinding, then relief—molten and fierce—floods in. It reminds me of wildfire, consuming and soothing all at once. His power pours into me, invasive and undeniable, weaving itself into the broken places I didn't even know I carried.

My visions, always a swirling chaos at the back of my mind, fall silent.

I understand now why I never saw this moment coming.

My fate wasn't mine to see. It was *his* to claim.

# CHAPTER
# THREE

Pain lances through my feet with each step, tiny rocks and broken twigs cutting into my bare soles. Every stride is agony, but I dare not slow. Ryker has shifted back into his massive wolf form, and moves beside me with liquid grace, his fur still wet with the blood of those who tried to claim me. Each time I stumble, his shoulder brushes my hip, steadying me. The heat of him burns against my naked skin like a brand, leaving bloody smears where we touch.

The claiming mark on my throat throbs in time with my racing heart, hot and raw. Ryker's power thrums through my veins, foreign and overwhelming. It moves through me like a serpent, making my human form feel too small and fragile to contain it.

I suck in a deep breath, fighting to control the fear churning in my gut, but even the air comes differently, carrying his scent deeper into my lungs.

Moonlight spills through the ancient trees, painting silver patterns across Ryker's scarred black coat. He stands taller than any wolf I've ever seen, his back level with my shoulders, his paws leaving impressions in the earth twice the size of a normal wolf's. When he turns his head to check our trail, muscles ripple beneath fur so black it seems to swallow the moonlight itself. The silver scar that slashes across his face catches the light, transforming from shadow to silver with each movement.

We return to the grove to find the air charged and heavy. The claiming circle hums with power, I can feel it vibrating through the soles of my feet, up through my bones, making my teeth ache. Torches line the ancient stones, their flames dancing in the wind, casting writhing shadows across the gathered wolves. The scent of blood, both fresh and ancient, rises from the earth, mingling with smoke and sweat and anticipation.

Other claimed pairs have already gathered, forming a crescent before the stone altar. The females wear their claiming marks proudly, pressed against their mates' sides, most having shifted back to human form for the ceremony. Only the Shadowmist wolves remain in their beast forms, dark shapes lurking at the edges of the firelight like living pieces of the night.

Each step toward the altar makes me more aware of my nakedness, my humanity. I can't stand proud like the other claimed females with their sleek wolf forms and easy shifts. I can only walk forward in this vulnerable shape, guided by the blood-stained monster who has chosen me.

The eyes of every wolf in the circle burn into my skin— judging, assessing, and finding me wanting.

"Step into the circle," Grand Alpha Thaddeus calls, his voice resonating with power that makes the ground vibrate beneath my bloody feet. "Let your union be blessed by moon and pack law."

One by one, the pairs approach. Each step is part of a dance as old as our kind. The males bow their heads, submitting to the Grand Alpha's authority. The females bare their claiming marks for inspection, tilting their heads to expose the vulnerable flesh of their throats. Thaddeus presses his fingers to the marks, infusing them with magic that binds the pairs for eternity.

I watch as Xavier Drake and his chosen mate receive their blessing, the magic visible as silver light wraps around them both like ribbons.

Then it's our turn.

Thaddeus's eyes narrow as we approach, his disgust a palpable thing that makes the air around us grow colder. "Shift, Alpha Ashmere. Show proper respect to the ceremony."

The massive black wolf beside me goes still. Through our new bond, I feel his contempt. For a moment, I think he'll refuse. Then his form begins to change.

When Ryker straightens to his full height beside me, his massive form subtly shifts to place himself between me and Thaddeus. It's not an obvious movement—nothing so blatant as to appear defensive—but the positioning is deliberate. He stands with his scarred shoulder slightly angled forward, creating a barrier of flesh and muscle that would absorb any attack before it could reach me. Through our new bond, I feel no fear in him, only calculating vigilance and a cold readiness to unleash violence at the slightest provocation.

"Fascinating," Thaddeus's cold voice cuts through the tense silence. "I see you still wear your beast's savagery even in this form."

Ryker's laugh is low and dark, a sound that sends shivers across my spine. "Better a beast than a puppet," he says, his teeth flashing. "At least I haven't forgotten what we are beneath our civilized masks."

Thaddeus ignores the jab. His cold gaze sweeps over me, then returns to Ryker. "You claimed the seer? You, who once swore to rebuild the strength of your pack, but you choose a mate who can't shift?" His voice carries across the grove, clear and cruel.

I shrink into myself, aware that even though I'm claimed,

we have yet to be bound. Ryker can still reject me as his mate, leaving me without a hope for a future.

Thaddeus shakes his head. "An alpha needs a strong partner. One who can lead beside him. Fight beside him. Your lack of judgment, Alpha Ashmere, is... disappointing."

There's a stirring in the wolves around us, a tension that threads through the gathered.

They smell blood.

Thaddeus's gaze lands on me. "You would ask your pack to bleed for you, to trust you with their lives, and you choose this? A broken wolf with a gift she can't properly wield?" He shakes his head, feigning pity. "Perhaps the Shadowmist Pack should ask itself whether its alpha is fit to lead it at all."

Ryker's laugh is sharp and dangerous. "If so concerned about her weakness, why allow the seer to run in the ceremony at all?" His question cuts through the Grand Alpha's posturing like a blade. "If she's such an affront, why would she draw alphas from five territories to hunt her? Why would you—as the one responsible for the good of all— not simply declare her unfit for claiming before the run began?"

Thaddeus's face tightens almost imperceptibly, but I see it —the flicker of calculation behind his righteous anger.

"Or perhaps," Ryker continues, his voice a silken threat, "you did want her claimed—just not by me. Perhaps you had another in mind, one who would be more... compliant with your demands for her gift and her offspring."

The temperature around us plummets. Ryker's hand finds the back of my neck, his fingers pressing possessively against his claiming mark. The touch sends jolts of electricity through my body, his power flooding my system in a rush of white-hot sensation.

Goose bumps erupt across my skin, sweeping down my spine in an erotic wave. My nipples tighten in the chill night air, painfully sensitive. And lower—gods, lower—my core clenches, a deep, pulsing ache building between my thighs. It's primal and wrong and new.

My breath catches. I have never felt anything like this—never known that power could feel like this. That pain and pleasure could collide in a single heartbeat, shattering me open.

He doesn't speak, but his scent changes—sharpening with the tang of violence waiting to be unleashed. "The laws are clear," the Grand Alpha says, voice ringing through the grove. "Both parties must be strong. Both must be fit to lead. An alpha cannot bind himself to weakness and expect the pack to follow."

The words strike like lashes across my skin.

Ryker's growl rumbles low against my back, but Thaddeus presses on, cold and relentless.

"She cannot shift. She cannot defend your line. What message does that send to your pack, Ryker Ashmere? That your blood will weaken? That your judgment already has?" He turns slightly, addressing the gathered wolves now, not just Ryker. "Would you follow an alpha who chooses fragility over strength? Sentiment over survival?"

A murmur ripples through the crowd. I flinch, shame burning under my skin. But Ryker's hand tightens—not punishing, but anchoring. Grounding me in him.

"She is a seer," Ryker growls, and the vibration of his voice against my back makes me shiver.

"She is weak!" Thaddeus claps back, his power flaring with his anger. "I will not endorse this mating. You will reject her, Alpha. Throw her back to the pack where she will become an *Ekballo*."

Gasps erupt around the circle. My blood turns to ice, freezing me from the inside out. *Ekballo*—the fate worse than death.

As *Ekballo*, I will be forced to breed, passed around to all unmated wolves until a pup takes root in my belly. And when it does, and I bring it into this world, it will be ripped from my arms to be raised by another. I would then be bred again and again until a pup shows signs of my gift. Once assured that my visions are able to be passed on, they will cast me out, burning the pack marks from my flesh. Without an alpha's power to ground me, my mind and wolf will fracture piece by piece until madness claims me completely.

The whispers slither through the darkness, each one a knife in my chest.

"They'll breed her to the alphas, even the mated ones."

"The gift must be preserved..."

"She'll lose her mind within months."

"Better death than that fate."

My legs start to give out beneath me, but Ryker's hand never leaves my neck. His power continues to pulse through the claiming mark, hot against my frozen skin. When he speaks, his voice is low and lethal, a predator's warning growl.

"You would name my mate *Ekballo*?" Each word drips with deadly promise. "You would shame the wolves under your command by forcing them upon her? You would steal her child—my rightful heir—and leave her to madness?" His fingers tighten on my nape. "Perhaps it's time to remind everyone why the Shadowmist Pack hunts alone."

The shadows around us deepen, and I realize with a start that Ryker's pack is moving closer, their massive forms materializing from the night like living nightmares. None have shifted to human form. All bear the same battle scars as their alpha. Their eyes gleam in the torchlight—red, gold, amber—predators waiting for the signal to attack.

Even Thaddeus seems to sense the shift in power dynamics. His silver eyes dart between the approaching wolves, his hands gathering more of that ancient magic until it coalesces around him like ghostly flames.

"The gift must be preserved. The pup will be raised by a proper pack, with a proper mother. You cannot defy—"

"Pack law?" Ryker's laugh holds no humor, only the promise of violence. "Your laws mean nothing to me, old wolf. We are what you fear becoming—what you and your *pathetic* laws try to hide." His other hand comes up to cup my face, the gesture startlingly gentle compared to the promise of death in his voice. His palm is warm against my cheek, calloused from a life of violence. "I claimed her. She's mine. Her gift is mine. Any pups she bears will be mine. And if you try to take what's mine..."

The threat hangs in the air, heavy with promise. Power crackles between the two alphas, and I feel it like static against my bare skin. Around us, other wolves begin backing away, creating space for the inevitable explosion.

"Then you choose exile." Thaddeus raises his hands, ancient magic gathering around him in visible swirls of silver light that twist and reach like hungry serpents. "No pack will trade with you. No territory will shelter you. Your name will be—"

"Save your threats for wolves who still fear you, old man."

I gasp as Ryker moves, sweeping me into his arms and tossing me into the air. I barely know what's happening before I land astride his wolf's back, my fingers instinctively buried in his thick fur. He's shifted faster than anyone I've ever seen, faster even than Thaddeus. The transformation so swift I couldn't track it with my eyes.

*What power does he possess?* I wonder, clutching at my mate's fur as the ground blurs beneath us. *Who is this wolf that has claimed me?*

Ryker doesn't wait for me to settle before launching us into the darkness; his powerful muscles bunch and release beneath my thighs. The friction of his fur against my bare sex sends shocks of unwanted heat through my core, even as fear tightens my throat.

The Shadowmist wolves melt into formation around us as howls of outrage split the night. I press myself low against Ryker's back, the heat of him burning against my naked skin as we race through the ancient forest. Every stride jars my bones, but his fur cushions the worst of it.

*See?* my she-wolf asks. *A mate cannot harm.*

I take small comfort in her words when Thaddeus's furious howls trail after us. His magic sits heavy in the air, making it taste like metal—charged and dangerous.

But Ryker's answering howl isn't defensive—it's triumphant. A challenge and a promise that echoes through the darkness and reverberates in my very marrow. I listen, easily translating his answer.

*Come for her—and I'll tear your world apart.*

My paws eat up the dark miles, my pack flowing through the shadows around me. The weight of my claimed mate on my back drives me faster, urging me deeper into Shadowmist territory. Her bare skin burns against my fur, her thighs clenched tight around my ribs, her fingers buried in my coat. Each point of contact sends her scent deeper into me, binding us together in ways beyond the physical claiming mark.

I scented her before I even saw her.

Long before the ceremony began, her presence hit me like lightning splitting the sky—an intoxicating thread on the wind that wound through my blood and rooted deep. I didn't understand it at first. But when I arrived at the grove and saw her standing there defiant and trembling and perfect, every part of me howled *mine*.

She should've been guarded like a treasure, courted like a queen. Instead, they threw a seer who can't shift to the wolves.

Threw her to me.

Dane lopes beside me, his thoughts touching mine in the

silent language of wolves. *The dens are secured. Hunting parties positioned along the borders.*

*Any movement from the other packs?* My thoughts are sharp, focused.

*Not yet. But they'll come. The Grand Alpha won't let this insult stand.*

*Let them come.* My territory is shadow and stone, death and darkness. My pack knows how to fight in the black spaces between moonlight and madness. And now I have something worth protecting—something more valuable than territory or power.

*My mate.*

The words thunder through me, and I have to fight to keep from howling my triumph.

She is *mine*. Not just by the laws of the Claiming, but in every breath, every heartbeat, every fractured place inside me that's never known peace. The bond pulls tight like a leash around my soul, dragging everything I am toward her.

There's a thirst in me I've never known. To kiss her. Lick her. Sink my teeth into the soft place where her neck meets her shoulder and mark her again—not for show, but because my beast needs to. I want her taste on my tongue. Her scent in my lungs. Her nails in my skin and her moans in my mouth.

Now that I've found her, I will never—never—let her go.

The little seer's grip loosens over the last hour of our journey, her body molding to my stride. I feel the moment exhaustion claims her, feel her cheek press against my neck as sleep drags her under. Still, her fingers remain tangled in my fur, holding on even in dreams. The trust in that unconscious gesture stirs a protective and primal need within me.

I slow as we approach the cliffs that house our dens, giving myself time to really scent my mate. Beneath the sharp tang of fear, she smells like the cusp of summer—warm, ripe, and reckless. I drag her scent deep into my lungs, memorizing it, letting it burn through me like wildfire.

*Run double shifts along the borders. I don't want any surprises.*

*As you wish, Alpha.* Dane turns to leave.

*And clear the main den,* I command. *Ready the pack for skirmishes. I don't want us caught unaware.*

As my pack melts away to follow my orders, I allow myself to focus fully on the female sleeping on my back. Gently, I lay down until I can shift without fear of losing her. The change ripples through me, bone and muscle reforming with practiced ease.

Upon returning to my human form, I catch her in my arms, watching her brunette hair spill over my arm like a waterfall. The moon paints her pale skin in shades of pearl and cream, making the marks of her run through the forest stand out—scratches from branches, bruises from her fall, the blood-edged claiming mark on her throat. My mark. My claim.

She's small for a wolf and holds none of the lean muscle of the women of my pack. Her body is an abundance of curves, so unlike my people that it seems almost taboo to observe her nakedness. She's to be savored in private, not exposed to others' eyes.

Her high cheekbones and full lips give her face an ethereal quality that makes her look more fae than wolf. Dark lashes fan against her cheeks, and I can see rapid movement beneath her eyelids. Dreaming or seeing? I'm unsure but I can feel whatever vision has claimed her touching the edge of my mind, such is our connection already.

I lean down, inhaling her scent again, imprinting it so I might always find her. My wolf rises, chafing under my skin to claim her in all the ways I have yet to do. The urge to mark her, to take her, to make her irrevocably mine pulses through me with each heartbeat.

Everything about her calls to my most feral instincts. Her

vulnerability makes me want to hunt for her, to kill for her, to wrap her in my power until nothing can touch her. My lips curl back from my teeth at the thought of anyone laying claim to what is mine.

Her gift makes her valuable enough to risk war over. But I would have claimed her regardless. She calls to me on a level deeper than reason or strategy.

My thumb brushes the mark I placed on her neck. *No one can take her from me.*

A growl rumbles through my chest. The other packs wanted to breed her gift into their bloodlines, to use her and then discard her. But I have claimed her. Any pups she bears will be mine—they will carry both her sight and my strength, and will rule the shadows with both power and prophecy.

I reach the entrance to my private den and duck carefully through the opening, mindful of my sleeping cargo. The cave system is vast, a maze of tunnels and chambers that humans have long forgotten. My own den lies deep in the heart of the caves. It is in this place of warmth and stone that I can finally breathe freely knowing she's protected.

My mate stirs slightly but doesn't wake, her body instinctively curling into my heat. Her fingers, now gripping my shoulder instead of my fur, hold on with surprising strength.

"Sleep, little seer," I murmur, laying her on the furs that cover my bed. "You'll need your strength for what's coming."

And come they will. The Grand Alpha will gather his forces—and then I will show them all exactly why the Shadowmist pack is feared in more than just name.

I glance back down at my mate. I have claimed the most valuable female in five territories. Now I must be vicious enough to keep her.

# CHAPTER
# FIVE

My dream releases me with a gasp, fragments of blood and moonlight still dancing behind my eyes. I blink awake, disoriented, my body heavy and warm against unfamiliar furs. Then memory crashes over me—the Claiming ceremony, Kieran's death, Ryker's teeth in my throat.

My hand flies to the claiming mark, finding it hot and tender under my fingers. The bond thrums with foreign power, his strength burning through my veins. It makes me feel both more and less myself, as though his wildness is seeping into my bones, reshaping me from the inside out.

As my eyes adjust to the dim light, I take in my surroundings. This is nothing like the bedrooms I'd known in my old pack—there's no sterile symmetry or forced elegance. This is a true den carved into the heart of a mountain.

For a beat, I wonder if Ryker's pack has rejected modern comforts altogether—until I spy the lights tucked into a recess strip in the stone ceiling. Sitting up slowly, I glance around, taking in the luxe finishes. Built into one wall, a state-of-the-art coffee machine perches next to a mini bar stocked with glass decanters—whiskey, scotch, something amber and old.

There's even a touchscreen tablet mounted into the wall near the bed.

But the rest of it? All wild.

A massive fireplace dominates the room casting dancing shadows across walls lined with weapons—knives, swords, and what looks like ancient battle axes. Each is well crafted and lovingly maintained.

The massive bed I'm lying in is a nest of luxurious furs and pillows that still hold Ryker's scent—earth and stone and predator.

I shiver as I gather them to me, breathing in his addictive aroma, grounding myself in his feral and masculine and terrifying scent.

"Welcome back."

His voice sends shivers down my spine, and I twist toward the sound. Ryker stands in the stone archway, utterly relaxed and completely naked. Dried blood maps dark lines over his chest, his arms, his thighs—savage brushstrokes across his skin. The firelight makes his scars shimmer, turning him into an ancient and untamed beast. He's a god of war, pulled from myth and dropped into my bedchamber.

Nudity is nothing in pack life. I've seen a hundred male wolves shift and stand bare in the open.

But this?

There is nothing casual about Ryker's nakedness.

My eyes betray me, roaming his towering frame—his broad shoulders, the cut of his muscles, the sharp lines of his abdomen that lead down. My breath hitches, heat coiling low in my belly. He's well-endowed—thick, heavy, and utterly unapologetic about it.

I've never cared to look before. Never wanted to. But now?

I can't not look.

He is heat and danger made flesh. Everything about him radiates power—sex and violence braided so tightly together

I can't tell where one ends and the other begins. My heart hammers in my chest, torn between fear and a feeling far more dangerous.

"I..." I clutch the furs to my chest, though they do little to hide my curves from his predatory gaze. "How did you know I was waking?"

"I felt it." He pushes off from the archway, moving toward me with fluid grace. "Through the claiming mark. I feel all my pack. Can you not?"

I shake my head.

"You will. Your power calls to mine now, little seer."

My heart thunders as he approaches. He moves like his wolf even in human form, all contained violence and lethal intent. But there's something else in his gaze too—a hunger that makes heat pool in my belly despite my fear.

"Tell me what you dreamed." It isn't a request.

"I..." The vision is already fragmenting in my mind, slipping away like water through cupped hands, but one image remains clear. "Blood on stone. Wolves fighting in darkness. But I couldn't tell if they were attacking or defending."

His laugh is dark silk against my nerves. "Both, my little mate. Always both." He reaches the edge of the bed, looming over me. "The Grand Alpha will come for you. And my pack will paint these stones with the blood of anyone who tries to take what's mine."

The possessive growl in his voice makes me shiver. "I won't be able to help you fight. I can't even shift—"

"No." His hand shoots out, gripping my chin with surprising gentleness despite the speed of the movement. "But you can see. And that's worth more than teeth and claws." His thumb brushes my lower lip, sending sparks of sensation down my spine. "Your gift will let us know where they'll strike. When they'll come. How they'll try to break us."

I shake my head, pulling away from his touch. "It doesn't work like that. At least, not for me."

"But it will." He tangles his hand in my hair, not painfully, but with enough pressure to command my attention. "We will train you."

"And if I refuse to use it for you?"

His smile is all fang, a predator's warning. "Then I'll have the mate I claimed."

The words steal the breath from my lungs.

I stare at him, unable to speak. *Mate*—the word is ancient, sacred, terrifying. My heart thunders against my ribs, the pulse in my neck fluttering like a trapped bird. My body is trembling, but not just with fear.

With want.

I force myself to meet his gaze, refusing to be cowed despite the feelings coursing through me.

He's staring at me with that dark, searing intensity that strips me bare. I can feel the truth of his words in the heat between us, in the way his thumb brushes against my lip like he's memorizing the shape of me. In the way his voice is still sharp, still dominant, but softer now; threaded with something close to reverence.

He doesn't see a mistake.

He sees his mate.

Gods help me, part of me wants to belong to someone who sees me like Ryker does.

But I can't allow myself to believe we can be more when I know exactly how much of a disappointment I am.

"I was born broken. My own mother couldn't look at me after my first failed shift." I look away, shame tightening my throat. "Do you know what it's like to feel your wolf pacing under your skin and never be able to reach her? To hear her howl and know you'll never run with her?" I wrap my arms around myself, retreating inward. "I'm not a wolf. I'm a mistake."

Silence stretches between us, thick with tension.

Then Ryker moves, one hand rises, not to grip, but to cup my jaw with surprising gentleness.

"You're not broken, Kitara. Your pack was just too small-minded to understand you."

I startle at both his touch and the use of my name for the first time. It lands with weight; the way he says it sounds like a caress.

"I don't want your gift," he continues, his voice rough. "I want *you*."

His mouth crashes down on mine, swallowing my words. The kiss is possession itself—all heat and demand and barely contained violence. His hand tightens in my hair, tilting my head back as his other arm wraps around my waist, dragging me up against his chest. The furs fall away, leaving nothing between us but the blood dried on his skin.

Power surges through the claiming mark, making me gasp against his lips. He takes advantage, deepening the kiss until I can taste his wildness, his rage, his need to possess every part of me. My hands come up to his chest, whether to push him away or pull him closer, I'm not sure. His skin burns beneath my palms, hard muscle and rough scars under my fingertips.

When he finally breaks the kiss, we're both breathing hard. His eyes have shifted, the gold one burning bright, while the red one seems to glow—a sign of how close his beast is to the surface.

"Mine," he growls against my lips. "You're mine."

A sharp scratch at the stone entrance makes Ryker's head snap up, a snarl building in his chest. I feel his arms tighten around me protectively before a voice calls out.

"Alpha," the male calls, his eyes averted respectfully. "Forgive the interruption, but the northern scouts have picked up movement. A large group is approaching the border markers. They're not even trying to hide."

Ryker's muscles coil beneath my hands. He doesn't

release me, but his demeanor shifts from passionate to lethal in an instant. "Numbers?"

"At least thirty. Mixed pack signatures. And..." The wolf hesitates. "They're carrying silver, Alpha. We can smell it on the wind."

The growl that rumbles through Ryker's chest is pure predator. He finally pulls away from me, though his hand lingers on my claiming mark sending pulses of warmth through the bond. "Get the enforcers in position. No one engages without my command." His eyes lock onto mine. "And post four guards outside this den. No one enters except yourself or Lithia."

"Already done, Alpha."

"Good. Now get Elias and his unit ready. If they want to play with silver, we'll remind them why we hunt in darkness."

The wolf retreats, and Ryker turns back to me. The heat from moments ago has transformed into something darker, more violent. "That was Dane. You allow only him or his sister in until I'm back. Her name is Lithia. She has a scar here." He runs a hand down his cheek in demonstration. "Rest, little seer. You're safe here." His thumb traces my lower lip, still swollen from his kiss. "And when I return, we'll finish what we started."

As he goes to pull away, another vision sucks me under without warning. My eyes roll back as the vision drags me into its depths. My fingers dig into his arm, holding him in place as power surges through our claiming bond.

Through the haze of images, I feel Ryker experiencing it too—the electric current of my gift. Somehow I know that he catches fragments of what I'm seeing—moonlight on silver arrows, wolves moving through hidden tunnels, a trap waiting in the darkness.

"No," I gasp, my body arching as the vision claws through me. "Not the northern border. It's a distraction. They're coming through the old mines. The silver scent... it's to mask—"

The vision releases me, and I collapse against his chest, my body shaking from the strain. Every muscle aches as though I've run for miles. A warmth trickles from my nose, and I touch it to find blood staining my fingertips. This is the familiar aftermath of a forced vision.

"You're bleeding." There's alarm in Ryker's voice, something I didn't expect from the savage alpha. His brow furrows as he examines the blood, then he glances toward the door. "Dane!"

The wolf appears instantly. "Alpha?"

"Bring water, cloths, and food. Now." The command is sharp. He leaves, and Ryker lifts me gently, cradling me against his chest as he moves to sit us on the edge of the bed. "Does this happen every time?" he asks, his voice soft as he cradles my head, holding my hair back.

He reaches over to his bedside table, pulling tissues from the drawer. Gently, he presses it to my nose, capturing the blood flow.

I nod. "The stronger the vision, the worse the outcome."

"And how did your pack treat this?" There's a dangerous undertone lurking behind the question.

"They didn't," I whisper.

A growl rumbles through his chest, but it's not directed at me. It's a sound of pure rage focused elsewhere. "And they called themselves wolves," he mutters, disgust evident in every word.

Dane returns with remarkable speed, setting a basin of water, clean cloths, and a tray of food near the bed before retreating without a word.

Ryker dips a cloth in the cool water and gently cleans the blood from my face. His touch is surprisingly tender, at odds with the hands that tore out Kieran's throat just hours ago. He wrings another cloth and folds it, pressing it gently to the back of my neck.

"The cold will help," he explains, supporting me with one arm while he uses his other hand to hold the compress in place. "My mother used to do this for my sister when her moon cycles were painful."

The mention of his family startles me. It's easy to forget that even the most feared alpha has a mother, a childhood, connections beyond violence and power.

"Eat," he urges, nodding toward the tray once my nose has stopped bleeding. There's meat—perfectly rare—fresh bread, and what looks like honey. "You need to rebuild your strength."

"But the tunnels," I protest weakly. "The ambush—"

"Will be handled," he assures me, his voice hardening again. "I'll send scouts to confirm your vision. But you"—he brushes a strand of hair from my face, his touch lingering—"need to rest. Your gift drains you too severely to ignore."

He gently lays me back on the bed, drawing the furs around me with surprising tenderness. "Rest, Kitara. You are safe."

With one fluid step he shifts, transforming into the giant black wolf. The change is so swift, so graceful, that I barely register the moment human becomes beast. He shakes his massive head, then throws it back in a howl that echoes through the den and into the caves outside.

It's a call to action. A call to defend.

A call to *kill*.

As the sound fades, I curl deeper into the furs that smell of him. It's not safety I feel—not yet.

But for the first time in a long time, I'm hopeful.

Blood sings in my veins as I prowl through the mining tunnels, twelve of my most lethal wolves following behind me. Their massive forms fill the narrow passages, dark fur swallowing what little light filters through the ancient support beams. Above ground, Lachlan and twenty others will be engaging the northern distraction—but down here, in the darkness where my pack rules, I will remind our enemies of why they fear the shadows.

I catch their scent before I see them. The sharp tang of silver mixed with the musk of foreign wolves—Moonclaw's elite hunters, by the smell of them. They've brought with them silver dust to mask their approach, thinking to use my pack's notorious sensitivity against us.

*Fools.* As if my wolves haven't learned to hunt through pain.

*Eight coming through the main shaft,* Leon's thoughts touch mine. *Another six trying to circle behind through the eastern tunnel.*

My answering growl is silent but felt by all. *Drive the six toward the Killing Chamber. The eight are mine.*

The tunnel ahead opens into an old mining junction, support beams creating shadows within shadows.

*Perfect.*

My wolves melt into the darkness, becoming part of it. Waiting for our prey.

The enemy pack moves with silent precision, silver-coated weapons gleaming. They're alert but relaxed, expecting no challenge. Until I launch myself from the shadows above.

My massive form crashes into their leader, fangs finding throat before the wolf can even yelp. Blood sprays across the tunnel walls as I rip and tear, using the dying wolf's body as a shield against the silver-tipped spears of the others. The taste of his lifeblood fills my mouth, hot and metallic and somehow sweeter for being an enemy's.

My pack erupts from every shadow, the junction exploding into savage violence. These aren't the controlled fights of pack challenges with their rules and restraint. This is old violence, primal and merciless.

A silver blade scores my flank, burning like molten metal against my skin. I turn on my attacker, lips pulled back from blood-stained fangs. The Moonclaw wolf has time for one startled yelp before my jaws crush his spine, the satisfying crack echoing off the stone walls.

The men begin to shift, dropping their weapons in a desperate attempt to save their hides.

It won't work. My people are too powerful for these runts. We are forged from shame and pain, tempered by brutal survival where they have grown soft with loving domestication.

I can feel Kitara's presence in my mind, our bond humming with shared sensation. I push the violence toward her, let her feel the savagery flowing through my veins. I need her to understand exactly the kind of monster who's claimed her. I need her to know the violence I will unleash to keep her by my side.

*Alpha!* Lachlan's thoughts cut through the battle-haze. *The northern group has been turned back. Our people await your command.*

I stand in the carnage of the junction, blood dripping from my muzzle, bodies broken around me. Only three of the original eight still breathe, pinned down by my wolves, their eyes wide with terror.

*Bring me the weakest*, I command. *Kill the rest.*

The survivor they bring me wears Thaddeus's personal mark—one of the Grand Alpha's own hunters.

*Good.*

I shift back to human form, my naked body painted in blood and silver burns that are already healing. The pain is nothing compared to the satisfaction of victory.

"Tell your Alpha what you found in these tunnels," I growl, crouching before the terrified wolf. "Tell him what happens to those who try to steal from the Shadowmist alpha."

"Please..." the wolf whimpers, his scent thick with fear. "We were only meant to scout—"

"Lie to me again and I'll take your tongue before I send you back." My voice is death itself. "You came for my mate. Thought to sneak in and steal her while the northern group kept us occupied." I grip his throat, feeling his pulse flutter beneath my fingers like a trapped bird. "Did you really think I wouldn't protect what's mine?"

"The Grand Alpha... he said she needs to be cleansed. Said she's a problem for the—"

My laugh is cruel. "Then he can come try to take her himself." I release the wolf's throat, shoving him away. "Run back to your Alpha, pup. Show him your wounds. Tell him what my pack did to his elite hunters." My smile promises violence. "And tell him that next time, I won't leave anyone alive."

The messenger scrambles away, leaving trails of blood in

his wake. As his scent fades, I feel the mood of my pack shift. Leon steps forward, still in wolf form but radiating concern.

"Alpha," he says upon shifting, facing me with the frankness that makes him a valued warrior. "The pack follows you without question. But this seer... she's brought war to our doorstep. Thaddeus won't stop. More will come."

Low growls of agreement ripple through the gathered wolves. Blood drips from their muzzles, silver burns scoring their hides. They've fought for me, bled for me. They deserve honesty.

"More will come," I agree, pitching my voice to carry through the tunnels. "They'll bring silver and fire and every weapon they possess." My smile is savage. "And we'll destroy them all. Because that little seer you doubt? She just saved every wolf in these caves."

I gesture to the bodies littering the junction. "They thought to catch us sleeping. Thought to slip through tunnels we've thought safe for generations. But she saw them coming. Her gift showed us their trap before it could spring."

I move through my wolves, touching scarred flanks, acknowledging their wounds with pride and gratitude. "For too long, we've been the outcasts. The feral pack others fear. But with her sight guiding us? We'll be untouchable. No one will dare move against us without her seeing it first."

"And if she turns on us?" Elias asks. "If she's as weak as they say—"

"She's mine." My growl echoes off the stone. "My mate. My responsibility. I claimed her knowing exactly what she was—what she could become with us." My wolf surges to the surface, in full agreement. "Question her worth again, and you question my judgment as alpha."

Silence falls. One by one, my wolves lower their heads, submission rippling through the pack bond. They may have doubts, but their loyalty to me remains unshaken.

Only Levi stares at me.

I arch an eyebrow.

"I'll say one thing," he says, his tone respectful even if his defiance is pushing my patience. "Lithia would have been a better choice."

Lithia, my second, would have been an easier choice as Alpha Female. She's strong, brave, and fierce. She loves our pack and would sacrifice herself for any member.

But she was never meant to be my mate, and robbing us both of the bond that true mates experience would have been the worst decision of my life.

"No. She wouldn't." I nod at the bodies around us. "Clean this mess. Double the patrols. I want to know the instant another pack even thinks about breathing in our direction." I turn toward the tunnel leading to my den. "And spread the word—the seer is mine. Anyone who doubts that answers to me."

THE JOURNEY back to my den passes in a blur of stone and shadow. I can feel Kitara through our bond—her anxiety, her awareness of the violence I've unleashed. Good. Let her understand exactly what kind of protection she's gained. What kind of monster will kill to keep her safe.

Four guards stand at my den entrance, stepping aside as I approach. Her scent calls to me, growing stronger with each step.

I pause, glancing down at myself—naked, blood streaked, and visibly aroused. The hunger in me isn't just for battle now. It's for her. To sink into her heat, to feel her mark me back, to have her whimper my name in the dark.

But not yet.

Not like this.

Soon, though. Very soon.

I snatch a length of cloth from a stack beside the door, wrapping it low around my hips. It barely hides the evidence of my desire, but it's enough. I need her to know I want her—but I will not scare her with it.

I find her exactly where I left her, curled in my furs. But her eyes... those blue eyes meet mine without flinching from my blood-covered form. She's felt what I've done. Has tasted my violence. And still she watches me with something more than fear.

"They came to take me," she whispers. Not a question.

"They died trying." The words are simple but heavy with promise.

"Was anyone hurt?" She twists a strand of dark hair nervously. "I felt... there was so much pain when the silver—"

"You're worried about my wolves?"

She lifts her chin. "They fought to protect me. Because you ordered it, yes, but they still bled. Still risked—"

"Minor wounds," I cut her off, but my tone softens. "A few silver burns. Nothing that won't heal by morning." My hand comes up to cup her face, thumb stroking her cheek. "But you feel it, don't you? Through the bond. My pack's pain. Their doubts. Their fury."

"Yes." She leans into my touch despite herself. "I feel everything. The silver burning. Their determination. Their anger. Even their..." She hesitates.

"Their what, little mate?" I coax the words from her, curious about what she senses.

"Their fear," she whispers. "Not of the fight. Of me. Of what claiming me will cost them."

My growl is possessive as I pull her against my chest, uncaring of the blood that smears her skin. "Let them fear. Let them doubt. You proved yourself tonight. The pack will learn."

"And if I'm not worth the cost?" Her hands press against

my chest, and I can feel my heart thundering beneath her palms. "If more come, if—"

My mouth crashes down on hers, silencing her doubts with a kiss that tastes of blood and victory. I pour my certainty into it, my absolute conviction that she belongs with us—with me. When I finally pull back, my beast is close to the surface.

"You're mine," I growl against her lips. "That makes you worth any cost."

# SEVEN

"Come." Ryker's voice is low but not unkind. "You need to wash, and I need these wounds cleaned."

He leads me through softly lit tunnels that spiral deep into the earth. The stone beneath my feet is smooth, worn down by generations of wolf-kind and lovingly polished to a warm shine. The air carries the faint scent of mineral-rich earth and something floral—lily, maybe? Or perhaps mountain thyme.

Crystal sconces glow softly along the walls, highlighting veins of quartz and amethyst like starlight frozen in stone. Some of the stone archways are clearly ancient—natural formations reinforced and carved with different images by skilled hands. Others are newer, smoothed into graceful curves that blend seamlessly with the old. Woven tapestries hang at intervals, stitched with symbols I don't recognize—wolves, moons, flames, and eyes.

Weapons line the walls in places, next to fire hydrants and emergency panels. Modern survival and ancient violence coexisting, like the wolves who walk these halls.

I trail my fingers along the cool stone as we walk, my

inner wolf quiet but watchful. Ryker's scent curls around us, and she presses closer.

*Mate*, she whispers, her certainty absolute.

But I'm not so sure.

She may trust, but I remember betrayal. I remember being paraded before the elders, told to shift until I collapsed from trying. I remember the disappointment in my mother's eyes, the muttered curses from the alpha when I failed to give them the seer they wanted in wolf form.

My wolf trusts. I remember.

*The man in him is more than capable of breaking me.*

"It's through here," Ryker says, interrupting my thoughts.

The bathing chamber takes my breath away.

A vast cavern opens before us, its ceiling arching high above like the inside of some forgotten temple. Crystals jut from the rock in jagged blooms, catching the soft lighting and amplifying it into a celestial glow. The entire space shimmers with cool silver, dusky gold, and the occasional glimpses of violet and green where the mist is thickest.

Steam coils from a series of natural pools, misting the air. As we move closer, I notice the water is an impossible shade of turquoise, clear and inviting. The air is thick with heat and the scent of minerals—salt, stone, and something almost sweet, like warmed honey.

Woven towels sit in thick, orderly stacks on a nearby bench. A low tray holds soaps shaped like pressed leaves, and small polished bowls of clay scrubs and herbal ointments.

It's... beautiful.

No. It's more than beautiful. It's decadent.

I freeze for a moment, unease curling through me.

Everything here speaks of ritual, comfort, and luxury. Of a life where care is not earned but expected. Where softness is not a weakness but a birthright. Where someone thought it was worthwhile to carve beauty into the walls and stock balms that smell like summer and silk.

I don't know how to exist in a place like this.

All my life I've lived on the edge of too little. Too little food. Too little kindness. Too little safety. I've washed in cold streams. Slept on the floor. Been told that pain was the price of being tolerated.

And now I stand here in a room designed for pleasure.

My chest tightens. My throat aches with an emotion I don't have words for. Grief, maybe—for all the years no one ever thought I deserved this.

I run my fingers over a towel. It's softer than anything I've ever touched.

"The waters have healing properties," Ryker explains, watching me. "Silver burns fade faster when treated in these pools."

I wrap my arms around my middle, wondering if they have the power to heal my wolf.

Ryker's gaze drops to my arms, and I'm once again painfully aware of my nudity. In my old pack, curves like mine were seen as a weakness—another sign I wasn't a true wolf. The females there are lean and athletic, their bodies honed for running and hunting. Here, in this chamber of stone and steam, I feel even more exposed, my weakness on display.

My wolf pushes forward, trying to nuzzle against him, to be close. She trusts him.

*He is ours*, she tells me.

"You're afraid," Ryker says.

"I'm cautious," I say instead.

He steps closer but doesn't touch me. "Why? Yesterday you were one of a pack of many. Today you're a queen."

I want to answer him but find myself without words.

He waits, the silence growing between us before sighing and turning away. "Help me clean these wounds?"

I'm surprised that his question is a request rather than an order.

"Okay."

I follow him into the water, the heat seeping into my muscles, easing aches I didn't even realize I had. The pool has natural ledges carved into its sides, allowing us to sit comfortably with the water at chest height.

Or at least chest height for him. It laps my collarbone, hiding me from his gaze.

Ryker hands me a cloth, turning so I can see the silver burns across his back. Some are already healing, but others look angry and deep, the skin blistered and raw. With gentle fingers, I begin to clean them, watching as the mineral-rich water washes away the remnants of metal and grit, seeming to soothe the worst of the damage.

My wolf is calm, tail curled around her paws. *Safe*, she tells me again. *He is safe.*

He may be tame now, but I have little doubt he could become feral quickly.

"Tell me about the Shadowmist Pack," I say softly, needing to fill the intimate silence. "I know so little about you."

"What do you know?"

"Barely anything at all. Alpha Varick rarely asked me to turn my vision your way, and we aren't taught your lore."

Ryker shakes his head. "Fool. Let me guess, he didn't see us as a worthy threat."

"You'd have to ask him." I dip the cloth back in the waters, then lift it, running it across his back. "Are you a threat?"

He glances behind him, our gazes meeting. "Yes."

I swallow, ducking my head as I concentrate on cleaning his wounds. "Thaddeus seemed angry with you. Why?"

"Because we are what they try to forget. We hunt as wolves are meant to hunt. We embrace the darkness they've tried to purge." He hisses as I find a particularly deep burn. "We are what they fear becoming."

"I'm not sure I understand."

He's quiet for a moment. "You will. In time."

I wring out the cloth, grimacing at the blood that falls.

He continues, his voice low. "Our pack were almost wiped out in the Blood Wars. Betrayed by the former Grand Alpha. The survivors live here now, underground. We welcome wolves who don't fit anywhere else."

I pause at the mention of the Blood Wars, my stomach tightening. It was a bloody time in our recent history—a time when wolves were dragged from their dens by fae magic, children turned into weapons, whole bloodlines erased in the name of balance. The fae courts wanted control over the were, and the former Grand Alpha opened our borders to them. Sold our kind in exchange for his own power.

"I was a pup when they happened," I say, lifting up on my knees to reach a cut near his shoulder. "You couldn't have been much older."

"I wasn't. But my wolf is large and fierce, and so we went to battle at the side of my pack." His shoulders tense under my hands. "I was in the final battle. When I became injured, I hid at the direction of my Alpha, surviving by huddling under bones and bodies."

My wolf makes a sound deep inside me, calling her sympathy and comfort to his wolf.

"I'm sorry—for both you and your pack."

He turns, slow and deliberate, and lifts a hand toward my face. I tense—but he only brushes a wet curl behind my ear.

"Thank you."

We're silent as he turns back and I continue to wash him, watching as the silver is removed and his natural healing takes over.

"Thank you," I murmur.

"For what?" he asks.

"For being honest. And for being patient with me."

Ryker moves so fast the water barely ripples. One moment

I'm cleaning his wounds, the next I'm pulled onto his lap, his large hands spanning my waist. The sudden heat of his skin against mine steals my breath.

Every nerve lights up as I register exactly how close we are. We're both naked. His chest presses against mine, his thighs bracketing me. And beneath me—gods—I feel him. His thickening length presses against my core, hard and growing harder by the second. The only thing separating us is the slick heat of the water and whatever thread of control he's still clinging to.

I've never been this close to a man before. Never wanted to be.

And yet, I don't move.

My hands are on his shoulders, braced there as if for balance. The muscle beneath my palms is iron-wrapped tension. His body hums with it—restrained strength, coiled and waiting. His jaw is clenched so tight I can see the muscle ticking beneath the stubble. His nose flares once, twice, drawing in my scent like it's the only thing anchoring him to reality.

His gaze locks with mine.

There's heat there, yes. Hunger. Claiming. But there's something else too. Something wild and reverent and deeply, achingly tender.

He's holding me like I imagine a mate should hold their heart.

"I'm not a patient wolf, Kitara," he says, voice low and ragged. "My instincts demand I claim what's mine. Completely."

It's too much. I start to pull away, but his hand catches my wrist—not painfully, but firmly enough to stop me.

"But I can smell your fear and hesitation on your skin," he continues, his thumb stroking the inside of my wrist where my pulse jumps beneath his touch. "And I want you willing. I won't take what isn't freely given."

"Why?" The question slips out before I can stop it.

His smile is dark and full of promise. "Because submission is sweeter when it isn't gained through coercion. And you will submit to me, little seer. When you're ready."

Heat blooms low in my belly at his words. My wolf stretches, eager and wanting, while the human in me remains wary.

"Until then..." His hand slides up my arm, leaving goose bumps in its wake. "I'll help you become comfortable with my touch."

The water laps around us as I shift in his lap, uncertain but drawn to his heat like a moth to flame. "I don't understand."

His growl vibrates through me as his hands tighten possessively. "When I look at you, I see power waiting to be unleashed. I see curves that make my wolf want to howl." He presses his forehead to mine, our breath mingling. "I see a mate who needs to be shown her own worth."

"How?" The word is barely a whisper, but it hangs in the steam between us.

His lips brush mine, teasing. "By proving that every part of you is precious to me."

The steam curls around us, making the moment feel dreamlike, detached from reality. His hands move over my skin beneath the water, discovering places that make my breath catch. When he finds a particularly sensitive spot at my waist, I arch instinctively, my body responding without permission from my mind.

"See?" His voice is rough with approval. "Your body knows what it wants. No hesitation."

"It's not that simple—" But my protest dies as his mouth finds my throat, teeth grazing the claiming mark. The sensation shoots straight through me, making my toes curl.

"It is that simple." Power pulses through our bond. "You're mine now. My mate. My woman. My wolf." His hands tighten possessively on my hips. "And I protect what's mine."

"Even from your own pack?" I ask, thinking of the doubts I felt—still feel even now—through our bond during his confrontation with his wolves.

He pulls back enough to meet my eyes. "If necessary. But they'll learn." His smile holds predatory promise. "Wait until they see what you can do. What we can do together."

"And that is?"

"Change everything." He catches my bottom lip between his teeth, then soothes the sting with his tongue. The contrast makes me gasp. "The old ways are dying. The civilized packs grow weaker with each generation. But us?" His hands slide up my back, pulling me closer until I can feel every hard plane of his body against my softness. "We'll show them true power."

The conviction in his voice makes me shiver. Or maybe it's the way his hands move over my skin, claiming every inch they touch. I should be terrified of this feral alpha with his blood-soaked reputation. I've seen what he's capable of, felt his savage joy through our bond as he tore apart his enemies. Yet instead of fear, I find myself melting into his touch, craving more.

"First," he growls against my lips, "you need to finish cleaning my wounds. Then I'm taking you back to our den." His eyes promise things that make heat pool low in my belly.

My heart thunders against my ribs. This is the Shadowmist alpha, the most feared wolf in five territories.

And yet...

The way he touches me is nothing like I expected. His hands move over my curves with reverence, not disgust. Where my old pack saw only weakness, he seems to find beauty. It makes my head spin—this contrast between his savage reputation and the gentle way he traces my softness.

But can I trust it? Trust him? Hours ago, he claimed me in

violence. Now he speaks of pleasure, of worth, of change. Part of me wants to believe him, to sink into the heat of his touch and let myself be claimed in every way he promises.

Another part remembers years of shame. What if he changes his mind once the thrill of claiming me wears off? What if my gift isn't enough to make up for my weaknesses?

Through our bond, I feel his response to my doubts—a surge of possessive protection that makes me gasp. His hands tighten on my hips, and I realize he can't just smell my fear, he can feel everything I'm feeling. Every fear, every longing, every hesitant spark of hope.

"Stop thinking so hard, little mate." His voice is rough silk against my ear. "Feel instead." His mouth finds my claiming mark, and power surges between us like a living current. "Feel how much I want you. How perfectly you fit in my hands. How right this is."

And I *can* feel it—his desire burning through our bond like wildfire. Not just for my gift, but for me. All of me. My curves, my softness, even my human form that can't shift. He wants me with an intensity that steals my breath.

"Turn around," he murmurs, nuzzling my neck. "Let me wash your hair."

The simple request catches me off guard. This isn't the savage claiming I expected. His fingers are gentle as they work through my dark strands, massaging my scalp with unexpected tenderness. No one has done this for me since I was a child, before my wolf failed to emerge.

"Your thoughts are too loud," he rumbles behind me. "I can feel them spinning through our bond."

"I'm not used to..." I gesture vaguely at his hands in my hair, at the way he handles me like I'm precious instead of broken. "People being gentle with me."

"Gentleness?" His laugh is dark honey. "The Shadowmist Pack isn't known for it. But a mate deserves careful handling." His fingers find a knot in my neck, working it loose with firm pressure. "At least until she's ready for something... rougher."

Heat blooms in my cheeks at his tone. Through our bond, I feel his satisfaction at my response, the way my body betrays my interest despite my uncertainties.

His arms wrap around my waist, pulling me back against his chest. The hard planes of his body make my softness feel somehow right instead of wrong. Like we're two pieces of the same puzzle, finally clicking into place after years of trying to fit where we didn't belong.

"Everything about you calls to my wolf," he murmurs against my ear. "Makes me want to protect and possess in equal measure."

"And when the novelty wears off?" I can't keep the tremor from my voice. "When I'm not new and exciting anymore?"

His growl vibrates through my back. "Not possible. Now, kiss me."

I hesitate only for a heartbeat before turning in his arms, the mineral-rich water swirling around us. His gaze holds mine with an intensity that robs me of all thought. When my lips meet his, the claiming bond between us pulses with power, sending waves of warmth cascading through my body.

The connection between us flares open, no longer just a tether but a flood of sensation. Through our bond, his desires rush into me, raw, primal, and overwhelming. I feel his hunger, not just physically. Images flash through my mind—his fantasies, his intentions—of me standing beside him before the pack, strong and respected, of my body beneath his, our limbs entangled, of me heavy with his child, a tangible symbol of our union.

Beyond those visions lies something that shakes me to my core—his fierce pride in claiming me. Not despite my human form, but because of everything I am. I feel his fascination with my curves, so different from the lean-muscled females of his pack. His admiration for my resilience after years of mistreatment. His almost obsessive need to protect what is his.

Most startling of all, I sense his respect for my gift. He doesn't see it as just a tool to be used, but as power in its own right. The Shadowmist alpha sees me as his equal in ways my old pack never could have imagined.

"You can feel it," he murmurs against my lips, not a question but a realization. "What you do to me. What I see when I look at you."

The kiss deepens, his hands finding their way to my face, cradling it with surprising gentleness from a wolf known only for violence. I feel the coiled strength in his body, the barely contained power of his wolf pressing against the boundaries of his control.

His fingers tangle in my wet hair, tilting my head back as his lips move from my mouth to trace the line of my throat.

"You belong with me. With us." His teeth graze my neck, raising goose bumps along my skin. "The pack will learn, just as you're learning."

When he kisses me again, there's a new urgency to it. His arms tighten around me, lifting me slightly in the water so that we're perfectly aligned. The mineral bath laps around us, steam swirling. His hand trails down my spine, leaving fire in its wake as our kiss intensifies.

A growl builds in his chest, vibrating against me. I can feel his control slipping, his wolf pushing forward, demanding more. His breathing grows ragged as he pulls back suddenly, pressing his forehead against mine.

"Enough," he says, his voice rough with restraint. "If we continue this here..."

The heat in his gaze makes me shiver despite the warmth of the water. Through our bond, I can feel his hunger, his wolf's impatience, and his human side's surprising determination to do this properly.

"Come." He lifts me from the water in one fluid movement, his strength making me feel weightless. "I'm taking you back to our den."

He sets me on my feet at the edge of the pool, reaching for the soft cloths we'd discarded earlier. With unexpected care, he wraps one around me, his hands lingering at my shoulders.

"Make no mistake, Kitara, I will claim you fully," he says, his voice a low promise that makes my heart race. "As my mate. My Alpha Female. Mine in every way a wolf can be claimed."

The possessiveness in his tone should frighten me, but instead, I find myself leaning into his touch, my body responding to the primal call of his. For the first time in my life, my inability to shift doesn't feel like a wall between me and the wolf world—not when Ryker looks at me with such hunger, such need.

"Yes," I whisper, the simple word feeling like a pledge.

His smile is predatory, satisfied, as he wraps his own cloth around his waist. "Yes," he echoes, taking my hand. "Now let's go back to our den, little seer, before my control breaks entirely."

# CHAPTER
# EIGHT

Ryker leads me through winding tunnels back toward our den, his hand a constant presence at the small of my back, warm and solid. The mineral waters have done their work—his silver burns now appear as faded pink marks rather than angry welts, and my own aches from the Claiming run have eased. We're both wrapped in soft woven cloth towels, though Ryker wears his slung low on his waist and with the casual confidence of someone who considers clothing optional at best.

He guides me back through via a different passage, pointing out various rooms—storage areas, a medical practice, children's playrooms, and communal kitchens that smell faintly of roasted meat and herbs. As we emerge into the main cavern, the atmosphere shifts. It's a vast, open space humming with low conversation and the thrum of pack life.

It's a massive space with a vaulted ceiling that rises high above us. There's a cluster of narrow crystal shafts carved into the rock overhead, light tunnels engineered so cleverly that no outside threat could ever slip through. It's dark now, but I can imagine how different this space must look in the light of the morning when beams strike the center of the cavern, turning dust motes to gold and illuminating a mosaic floor patterned with lunar phases and pack sigils.

Wolves gather in quiet groups around stone hearths and on elevated platforms. The moment they see Ryker, a ripple passes through the room—spines straightening, heads dipping in subtle deference. Some nod respectfully, acknowledging him with the quiet reverence reserved for dominant predators. Others pause mid-task, their gazes flicking to me with open curiosity, suspicion, or worse—thinly veiled hostility.

The air thickens around me, prickling with unspoken questions. I catch whispered words, *seer… human-born… can't even shift*—before Ryker's presence silences them. He doesn't speak, doesn't growl. He doesn't need to. The way he walks, the raw power in his frame, the weight of his gaze—it's enough.

His hand presses more firmly to the small of my back, a silent claim and warning in one. *Mine,* the touch says. *Look, but don't forget who stands at her side.*

"They don't know what to make of me," I murmur, keeping my voice low as we pass a group of females who make no effort to hide their stares.

"They'll learn," he replies simply, guiding me toward a carved stone stairway that spirals upward. "My quarters are above most of the pack dens. Better vantage point."

We've barely started climbing when I feel it—a sudden shift in the air, a tension that makes the fine hairs on my arms stand on end. Ryker stiffens beside me, his body coiling with instant alertness.

"What is it?" I ask, though part of me already knows. Through our bond, I can sense his wolf's immediate response, territorial, protective, angry.

"Stay behind me," he orders, his voice dropping to that dangerous growl that promises violence.

At the top of the stairway stands a woman, tall and lean,

with striking white-blonde hair and eyes so pale blue they appear almost silver in the dim light. She's beautiful in the way of wolves—all predatory grace and deadly efficiency. A jagged scar runs from her right temple down her cheek, disappearing beneath the high collar of her fitted black shirt.

Even from this distance, I can feel the power radiating from her. She's not just any wolf—she's an enforcer, maybe even Ryker's beta.

"Lithia," Ryker acknowledges her, his tone giving nothing away.

This must be Dane's sister, one of the two wolves Ryker told me I could trust. The hostility pouring from her suggests Ryker's confidence may have been misplaced.

Her eyes fix on me with cold intensity. "This is what you bring us?" Her voice is as sharp as broken glass. "A wolf who can't shift?"

Ryker's growl vibrates through the stone beneath our feet. "Choose your next words carefully, Lithia."

"You cannot punish me when I speak truth, Alpha." She descends three steps, her movements controlled. "The pack whispers. They say you've claimed a broken wolf for her parlor tricks. They say you've endangered us all for a female who can't run with us, can't hunt with us, can't—"

"She saved lives tonight," Ryker cuts her off, his voice deadly quiet. "Her 'parlor tricks' prevented an ambush that would have killed half our enforcers."

Lithia's lip curls. "There wouldn't have been any bloodshed if not for her. One lucky vision doesn't make her worthy of being Alpha Female."

My breath catches at the challenge in her words. Through our bond, I feel Ryker's fury building, a storm gathering force.

"She bears my mark," he says, each word precise and heavy with threat. "That makes her Alpha Female. The matter is settled."

"Nothing is settled." Lithia takes another step down, and I notice she's not wearing shoes, her bare feet silent against the stone. "The laws are clear, even for us. The role of Alpha Female may be granted, but it must also be earned."

I step out from behind Ryker, ignoring his warning growl. The moment I move forward, something shifts inside me. The world tilts, colors bleeding together. I've experienced enough visions to recognize the signs, but this one comes without the usual pain, flowing naturally like water finding its path.

Through our bond, I feel Ryker's surprise as my gift surges, pulling me under while leaving me strangely conscious. It's different from before, more controlled, more focused. I remain standing, my eyes meeting Lithia's defiant gaze, but I'm seeing beyond the present moment.

*I see her, younger, barely more than a child. She's crouched in darkness, covering the mouth of an even smaller boy—Dane. Fae hunters move through the forest above them, silver weapons gleaming in moonlight. They're hiding. Surviving.*

*Another flash, Lithia standing before Ryker, her face unmarked by the scar she now bears. "I failed them," she's saying, voice breaking. "My family, my responsibility...."*

*And then, shockingly clear, Lithia throwing herself between a silver blade and Ryker, taking the wound that now marks her face. Saving her alpha without hesitation.*

The vision releases me gently, and I feel a little like driftwood being carried to shore. I find myself still standing, still facing Lithia, but with new understanding.

"You bear the scar meant for him," I say softly.

Lithia freezes, her body rigid. "What did you say?"

"The silver blade," I continue, the vision's details crystal clear in my mind. "You stepped between it and Ryker. You weren't fast enough to stop it completely, but you turned the killing blow into..." I gesture to my own cheek, mirroring the path of her scar.

The hostility in her eyes transforms into wary disbelief. She flicks a glance at Ryker. "You told her?"

Through our bond, I feel Ryker's mixture of surprise and dawning realization. He steps beside me, no longer shielding me but standing as my equal.

"I told Kitara nothing of your sacrifice. All she knows is that she could trust you." He glowers. "Are you proving me wrong?"

Without thinking, I lay a hand on his arm, halting his words. "You protect what matters to you," I tell Lithia. "Your brother when you were children, hidden in a hollow beneath a fallen oak while hunters searched above. Your Alpha, taking the silver that was meant for him." I take a step toward her. "Now you think you're protecting your pack from me."

A low murmur of voices reaches us, and I realize we've gathered an audience. Wolves line the upper walkways and lower platforms, drawn by the tension radiating through their pack bond.

A bond I've yet to fully establish, but one I crave more than ever.

Lithia's expression shifts, confusion replacing hostility. "You saw my past?"

I nod slowly. "My visions… they're not just about what's coming. Sometimes they show me what I need to understand." I swallow, trying to hold her gaze. "I understand your loyalty. I understand why you'd question me. And… I'm grateful you protected Ryker."

The gathered wolves watch in silence. The weight of their eyes drapes over me like chains, not yet oppressive but heavy enough to remind me I don't belong.

"I don't ask you to accept me recklessly," I tell Lithia, aware that I'm speaking to the entire pack now. " Just… give me a chance. Judge me by what I *can* do. Not by what I was born without."

I shift my hands in front of me, unsure what to do with

them. "I'll never run as a wolf, I know that. But I can see threats others miss. I'll never draw blood with claws, but I'll bleed for this pack if I have to. The Moon Goddess gave me *something*, even if it's not what you're used to."

Lithia studies me for a long moment, her gaze searching mine for deception. Finally, her posture shifts, not quite relaxed but no longer openly hostile.

"The Alpha has chosen," she says, inclining her head slightly. "Time will prove your worth... or your weakness."

It's not acceptance, not yet. But it's an opening—a chance to prove myself through actions rather than words.

"Fair enough," I reply, matching her formal tone.

Ryker steps forward, his presence commanding immediate attention. "Kitara is my mate and your Alpha Female," he announces, his voice carrying through the cavern. "Her gift has already saved Shadowmist blood. Remember that before you whisper challenges."

The gathered wolves disperse, conversations already buzzing with what they've witnessed. Lithia gives me one last measuring look before turning away, her movements still predatory but lacking the open aggression from moments before.

As Ryker guides me the rest of the way up the stairs, his hand returns to the small of my back.

"Are you okay?" he asks once we're alone in the corridor leading to our chambers.

I shake my head, still processing what happened. "I've never had that happen before. Usually, my visions are either vague glimpses that come in dreams or forced visions that leave me bleeding and weak." I look up at him, wondering. "Could it be the claiming bond? Your power somehow stabilizing mine?"

"Perhaps." His finger traces the line of my jaw. "Time will tell."

Inside our room, I let myself embrace the hope that I've so coveted.

"What did you see?" Ryker asks as he closes the heavy door behind us. "About Lithia?"

"Everything that makes her loyal to you," I answer honestly. "Everything that makes her dangerous to your enemies."

His smile is slow and satisfied. "Then you understand why you can trust her."

"Yes."

Through our bond, I feel his certainty—warm and absolute. "She now understands your value as well, little seer. Whether she admits it yet or not."

As Ryker moves toward me, his intentions clear in the heat of his gaze, I realize that I've won something more significant than Lithia's grudging acceptance. I've glimpsed what I could become here, with this pack, with this mate.

*See?* my wolf asks. *He is a mate to stand beside.*

The air inside the den is warm, faintly spiced with cedar and smoke. Ryker's scent. Comforting. Commanding. Entirely him.

The silence stretches between us as I wrap the towel tighter around my body, damp tendrils of hair curling along my neck. I can feel his gaze like heat on my skin, tracking every breath, every shift of fabric.

"You handled Lithia well," he murmurs, stepping toward me with the slow certainty of a predator who already knows his prey won't run.

"I didn't know I could," I admit. "The vision came… clean. No pain or confusion."

He stops in front of me, lifting a hand to brush a strand of hair from my cheek. "Because you weren't alone in it."

My breath catches. The bond between us hums, a pulse under my skin that responds to his nearness. There's a pull between us that goes far deeper than attraction.

His fingers trail from my cheek down the line of my jaw, then lower, grazing my collarbone where the cloth begins to dip.

"Ryker," I whisper, unsure if it's a warning or a plea.

"Tell me to stop," he says, voice low and rough. "And I will."

I don't. I can't.

Instead, I tilt my face up, lips parting slightly. His eyes flash with hunger. But he's restrained, balancing on the edge.

His hand slides down, warm against my waist as he steps closer, chest nearly brushing mine. The damp fabric we wear are barriers in name only. I can feel the heat of him, the strength, the hunger beneath the surface.

"Your eyes are saying yes," he murmurs, his mouth so close to mine I can taste the promise, "but your body's saying no, little wolf."

I shudder. Not from fear, but from the sheer force of his control.

"And I will not force my mate." He steps back, just a breath, but it might as well be a mile. "You'll want me just as much as I want you. You'll come to me because you need to, not because the bond tells you to."

It shouldn't undo me. Shouldn't make something inside me tremble more than any kiss could. But it does. That he *wants* me but won't *take* me. That he sees my hesitation and meets it with patience.

My throat tightens. "I don't know how to give myself without breaking."

Ryker smiles, slow and dangerous, but not unkind. "Then we'll go slow."

He turns away, giving me space. Control.

"Sleep in my bed tonight," he adds, glancing over his shoulder. "Just sleep. Let your body learn me without fear."

And damn, if that isn't the most seductive thing he's said all night.

# CHAPTER
# NINE

I wake to unfamiliar softness, my body cradled in furs that smell of earth and stone and *him*. Ryker. My mate. The claiming mark on my throat pulses with his power, a constant reminder of our bond. Sunlight filters through crystal formations in the ceiling, casting rainbow patterns across the stone walls of our den.

*Our den.* The thought still feels foreign—like a secret I've stolen and will eventually be punished for keeping.

I reach for Ryker but find cooling furs beside me. The events of last night rush back, and I remember his amused rumble as I'd struggled to keep my eyes open, his lips brushing my forehead as he'd tucked me against his chest.

"Rest," he'd murmured. "You are safe here, little wolf."

Now I stretch, taking inventory of my body. The aches from the claiming have faded, leaving only a pleasant soreness in muscles unused to such exertion.

I roll and close my eyes, sinking back into the furs only to feel a tickle in the back of my mind. A whisper-light touch that stirs my she-wolf.

*What is it?* I ask her, unsure.

*Our mate. Feel him.*

I keep my eyes closed, following the whisper. We walk together, my wolf and I, along pathways where Ryker's voice grows stronger, his presence more clear.

*Is this normal?* I ask my wolf.

*This is the way of all wolves.*

*But it wasn't in our old pack.*

She shakes her head, letting out a whining growl that articulates clearly what she thinks of our previous pack.

We move along and suddenly all the whispers and white noise snap into focus.

I startle, sitting up as a hundred voices dance in my head.

*….need to order more apples for pie…*

*…have you seen my red socks?*

*…homework is late again, you'll…*

*Kitara.*

I stiffen, hearing Ryker as loudly as if he were beside me. The other voices abruptly disappear, until it's just me and him.

*You're oversharing. I'm closing you off from the pack to protect your secrets from them.* He sounds amused. *Eat and dress. I'll meet you once my morning brief is complete.*

*Yes, Alpha.*

His displeasure rolls toward me with the swiftness of a wave, crashing into me.

*Ryker,* he corrects. *I am never Alpha to you.*

Our connection weakens, leaving me alone in our bed. I slip from under the covers to find a soft robe laid out. The material feels rich against my skin, nothing like the threadbare hand-me-downs I'd been provided in the Silvercrest Pack.

The main chamber beyond the bedroom is empty, but evidence of Ryker's morning remains—a cup on the stone table, maps spread across its surface, markers showing territories and borders. Looking closer, I see they're planning documents, defensive positions marked in what looks like dried blood rather than ink.

War preparations.

I'm studying them when the door scrapes open. I turn, expecting Ryker, but instead find a tall female with copper-auburn hair and striking amber eyes. She carries a tray of food, steam rising from a bowl that fills the air with savory aromas that make my stomach growl embarrassingly loud.

"Oh!" She startles slightly upon seeing me, then recovers with a formal nod. "Alpha Female. I didn't realize you were awake."

The title makes me tense. "Please, call me Kitara."

She hesitates, clearly torn between protocol and my request. "I'm Nora. The Alpha asked me to bring you breakfast and show you around." She sets the tray down, keeping a respectful distance. Unlike Lithia's open hostility, Nora's manner is carefully neutral—professional courtesy rather than personal welcome.

"Thank you." I approach the table as she arranges the meal. "Where is Ry—the Alpha?"

"Patrolling the borders with the enforcers." She doesn't look up as she works. "After last night's attack, he's strengthening our defenses."

My fingers find the claiming mark automatically. Through our bond, I can sense Ryker's presence—distant but focused, alert, his attention focused on pack business and constant awareness of me.

"How many died in the attack?" I ask quietly.

Nora's hands pause. "None of ours. Many of theirs." Her amber eyes finally meet mine. "Thanks to your warning."

The memory of the tunnel vision returns—blood and silver. "It wasn't—"

"It was exactly what we needed," she interrupts, her tone firm. "The Alpha explained what happened."

I duck my head, uncomfortable with the implication that I

had somehow saved them. My visions have always been treated as a tool at best, a burden at worst. Never as something worthy of gratitude.

Nora gestures to the food. "You should eat. The Alpha was clear about keeping up your strength." Her eyes flick to the claiming mark, then away. "He said your gift drains you."

I sit, aware of the hollow feeling in my stomach. The meal is simple but hearty, some kind of sweet oat mix with chunks of fruit and berries. I take a tentative bite and have to stifle a moan at the explosion of flavor.

"This is delicious," I manage between bites.

Nora's expression softens fractionally. "Marta is our cook. She insists on only the best produce." She watches me eat with a thoughtful expression. "The Alpha said you're to have your own quarters prepared, if you wish."

I nearly choke on my mouthful. "My own quarters?"

"Adjacent to his, of course." She tilts her head. "Is that not customary in your old pack? For the female to have her personal space?"

I set down my spoon, gathering my thoughts. In the Silvercrest Pack, females—especially claimed ones—had no such luxury. They were expected to be available to their mates at all times, their personal space limited to whatever corner they could carve out in their mate's den.

As for me, I was offered a small room in the rear of Varick's house. It had been big enough for a small pallet on the floor, and one bedside table filled with my clothes. I'd owned three books, none of which I could read, and nothing else.

"No," I admit. "It isn't customary."

A look of pity passes across Nora's face before it's quickly masked. "Shadowmist ways are different. The Alpha Female has her own territory, just as the Alpha has his." She moves toward a doorway I hadn't noticed before. "Would you like to see the space?"

I finish eating then follow her through a short corridor at the rear of our den, emerging into a chamber that takes my breath away. Like Ryker's rooms, it's built into the natural rock formation, but where his quarters are masculine, this space is infinitely feminine.

A bed smaller than Ryker's but still luxurious rests against one wall. Shelves have been carved directly into the stone, holding books, crystals, and what look like scrying tools. A natural skylight brings in streams of sunlight, while a small waterfall trickles down one wall into a basin, the sound soothing and peaceful.

"This is…" I start, then stop, overwhelmed.

"It hasn't been used in some time," Nora explains, running a hand along one of the shelves. "Not since the Alpha's mother."

"His mother lived here?" I ask, surprised.

Nora nods. "The Alpha will tell you about her in time, I'm sure."

I step farther into the room, drawn to a small alcove where a silver bowl rests on a raised stone platform. The bowl's interior is polished to a mirror finish, its rim etched with symbols I don't recognize.

"A scrying basin," Nora explains, keeping her distance. "For focused visions."

I barely resist the urge to touch it, feeling the latent power humming from its surface. "Ryker's mother used this?"

"No, our previous seer, Cheyenne, did."

"Is she alive?"

Nora chuckles. "No. She was old before I was born. She passed when I was but a few summers old." She touches the bowl. "But I remember her. She had a kind spirit, and when she wanted to see specific things rather than wait for visions to come naturally she used these tools." Nora gestures to the books. "Her journals are there as well. I'm sure the Alpha would want you to have them."

My heart stutters at the thought, the pleasure of this room quickly shadowed by shame. I'd never been taught to read. Knowledge had always been kept just out of reach, a tool wielded against me rather than gifted freely. And my visions weren't seen as a trainable skill, they'd simply been ripped from me when needed, leaving me to deal with the aftermath alone. The idea that there might be guidance, methods, even a community of knowledge around seers leaves me dizzy with possibility, and wretched with shame at yet another of my failings.

"All these are mine?" I ask, running my fingers along the spines of the ancient books.

"This is your space," Nora confirms. "But you'll continue to share the Alpha's chambers. He was quite clear about that." There's something in her tone, not quite judgment, not quite amusement. "The library is yours to use as you wish. A place for study and reflection."

I nod, overwhelmed by this bounty.

"Thank you for showing me," I say, my voice thick with emotion.

Nora inclines her head. "The Alpha said you'll begin training today to strengthen your control."

"Training?"

"He believes your gift can be honed, like any other weapon." She reaches down to fluff a pillow on the bed. "We've never had a seer who couldn't shift. It will be interesting to see what you're capable of."

The words aren't unkind, merely factual. But in them, I hear what she doesn't say.

*Prove your worth. Show us why our Alpha chose you.*

I lift my chin. "When do we start?"

"As soon as you're ready." Ryker's voice fills the chamber, and I turn to find him leaning against the doorway, watching us with those mismatched eyes. His body still carries the wild energy of the forest, like he's brought part of the hunt back with him.

Nora lowers her gaze, tilting her head to expose her neck in deference. "Alpha."

"Thank you, Nora, you may leave us."

When she's gone, Ryker pushes off from the doorway, moving toward me with that predatory grace that still makes my heart race. He's dressed now, though the fitted black pants and open vest do little to conceal the scars mapping his torso.

"Did you sleep well?" he asks, his eyes tracing me in my borrowed robe.

I nod, holding the edges closed. "Yes. Thank you for—" I gesture around the room. "—for this. I've never had access to knowledge about my gift before."

His fingers brush the claiming mark, sending warmth cascading through me. "The library is yours. But your place is with me, in our chambers." The possessiveness in his voice should frighten me, but instead, it sends a thrill down my spine. "You need to get used to my presence, my scent... my touch."

The claiming bond hums between us, carrying the truth of his words. He believes what he's saying, even if I still struggle to accept it.

I look past him, my fingers drifting toward one of the books again. I swallow, knowing I need to confess my failure but terrified of what he might think.

Ryker's fingers are gentle on my chin as he turns my face toward his. "I can smell your fear, Kitara. Talk to me."

"I can't read," The words feel heavier than they should. "I was never taught."

The shift in him is immediate. Subtle, but sharp. His jaw clenches. His body goes still, taut with something that looks like fury. His eyes flare—wild, feral, dangerous.

My stomach drops.

*He regrets claiming me.*

Of course he does. What alpha ties himself to a female who can't even read her own name? I look away, shame prickling across my skin.

He exhales hard through his nose as his hands come up to cup my face.

"Calm, Kitara," he murmurs, voice raw. "I'm not angry at you. I'm angry at them. At those fucking bastards who kept you small. Who used your gift and gave you nothing in return."

A beat of silence stretches between us, thick with things I don't know how to say.

Then he softens, the storm in his eyes ebbing.

"I'll teach you," he says simply. "Every night, if you want. Or I'll ask Lyra, one of the elders. She's taught many of our pack. Then you can read the journals and know how to control your power."

I stare at him, throat tight, heart thudding like it's trying to escape the cage of my ribs. No one's ever offered to build me up before. Only to tear me down, use what they needed, and leave the rest.

This... this is something else entirely.

I shake my head, not in refusal, but because I don't know what to say. It's too big. Too kind. Too much.

"I don't even know where to start," I whisper, ashamed of the wobble in my voice.

Ryker brushes a knuckle down my jaw, his touch grounding. "You start by showing up. That's enough."

My eyes burn. I blink hard, holding them back by sheer force of will.

He doesn't flinch. Doesn't tease. Just cups my cheek and lets me have this moment. Lets me be.

I nod once, fiercely. "Okay."

He grins, pressing a kiss to my forehead. "I think I'll like teaching you new things." There's a husky tease in his tone but he lets me go, moving away to walk around the room, examining the various trinkets and tools on the shelves.

"Nora mentioned your mother lived here," I say, watching his expression carefully.

An old pain flickers across his face. "She did. For many years before she left to join another pack."

"Was your father the alpha?"

"No." He doesn't elaborate.

I stand awkwardly, waiting for him to explain further, but instead he turns away from the room, walking toward the door.

"Get dressed," he says over his shoulder. "Your training begins in the East Chamber."

After he leaves, I find exercise clothing laid out for me, practical but well-made. Leggings and a shirt in deep forest green, with soft shoes that fit perfectly. Everything seems tailored to my size, which raises questions I don't have time to consider.

I move about our chambers, feeling half a thief in borrowed finery. The clothing, his mother's room, the freedom to explore—it all feels like a dream from which I'll wake at any moment. For twenty-five years, I've been the broken wolf, the failed shifter, useful only for a gift I can't control. Now I'm being offered tools, training, respect. The sheer difference between my old life and this new one feels too vast to comprehend.

I return to the library, running my fingers along the spines of the ancient books. Some are written with symbols I don't recognize, their bindings cracked with age. Others appear newer, journals filled with handwritten notes. Knowledge from one seer to another, preserved for a future she may have foreseen.

As I prepare to leave, I catch sight of myself in a polished silver mirror. The woman who looks back is someone I barely recognize. She stands straighter, color in her cheeks, a claiming mark vivid against her throat. There's something different in her eyes too, the faintest glimmer of hope.

I touch the mark, feeling Ryker's power pulse in response. Through our bond, I sense his impatience, his eagerness to begin whatever training he has planned. But beneath that runs a deeper current—determination.

Taking a deep breath, I leave our chambers, following the pull of our bond through the stone corridors. Whatever comes next, I am no longer the broken wolf of Silvercrest Pack.

I am Kitara, Female Alpha of the Shadowmist Pack, and mate to the Shadowmist alpha. And for the first time in my life, that might be enough.

# TEN

The East Chamber is yet another cavern. Unlike the residential areas with their polished floors and comfortable furnishings, this space feels ancient and raw. The unfinished stone walls rise to a natural dome high above, where a circular opening allows a beam of sunlight to pierce the dimness. The light creates a perfect circle on the chamber floor, illuminating a design carved into the stone—a crescent moon embracing a starburst pattern.

Ryker waits in the center of the light circle, his massive frame seeming somehow larger in this space. Around the chamber's edges, I spot other wolves. Lithia stands with arms crossed, her silver eyes watchful. Dane leans against a column, his gaze steady, his posture deceptively relaxed. He shares his sister's height and elegance, the same striking bone structure, the same pale silver-blue eyes that gleam like frost under moonlight. But where Lithia is carved from ice and discipline, Dane radiates a gentle warmth.

His hair is the same white blond, though shorter, and tousled rather than slicked back. He watches with the intensity of someone who's always listening.

I turn my attention to the others in the room; I don't recognize those that observe from the shadows.

An audience. My stomach tightens with anxiety.

"Don't mind them," Ryker says as I approach, reading my hesitation. "They're here to learn, not judge."

I'm not convinced, but I step into the circle of light regardless, feeling exposed under the gazes of so many wolves.

"What exactly are we doing?" I ask, keeping my voice low.

"Testing boundaries." Ryker circles me slowly, his movements deliberate. "Your gift has been abused for years, ripped out when convenient, ignored when not. We're going to see what happens when it's actually nurtured."

The way he says it makes my chest tighten. No one has ever described my treatment in such terms—*abuse*. It was always *necessity* or *duty* or *service to the pack*. Never something done to me, but rather something expected from me.

"How?" I ask.

"By learning to access your gift voluntarily first." He stops behind me, close enough that I can feel the heat of him against my back. "No more bleeding. No more pain."

I can't help my skeptical laugh. "That's not how it works. The visions come when they want to, or they're forced. There's no middle ground."

"There is." His hands come to rest on my shoulders, firm but gentle. "Cheyenne found it. You will too."

Before I can process this, he continues, his voice pitched for the entire chamber to hear. "A seer's gift operates on three levels. First, passive visions, dreams, flashes, impressions that come unbidden. Second, focused sight, deliberately turning your attention to a specific person, place, or event to see its possible futures or pasts. Third, immersive vision. Completely entering a prophetic state to witness events in their fullness."

His hands slide down my arms, leaving fire in their wake. "You've experienced the first naturally. The third has been forced from you, at great cost. Today, we'll work on the second."

"How?" I ask again, my voice barely a whisper.

I feel his smile against my hair. "By giving your wolf something to protect."

Before I can question this cryptic statement, he steps away. The sudden absence of his warmth makes me shiver.

"Lithia," he calls. "Come forward."

The scarred enforcer approaches, her movements liquid and predatory. Up close, her beauty is even more striking, all sharp angles and deadly grace.

"The Alpha Female will attempt to see your next move," Ryker explains. "Nothing lethal."

Lithia's smile is all fang. "Of course, Alpha."

My heart pounds against my ribs. "I don't understand. What am I supposed to—"

"Focus on her," Ryker instructs, circling behind me again. "Don't look at what she is doing, try to see what she *will* do next."

Lithia begins to circle me, her silver eyes never leaving mine. I've seen that look before—a predator sizing up prey.

"I can't just—" I begin.

"You can," Ryker interrupts, his voice a low command. "Your gift is part of you, not separate. Stop waiting for it to arrive and start reaching for it."

Easier said than done. I've never been able to control when the visions come or what they show. They've always been wild things, untamed and unpredictable.

Lithia moves closer, and instinctively I step back. Through our bond, I feel Ryker's disapproval.

"Don't retreat," he growls. "See."

Swallowing hard, I force myself to stand still as Lithia circles. I try to focus on her, to see beyond the present moment, but nothing happens. No visions, no flashes—just my own hammering heart and the enforcer's predatory smile.

"This isn't working," I mutter.

"Because you're thinking too much," Ryker says. "Stop trying to force it. Let it come naturally."

"That's what I've been doing my whole life!" Frustration makes my voice sharp. "Waiting for visions to come naturally while people demand I produce them on command!"

Lithia's smile widens as she senses my distress. Without warning, she moves, a blur of speed leaving me no time to react. Her hand shoots out, grabbing my wrist and twisting, not hard enough to hurt but enough to demonstrate how easily she could.

"Too slow, seer," she taunts softly.

Pride stings, but before I can respond, Ryker is there. His hand wraps around Lithia's wrist, applying just enough pressure to make her release me.

"Again," he says, his voice carrying an edge of warning. "And remember who she is to me."

Lithia steps back, inclining her head in deference. But when her eyes meet mine, they hold a challenge that makes my blood heat.

"Again," Ryker repeats. "But this time, don't think about seeing. Feel it."

I take a steadying breath and focus on Lithia again. She resumes her circling, more cautious now but no less predatory.

"Close your eyes," Ryker instructs, surprising me.

"But then I can't—"

"Trust me," he cuts me off. "Close your eyes."

Reluctantly, I do as he asks, plunging myself into darkness. Immediately, my other senses heighten. I can hear Lithia's measured breathing, the soft pad of her feet against stone, the rustle of fabric as she moves.

"Now," Ryker says, his voice close to my ear, "reach for our bond."

The claiming mark pulses at his words. I focus on it, feeling the connection between us humming with energy.

"Our bond connects us on every level," he continues, his voice a low rumble that vibrates through me. "My strength flows to you through it. Use it. Anchor yourself in it."

I reach mentally for the bond, imagining it as a tether between us.

"Good," Ryker murmurs, and I feel his approval through the bond like sunshine on skin. "Now, keeping that anchor, reach for your gift. Invite it."

I've never thought of my visions as something to be invited rather than summoned or endured. The concept feels foreign but somehow right. I imagine my gift as a wild creature requiring coaxing rather than capture.

*Show me*, I think, focusing on Lithia's presence. *Help me see what she will do.*

For a moment, nothing happens. Then, like water seeping through cracks in stone, I feel it—the familiar shift in perception that precedes a vision. But unlike the painful flood that usually overwhelms me, this is controlled. Manageable.

The world behind my closed eyelids changes. I see Lithia, but she's moving in slow motion. I watch as she feints left, then shifts her weight to her right foot, preparing to—

My eyes snap open just as Lithia launches her attack—the same feint and right-side lunge I'd seen. Without conscious thought, I step to the left, neatly avoiding her grasp.

The chamber falls utterly silent.

Lithia recovers, surprise crossing her features before she masks it. "Lucky guess."

"That's good, Kitara," Ryker counters, and when I turn to look at him, I find his mismatched eyes blazing with triumph. "Try again."

The realization crashes over me. I did it. I called a vision deliberately, controlled what I saw and used it, all without pain.

"How?" I ask, staring at Ryker as if he might hold the answer.

"You stopped fighting your nature." His hand comes up to cup my face, thumb brushing my cheekbone. "Your gift isn't separate from you, Kitara. It's woven into everything you are."

"Again," I say, surprising myself with my eagerness.

Ryker's smile is slow and satisfied. "Lithia, continue. Dane, join her."

As the two enforcers move to circle me, I hesitate, my nerves catching up to my courage.

"What if that was a fluke?" I ask quietly. "What if I can't—"

Ryker steps closer, pressing his palm to the center of my back, fingers splayed wide. "Then we try again until it becomes natural. I'm not going anywhere."

I nod, then close my eyes. I reach first for our claiming bond. It's easier now—less effort and more instinct. Ryker's presence threads through me, steady and warm, grounding the chaos that usually threatens to unravel me.

I focus on Dane and Lithia, listening to the soft pad of their feet, feeling the shift in air as they circle me.

I focus, waiting for a blow but nothing comes. Frowning, I push toward my visions, searching for the same instinctive feeling that overtook me before. A headache blooms behind my eyes. My breathing stutters, and the familiar sharp edge of fear curls through my belly.

*I can't fail. Not now.*

The pressure builds. My hands shake as I try harder, pushing, straining, desperate to prove myself.

"Stop." Ryker's voice cuts through my panic.

I gasp, slumping. He catches me, his chest pressing against my back.

"Breathe," he instructs, holding me close. "Just breathe."

One of his hands settles over my racing heart, the other cups my forehead. Slowly, I calm, and the headache begins to recede.

"You're trying too hard," he murmurs against my ear. "You're forcing what should flow."

"But I—"

"Shh." His thumb strokes my temple. "Feel me through our bond. Let me guide you."

His presence wraps around me, strong and steady. Through our connection, I can sense his calm certainty, his patient strength. He's offering himself as an anchor.

"Don't grasp for your gift," he instructs softly. "This is not a desperate act, Kitara. It's already part of you. Like your heartbeat, like your breath."

I want to argue, to explain that it's never been like that for me, but I bite my tongue, desperate to try again.

"Watch first," he murmurs. "Lithia, Dane—demonstrate."

The two enforcers move until they're facing each other. Without warning, Lithia strikes—a blur of motion that would have caught me completely off guard. But Dane is already moving, sliding left as her practice blade cuts through empty air. He counters with a low sweep that she leaps over, landing in a crouch before spinning away from his follow-up strike.

They flow like water, each attack shifting into defense, each defense becoming an attack. There's a rhythm to it, a dance of violence that's almost beautiful.

"See how they move?" Ryker's voice is low in my ear. "They're not thinking about each strike. They're feeling the flow of combat, letting instinct guide them."

Lithia feints right, then strikes left, but Dane is already turning, his blade meeting hers with a sharp crack. They separate, circling each other like predators.

"Your turn," Ryker says. "Let them circle you. Don't think. Just feel."

His hands settle on my shoulders, grounding me. He signals to Lithia and Dane, who begin to circle us, their movements predatory and smooth. I close my eyes, trying to do as Ryker instructed, to feel rather than force.

And then... there it is. Not the violent visions I'm used to, but one far gentler. A knowing that encourages me to move.

I open my eyes and shift, as Lithia's practice blade whistles through the air where my head would have been.

"Excellent," Ryker murmurs. "Again."

The knowing feeling comes easier now. I sidestep Dane's strike, duck under Lithia's swing, feeling their movements a heartbeat before they happen.

"Better," Lithia calls out. "But you'll need to be faster if you want to avoid getting pinned like a fish."

I successfully avoid three more attacks before falling under Lithia's fist. My head spins as I lie staring up at the ceiling, wondering how I got there.

"Sorry, Alpha," she says, laughter in her voice as she helps me up. "Did I scramble your brains?"

I press a hand to the throbbing in my temple. "Maybe a little."

"That's enough for today," Ryker announces, cupping my cheeks in his hands as he examines me.

"I can keep going," I protest, feeling alive for the first time in my life. The sensation is intoxicating.

"No, you've had enough for today," Ryker announces. "We don't want to overtax a new muscle."

The gathered wolves disperse, but not before I catch their evaluating looks.

When we're alone in the circle of light, Ryker leans down to nuzzle my neck.

"You did well," he says, dragging his lips over my pulse point.

"Thank you." I tip my head, surprised that I'm enjoying his attention. "You really helped me."

His fingers trace the claiming mark on my throat, sending sparks of heat radiating from the touch. "The bond works both ways, little mate. My power flows to you, but your gift adds to mine as well." His lips trail down to my collarbone. "Together, we are stronger than either of us alone."

My breath catches. Through our bond, I feel his pride, his satisfaction, and beneath that, a hunger that has nothing to do with training and everything to do with carnal need.

"Is that why you sought a mate?" I ask, needing to know. "For the power a bond creates?"

His laugh is dark honey. "I have no need of a mate. But I saw you, my wolf knew you were ours." He shifts backward, standing straight as he slides a hand to cup the back of my neck. "The power is a bonus, sure. But make no mistake, Kitara—I would have taken no mate but you."

I'm not sure I believe him, but I want to—badly. His thumb strokes the sensitive skin beneath my ear, making me shiver.

"We'll keep working on this, and tomorrow we'll start measuring what distance you can achieve," he says, shifting to more practical conversation topics, though his touch remains intimate. "We need to make sure you're fighting fit if the worse should happen."

I don't need to ask what worse might mean; I've already foreseen blood and battle.

"Okay." My easy response seems to please him.

"Good girl." His praise sends heat pooling between my thighs.

His thumb strokes the skin beneath my ear, and I shiver, the sensation shooting straight down my spine. He leans in again, and this time I meet him halfway, our bodies brushing —his chest against mine—our breaths tangling.

I don't know who moves first. Maybe it's both of us. But suddenly we're pressed together, mouths colliding in a kiss that's all heat and hunger and dangerous desire. His hand tangles in my hair, mine fisting in the fabric at his back.

The bond flares between us, bright and consuming, and I feel his restraint slipping.

Ryker groans, deep in his throat, and abruptly pulls back. His breathing is ragged, eyes blown wide with need.

"Fuck," he mutters, dragging a hand through his hair. "We keep this up, I'm going to forget we're still in the training ring."

I blink, dazed. Lips swollen. Body thrumming.

"Is that a bad thing?"

He grits his teeth. "Are you really ready for me to claim you?"

I swallow, desire now at war with fear.

"That's what I thought." He turns away, running a hand over his hair. "Go explore your chambers, Kitara. Examine Cheyenne's things. Or get one of the wolves to show you around our den."

"Where will you be?"

Seemingly back in control, he turns full to me. "I have pack business to attend to."

"Can I come? Can I help?"

He chuckles. "Not yet. I've no control around you and more work will be made than achieved." He brushes a stray strand of hair behind my ear. "Soon, though. I promise."

His words only slightly soften the blow.

# CHAPTER
# ELEVEN

After the training session, exhaustion and hunger gnaw at me. I follow the mouthwatering scent of food through the winding stone corridors. Unlike the polished formality of my old pack's dining hall, which is rarely used, this space is bustling and alive with energy. Stone tables of various heights fill the room, with some designated areas designed for wolves who prefer to eat in their animal forms. Torches and crystal formations provide warm, dancing light that create pockets of intimacy despite the hall's size.

I hesitate at the entrance. In my old pack, mealtimes were taken alone unless during special occasions. When we did have a feast, the eating order was rigidly hierarchical— omegas and "undesirables" like me ate last, often receiving only scraps, while Alpha Varick and his inner sanctum gorged on fresh kills, sweet desserts, and multiple courses perfectly cooked.

Now, all eyes turn to me, conversations hushing. I'm suddenly aware of my status, the Alpha's mate, marked and claimed, yet still a stranger.

A tall wolf with auburn hair rises from a nearby table and

approaches. His movement is measured, deliberate, his eyes —a striking amber—are assessing but not hostile.

"Alpha Female," he greets with a slight bow of his head. "I'm Elias, head of security. Second to Lithia."

"Please, call me Kitara," I say, feeling awkward in the silence that's fallen over the hall.

His smile is surprisingly warm. "Of course. Welcome, Kitara." He gestures toward a raised platform where a single table sits. "The Alpha's table awaits you."

The elevated table, carved from dark stone, is set a few steps above the rest of the dining hall. From here, it commands the room. It's a show of dominance and separation, a visible reminder that the one who sits there leads.

I glance around, noting the wolves sharing meals and laughter, their bodies pressed close as stories fly back and forth across the long benches.

I look back to the black table, my stomach twisting.

*I hate it.*

My wolf stirs, watching with sharp, steady eyes. *We are pack. We should not be separate.*

I agree. *I don't want to be stared at.*

*Then be with the pack.*

Relief curls in my chest as I turn to Elias. "If it's okay, could I join you?"

Surprise flickers across his face, followed by a look that might be approval. "Of course." He indicates his table, where several wolves watch our interaction with undisguised curiosity.

The choice feels significant somehow, my first real decision as Alpha Female. I nod, following him back to his table. The wolves seated there rise in respect, though their expressions range from open interest to careful neutrality.

"My hunting unit," Elias explains. "Zella, our tracker." He indicates a woman with pale-cream skin, delicate features, and warm-chestnut hair that frames her face in soft waves. Her eyes, a striking forest green, light up with genuine warmth when they meet mine. She offers a brilliant smile that immediately puts me at ease.

"Heath, weapons master." A massive Black man with a bald head and scar bisecting his left eyebrow nods solemnly. His shoulders are broader than Ryker's, though he lacks the alpha's predatory grace.

"And Kaden, our resident troublemaker." Said with a gesture toward a lean wolf with mischief in his green eyes and silver-streaked-black hair that seems at odds with his tan, youthful face.

"I prefer comedian," Kaden corrects with an easy grin that reveals slightly crooked canines. "Someone has to keep things interesting around here."

I slide onto the bench, hyperaware of the space they make for me. In Silvercrest, no one would have willingly sat beside me.

"We saw your training session," Zella says, leaning forward with an encouraging smile as she helps herself to what looks like roasted venison from a central platter. "Very impressive."

I blink in surprise at her unexpected praise. "You were there?"

"Even if we weren't we already know about it," Kaden says, pushing a plate toward me. His movements are casual but there's an intensity to his gaze when it meets mine. "For most it's our first time seeing a seer work. Plus, you know, curiosity about the Alpha's new mate."

Zella gently nudges a basket of freshly baked bread in my direction. "You have to be starving after that workout. The kitchen made blackberry honey butter today—it's perfect on the warm bread."

I take the plate, unsure how to respond. Through the

claiming bond, I sense Ryker's distant awareness spike. I force myself to calm, turning away from his questing mind.

*I need to stand on my own.*

"What they're failing to say," comes a new voice, cool and precise, "is that they wanted to see if you're worthy of the Alpha's mark."

A slim woman slides onto the bench across from me. Unlike the others, who wear jeans or sweats suited for hunting and fighting, she's dressed as if she's about to go to a party. Her coppery hair is pulled into severe braids, while her deep-burgundy dress complements her milky skin perfectly.

"Sara," Elias acknowledges, his tone neutral but with an undercurrent of tension. "I didn't realize you were joining us."

"Of course I am," she replies, her eyes never leaving mine. "I'm the pack historian and record-keeper. Your claiming is the first time a Shadowmist alpha has taken a mate who can't shift. It's a historic event."

There's something in her tone, not quite hostility, but a clinical detachment that makes me feel like a specimen being examined. I straighten my spine, meeting her gaze directly.

"It's a pleasure to meet you."

"We'll see."

Kaden chokes slightly on his drink, eyes widening at her boldness. Heath's massive hand tightens around his fork, while Zella watches the interaction with sharp interest.

"Sara," Elias says, his voice carrying a warning.

She shrugs one elegant shoulder. "I merely speak what others think. Our pack survives on strength. The Alpha's mate must embody that strength."

My wolf stirs, her teeth baring. *I don't like this one.*

*Me either.*

"Are you saying strength only comes in one form?" I ask, surprised by the steadiness in my voice. I reach for some food, trying to appear casual as I serve myself venison and roasted vegetables. "That only fangs and claws matter?"

"They've kept us alive for centuries," she counters. "History shows that seers rarely bring anything but trouble with them."

An uncomfortable silence falls over the table. I can feel other wolves watching, listening, gauging my response. This has become as much a test as the training session.

I spear a piece of meat, chewing slowly as I consider her statement.

The meat is tender, perfectly seasoned—someone's worked hard on this meal.

"Tell me," I continue, voice soft but pointed, "when an elder can no longer hunt, does their worth to the pack vanish?"

Sara frowns, her brow furrowing. "Of course not."

"Why?"

"Because they hold knowledge. Wisdom. They guide the young. Teach the old ways."

"And when a wolf is injured, what value do they hold?"

She bristles. "Of course they are valued by the pack. They might serve as advisors or makers, looking after children or helping the frail. There's always a place in our pack."

I nod, swallowing another mouthful of perfectly seasoned meat. "In my experience, what makes a pack strong isn't just fangs and claws. It's the bonds between us." I see the understanding flicker across her face but continue to gently make my point. "The elder who comforts a frightened pup. The injured wolf who shares hard-won wisdom. The ones who can't fight but tend the hearths, keeping home fires burning for those who do. Strength comes from many places. Compassion creates loyalty. Kindness builds trust. Without those bonds, a pack might survive—but it will never thrive."

Kaden lets out a low whistle, leaning back in his seat.

Even Heath's stoic expression cracks slightly with the tiniest flick of a smile.

Sara studies me for a long moment, then inclines her head in acknowledgment. "Well said, Alpha Female."

"Tell me about your records," I say, genuinely curious. "What exactly does your pack know about seers?"

"Less than we should," comes another voice, and I turn to find a weathered older woman approaching our table. Her once-black hair is now mostly silver, but her movements remain fluid and strong. Deep lines mark a face that has seen decades of pack life, and her eyes—an unusual amber gold— hold wisdom and assessment in equal measure.

The respect with which the others make room for her tells me this is someone of significance.

"Elder Lyra," Elias greets her, bowing his head deeply.

"Save the formalities for public ceremonies." She waves him off, settling her gaze on me. "So you're the seer who's turned our pack upside down."

I swallow hard. "I didn't intend to cause disruption."

Her laugh is unexpectedly bright. "Disruption is precisely what this pack needs. Stagnation kills faster than any enemy." She studies me openly, her gaze lingering on my claiming mark. "The Alpha chose well. Though many still doubt."

"With respect, Elder," Sara interjects, "the concern isn't about the Alpha's choice, but about what her presence means for our future. A broken seer is hardly a threat. The Grand Alpha won't—"

I flinch. The word *broken* lands like a brand. I've heard it all before, of course. Broken, damaged, useless. Only good for my visions. My old pack treated me as if I were a half-wolf just because I couldn't shift.

I shouldn't be surprised or hurt, but I am. Ryker treating me as a whole being doesn't wash away the perceptions others have of me.

"The Grand Alpha, bah!" Lyra cuts her off sharply.

"Thaddeus has been looking for an excuse to bring us to heel for decades. He'll simply use the Alpha Female as his latest excuse." Her gaze returns to me. "No offense intended, child."

"None taken," I assure her. "You're right. I think Thaddeus wanted me claimed by someone he could control."

"And instead, you were claimed by the one wolf he fears most," Lyra says with evident satisfaction. "It seems the Moon Goddess has different plans for you."

I rise, gesturing at the seat next to mine. "Will you join us?"

She quickly settles in next to me, patting my arm. "You're a good girl. You'll do well."

The conversation shifts as food is passed around, but I notice how the others defer to Lyra, seeking her opinions, respecting her wisdom. She must have been formidable in her prime—still is, judging by the sharpness of her mind and the strength evident in her movements despite her age.

Unfortunately, age has also brought with it a directness that doesn't hold back.

"How are you settling into the bond, child?" Lyra asks. "The first heat often comes within the week for strong matches like yours."

I blink, caught off guard. "The first... what?"

Lyra tilts her head, expression unreadable. "Heat. It's nature's way of reinforcing the bond—especially when the connection is deep and the pairing is powerful. Surely you know. It's the calling of the wolf from one mate to the other. A female goes into sexual heat and the male must answer her call."

My cheeks flush instantly, heat climbing my neck. "Oh. I— uh, that's... unlikely, given I've never shifted."

Lyra lifts one eyebrow, amused. "And why would that matter?"

"I don't think it works the same for me. Nothing else ever has."

"Mm." Lyra leans back. "We'll see."

"You should join us for the full moon gathering," Kaden suggests, changing the subject. He twirls the liquid in his cup with the lazy familiarity of someone used to nursing their drinks. "It's three nights from now."

"I'd be allowed?" In the Silvercrest Pack, I'd been prohibited from attending moon ceremonies, my human form considered an affront to sacred rituals.

"The pack runs together," Zella says, touching my arm with gentle reassurance. "We hunt together. It's tradition." Her eyes sparkle with genuine excitement. "It's magnificent, all of us under the moon. Even the pups attend. You'll love it."

"But I can't—"

"So you'll watch," Kaden shrugs, his easy smile returning. "From what I hear, you're good at that." He wiggles his eyebrows suggestively.

There's a groan around the table, and my cheeks flush at his implication.

"Ow!" Kaden jumps, rubbing the back of his head. "Lyra!"

"Your parents should be ashamed of you," she tells him primly.

"I'll stay with you," Zella offers. "I can guide you through the evening. No one should experience their first Shadowmist moon ceremony alone."

"I've never been allowed to attend a run before," I admit.

Lyra's expression hardens. "Silvercrest always was a pack of nitwits." She fixes me with a pointed look. "Everyone belongs at such gatherings, especially the Alpha Female."

As the meal continues, I find myself relaxing. The conversation flows around me, sometimes including me, sometimes moving to pack matters beyond my knowledge. I observe the dynamics carefully, Elias's quiet authority,

Heath's grudging participation, Kaden's carefully crafted lightness that seems to mask a sharper intelligence than he first presents.

Zella proves especially attentive, ensuring my plate is never empty and skillfully steering the conversation toward topics that might provide me with an insight into my new pack. There's something inherently likable about her, a genuine warmth that stands out among the more reserved Shadowmist wolves.

"You should join me on a perimeter walk sometime," she suggests during a lull in the conversation. "I know all the best viewpoints in our territory. And it would give us a chance to talk more... privately." She glances around the table with a conspiratorial smile. "Away from all this testosterone."

Sara remains reserved but engaged, her historian's mind evident in how she catalogs information and references past events. And Lyra, the elder, commands respect without demanding it, her perspectives carrying the weight of experience and trust.

I'm so absorbed in these observations that I nearly miss the new arrival until a shadow falls across our table. The conversations halt as a tall, imposing male approaches. His dark hair is pulled back from a face that is startlingly good-looking. Unlike the others, whose power feels contained, his radiates outward aggressively, demanding recognition.

*Beta,* my wolf whispers. *Would-be Alpha.*

"Levi," Elias acknowledges, his tone carefully neutral.

I tense at the newcomer's dominating presence, his energy so different from the others I've met.

"So the rumors are true," the newcomer says, his eyes raking over me with undisguised assessment. "The Alpha has taken a human as mate."

"Watch your tongue," Lyra warns. "She bears your Alpha's mark."

"A mark wasted on skin that can't shift," he retorts.

There's calculation in his gaze that I don't like at all. "The Shadowmist bloodline deserves better."

Even though my stomach is far fuller than it's ever been, I force myself to lift a final forkful to my lips, chewing slowly as if his words have no power over me.

Lyra watches me, her gaze narrowed. "Have you nothing to say to this welp?"

"No," I say, drawing on every ounce of courage I have. "I don't know him, and I don't care to. I never asked for his opinion on my worthiness, therefore it is of no value."

A surprised laugh escapes Kaden, quickly smothered.

"She has fire, at least," Levi concedes, his lip curling slightly. "Only time will tell if that will compensate for her limitations."

"Perhaps you should concern yourself with your own limitations," comes Ryker's voice, cold and dangerous, from directly behind Levi.

The entire hall falls silent as the alpha stalks through the doors. He moves across the room to stand behind me, his hands coming to rest possessively on my shoulders. Through our bond, I feel his tightly controlled fury.

"Alpha," Levi acknowledges, bowing his head though his posture remains stiff. "I meant no disrespect to you."

"But you meant it toward my mate," Ryker's voice is deceptively soft. "Which is the same thing."

A tense silence stretches between them. I can feel the power dynamics shifting, other wolves watching with bated breath. This confrontation carries meaning beyond the immediate moment. It's about establishing boundaries, about Ryker making clear where I stand in the pack hierarchy.

"My apologies, Alpha Female," Levi finally says, the words extracted rather than sincere. "I spoke without appropriate consideration."

I incline my head slightly, neither fully accepting nor

rejecting his apology. There's a whisper of Ryker's voice in the back of my mind.

*Nicely done.*

"See that it doesn't happen again," Ryker says, his hands squeezing my shoulders gently. "Remember this the next time you question my mate's worth—you're questioning my judgment as Alpha. Consider carefully if that's a challenge you wish to make."

Levi's jaw tightens, but he bows his head deeper. "Understood, Alpha."

As he retreats, the tension in the hall gradually dissolves, conversations resuming in hushed tones. Ryker slides onto the bench beside me, his thigh pressing against mine, his presence a tangible claim of territory.

"Making friends?" he murmurs, just loud enough for those at our table to hear.

"I hope so," I reply honestly.

He leans in, his lips a fraction of an inch from mine. His smile is slow and predatory. Languid heat pools in my belly, and I wait for him to kiss me—heart thudding, breath caught.

Instead, he swipes a piece of venison clean off my plate with his fingers and pops it into his mouth.

"Hey!" I protest, sharper than I intended. "I was saving that."

He grins, unrepentant. "You're full."

My hand tightens around the edge of the table as I try not to allow my distress to transmit through our bond. "I just— no, you're right. You should eat."

His brow furrows slightly, but he keeps his voice teasing. "Kitara, there's more meat in the kitchens."

"I know," I lie, looking everywhere but at him.

Intellectually, I do know there's more food in their kitchens. That no one's going to yank the bowl away from me or ration out my portions with suspicion.

But knowing it doesn't change the instinct.

I've learned that lesson far too many times. Food is precious. Scarcity is real. And having extra stored away means I'll rarely go to bed with a gnawing, empty stomach—something I did far too often as a pup. Hunger carves its habits deep.

"Kitara," Ryker says, his voice low, "tell me you do know you have free access to everything in this pack."

I lift my head, forcing myself to meet his gaze.

His eyes aren't hard. They're not angry, not even a little. There's no judgment in them, just a deep, quiet understanding that somehow cuts even deeper.

He sees me.

"I know," I say again, forcing myself to sound casual. "I was just playing."

The other wolves are watching our interplay, judging us.

"Do you want more venison?" Ryker asks slowly.

He's angry at what was done to me. I can feel it simmering under the surface like a storm held back on my behalf.

I should feel shame or fear; instead, his anger feels safe.

I shake my head. "No, you eat." I push my plate toward him. "Please."

He accepts, still watching me as he begins to bring his fork to his mouth. I turn from him to Lyra, forcing myself to act naturally.

"Tell me, Elder, what was the Alpha like as a pup?"

"Ryker?" Her eyes twinkle with amusement. "A little shit, truth be told."

I snort, delighted.

Ryker groans. "I'll thank you not to fill my mate's head with lies, Lyra."

"Your mate deserves to know what she's gotten herself into," Lyra says primly, but there's a wicked twinkle in her eye. "Used to steal pies right out of the oven and blame it on the younger pups. Had everyone convinced poor Finn was possessed."

"That's hardly a crime," Ryker mutters, stabbing a piece of meat with more aggression than necessary.

"Not a crime, my ass," Lyra fires back. "You tried to stage a coup at age nine because someone told you pups didn't have to bathe and yet there you were every night, being forced into a bath against your will."

A chorus of laughter bubbles around the table.

"Did it work?" I ask, grinning at Ryker.

"Temporarily," Lyra deadpans. "Until he got tackled into the river."

"I was making a point," Ryker says, biting into the venison like it personally offended him.

"A stinking point," Lyra adds, patting his arm fondly.

The tension in my chest loosens. But it's replaced by a new ache, one that wishes I could be part of this easy history and laughter someday.

*You already are*, my wolf tells me.

I don't correct her. Her concept of pack dynamics is vastly different than my own.

As the meal continues, I observe how Ryker's presence changes the dynamics. Sara becomes more formal, Elias more deferential. But the others are at ease, treating Ryker with respect but easy familiarity.

His interaction with his pack is so different from my experience that I find it hard to reconcile that he is the alpha. He's not obeyed out of fear, but followed out of respect. My mate is well-liked. He doesn't command loyalty. He *earns* it.

*We chose well*, my wolf tells me.

*We had no say in our choosing*, I answer her dryly.

The one dark spot on my meal is Levi. I notice him watching from across the hall, his expression unreadable. When our eyes meet briefly, he doesn't look away. Instead, he inclines his head fractionally, acknowledgment without submission.

*Remember his face*, my wolf whispers. *Remember his scent, his manner, his place in the pack.*

I file the impression away carefully, uncertain why it's important but trusting her intuition nonetheless.

As the meal winds down, Ryker's hand settles at the small of my back, warm and possessive. "Training continues tomorrow," he says, his voice pitched for my ears alone. "Tonight, you rest."

I glance at him. "Do you have a busy afternoon?"

He tangles his fingers in my hair. "Back-to-back meetings with packs who weren't represented at the Claiming—they're also not fans of Thaddeus. I'm optimistic we might come to some kind of allied agreement."

"Do you want me there?"

"Not today. I'd rather you familiarize yourself with the pack before I throw you into the political mess that is pack dynamics."

I chuckle, rising with him. "You'd be surprised what I know about pack dynamics. Varick was a particular fan of me spying during important meetings. He thought it would help my vision."

"Did it?" Ryker asks, gathering cutlery and plates. I help him, collecting my own ensemble of items.

"When my visions showed political discussions I wouldn't have otherwise understood."

He chuckles. "Are they meant to be understood? Sometimes it feels like I'm speaking in circles."

I lift my pile of plates and follow him toward the kitchens, acutely aware of the eyes following our departure. This has been my first real introduction to the pack and its complex web of relationships and power dynamics that will shape my life here.

"In my experience good leadership isn't about who speaks

the loudest," I say as we stack the plates near the wash bins. "It's about who listens best. Most alphas I've watched treat politics like a performance. They posture and puff, and forget the fundamental reason they're in the room together."

"And that is?" Ryker asks, sliding cutlery into a standing basket.

"Their role is to be a service to the pack."

He hums his agreement. "And that is the hardest part of my role—knowing what will be best for the pack."

I lay a hand on his arm. "From what I've seen, you're doing an excellent job."

His gaze meets mine, and in a flash a vision hits me—this one isn't of a future or a past, it's of a desire unspoken.

Ryker doesn't want a mate. He wants a partner.

The vision releases me, and I blink, shaking my head.

"Are you okay?" he asks, balancing me with one hand on my shoulder.

"Yeah, I just..." I don't know what to say. I want to be what he desires—more than anything. But I know in my heart I can't. I'm in all ways his inferior. "It's nothing," I lie, forcing a bright smile. "Shall we go?"

He hesitates, and I tense, wondering if he'll push. Instead, he captures my hand in his, intertwining our fingers.

As we walk back toward our chambers, Ryker's hand remains in mine, his presence both protection and possession.

"Your thoughts are loud," he murmurs. "Tell me what troubles you, Kitara."

"I'm just processing," I reply honestly. "This place is so different to where I grew up."

"Is that a bad thing?"

I laugh. "Not at all. Back there no one wanted to hear from me unless I had a vision to share. Here, all you seem to want me to do is share."

His growl is low, barely audible but vibrating through his entire chest. "That life is over. No one silences you."

"Not even you?" I can't help asking.

His laugh is dark and rich. "Especially not me." He glances at me and the heat in his gaze makes my cheeks flush. "Though I might ask your silence for other reasons sometimes."

A thought slips through the bond between us—me crouched before him, staring up at him, as I lean forward, my mouth open and ready for his—

"Sorry," he mutters, shutting down the thought. "I didn't mean for you to see that."

I swallow, fighting the drag of desire his thoughts sparked in me. "That's okay. I..." I don't know what else to say, but I'm saved from saying anything by a man calling Ryker's name.

"Alpha," the young wolf interrupts. "We need you urgently. It seems Genop and Rue are at it again."

With a sigh, Ryker presses a kiss to my temple and lets me go.

"Rest," he orders over his shoulder. "I'll see you tonight."

I watch him go, my fingers absently brushing the spot where his lips touched my temple.

*What have I gotten myself into?*

# TWELVE

Over the next three days, our training sessions intensify. Each morning, Ryker and I work in the East Chamber, refining my control over the visions. Each afternoon, I work with Lyra to learn to read the journals, absorbing Cheyenne's wisdom. The pattern is broken only by meals shared with the pack, where I'm gradually becoming a recognized—if not yet fully accepted—presence.

Zella has become a friend, often finding me between training sessions to share pack stories or offer insights into Shadowmist customs. Her easy warmth is welcome after so long without any kind of friendship.

"The full moon ceremony is tonight," she says as we walk along one of the upper corridors overlooking the main cavern. "Are you nervous?"

"A little," I admit. In the Silvercrest Pack, I'd spent every full moon locked away, forbidden from participating in what they considered sacred rituals. "I'm not sure what to expect."

Her smile is reassuring. "It's beautiful. The entire pack gathers at the rocks. We shift, we run, we hunt together under the moon's blessing." She hesitates. "I know you can't shift, but—"

"Ryker has made arrangements. I'll be joining you in the run."

Curiosity flashes in her eyes, but she doesn't press. "Well, whatever happens, I'll be there if you need anything." She squeezes my arm gently. "That's what pack is for."

The simple gesture of inclusion nearly undoes me. After a lifetime of rejection, these small moments of acceptance feel almost too precious to bear.

"Thank you," I manage, my voice rougher than intended.

She seems about to say more when a shadow falls across us. We turn to find Lithia approaching, her scarred face impassive but her silver eyes alert.

"Alpha Female." Despite my efforts, she's maintained a professional distance. Not hostile, but not friendly either. "The Alpha requests your presence."

I nod, touching Zella's arm in farewell before following Lithia through the winding corridors. She moves with predatory grace, her footsteps nearly silent on the stone floor.

"How are the patrols?" I ask, attempting conversation.

Her gaze flicks to me, surprise briefly visible. "Doubled on the northern boundary. Increased along the river territories." She hesitates, then adds, "No sign of any further forces since the tunnel attack."

"That doesn't mean they've given up."

"No," she agrees. "It means they're planning something bigger."

We fall silent as she leads me to a part of the den I haven't visited before. It sits well away from the main den, down a long corridor that slowly tilts down. I follow her as the passage narrows, forcing us to walk single file until it opens into a room quite unlike any I've yet seen.

It's a round room, the stone walls rough and covered in vines and moss. Where a ceiling should be, instead there is a hole open to the sky—a natural oculus. Afternoon sunlight streams through, illuminating a pool of crystal-clear water at the chamber's heart. The pool's surface is unnaturally still, reflecting the light like a perfect mirror. Around its circumference, ancient runes are carved into the stone floor, their patterns flowing in spirals toward the water.

Ryker stands at the pool's edge, his back to us, power radiating from him in almost visible waves. He wears only loose black pants, his upper body bare. His hands rest on an ornate stone bowl positioned at the pool's rim.

His scent seems stronger today, more distracting. My wolf stirs under skin, demanding I press close to him.

*Settle*, I admonish.

She bares her teeth but does as directed, though she's still on edge.

"Alpha," Lithia announces our presence, though I'm certain Ryker's aware of exactly when we entered. Through our bond, I feel his focus—sharp, intense, tinged with an emotion I can't quite name.

"Leave us," he says without turning.

Lithia bows and withdraws, the sound of her footsteps fading quickly.

I approach slowly, drawn to Ryker yet cautious of disturbing whatever ritual I've interrupted. The stone beneath my feet feels charged, humming with an ancient power that makes the fine hairs on my arms stand on end.

"What is this place?" I ask softly.

"The Vision Well," he answers, finally turning to face me. His mismatched eyes gleam with reflected light from the pool. "It's where Shadowmist seers have come for generations to seek clarity when ordinary visions have failed."

I glance at the still water, feeling its pull. "Cheyenne used this?"

"Yes." A look flickers across his face—old pain, quickly

masked. "It was her sanctuary." He gestures to the elaborate bowl. "And this was her scrying vessel."

"She had one in the other room too," I murmur, remembering the smaller bowl.

Ryker nods. "That one was for regular readings. This…" He glances around the cavern. "This is different. When a seer's power wasn't enough, when the visions were too clouded or dangerous, they came here."

I move closer, examining the bowl. It's carved from a single piece of black stone, its interior polished to mirror brightness. Symbols similar to those on the floor encircle its rim, though these are inlaid with what looks like gold.

"It's beautiful," I murmur.

"It's dangerous," he corrects, his hand covering mine as I reach toward it. "The Well amplifies a seer's gift, but at a cost."

The warning in his voice is unmistakable. "What cost?"

"Control." His fingers tighten on mine. "Once you enter a vision here, it doesn't release you until it's shown what you need to see—whether you're ready for it or not."

I swallow hard, remembering the visions that had nearly broken me in the Silvercrest Pack. "Why show me this now?"

"Because tonight is the full moon. Our first ceremony together." His expression softens slightly. "And because you're getting stronger. Your control is improving faster than I expected."

Pride blooms in my chest at his acknowledgment. Over the past days, I've learned to summon visions without pain, to direct my sight toward specific targets, to remain conscious and functional even as the images flow through me.

"Thank you for—" I begin.

"Don't thank me for what's rightfully yours," he interrupts, his thumb brushing my pulse point. "Your gift was always meant to be used this way."

The familiar anger he feels that surfaces whenever he

references my treatment in the Silvercrest Pack ripples through our bond. Just as quickly as it arrives, he pushes it away, hiding it from me.

*I wish he wouldn't. I wish he'd let me see everything.*

"Tonight," he continues, "you'll be formally presented to the pack as my mate."

My stomach tightens with nervousness. "I've never attended a full moon ceremony before. I don't know the traditions—"

"You'll be with me," he says simply, as if that resolves all concerns. And in a way, it does. "I'll carry you."

The image forms in my mind. Ryker in his massive wolf form, me on his back. The Alpha Female who can't shift, carried by her mate's strength.

"Will they accept that?"

"They'll accept what I decree." The words carry absolute authority, but he softens them by adding, "The Alpha Female attends all ceremonies. That you can't shift is irrelevant."

His certainty eases some of my anxiety. Through our bond, I feel his confidence flowing into me like warm honey, steadying my nerves.

"I've brought you here for another reason," he says, gesturing toward the Vision Well. "The full moon strengthens a seer's gift. Combined with the Well's power, it might let us see what Thaddeus or the other packs are up to."

For a second, I freeze.

His words are soft, gentle even, but I recoil. My jaw tightens. My spine locks. Suddenly I'm back in Varick's chamber, eyes ringed with shadows, throat raw from screaming through a forced vision while he stood watching, satisfied.

My heartbeat spikes. My instinct is to step back, to shut down. To do as I've been told.

But then I feel it—his regret and his concern.

"I… sorry," I say quietly, forcing air back into my lungs. "I thought—I thought you were going to force me to—"

Ryker's gaze darkens, not with anger, but with fury on my behalf.

"I'm not," he says. "And I never will."

It's a struggle, but I lock down my fears. "You want me to scry the Grand Alpha. You want me to see if he's planning another attack." It's a statement rather than a question.

Ryker nods slowly. "Thaddeus won't let our rebellion stand. I'm sure he's gathering forces and building alliances. I'm sorry to ask this of you, but I'm operating at a deficit. Our spies have gone silent, and anyone we've sent since hasn't made any inroad into Thaddeus's inner sanctum."

I study the still water.

"I don't ask this of you lightly, Kitara. And unlike your former Alpha, I won't force visions from you. This is your choice. There's no pressure here."

The distinction means more than he can possibly know. For so long, my gift has been something others demanded I use, regardless of the cost to me. To be given a choice, to be asked rather than commanded, feels revolutionary.

"No," I say, wanting to see his reaction. I don't raise my voice, don't lash out, but the word lands heavy between us.

Without a beat, he nods once. "Okay."

No challenge. No persuasion. Just… acceptance.

And gods, that undoes me. Not because he gave in, but because he *meant* it.

I study him, heart beating fast, throat tight. No one's ever heard my "no" before without turning it into a reason to push harder. To punish. To pry.

But Ryker takes my answer in his stride, making no efforts to change my mind. It's a heady powerful thing to realize that someone respects you enough to honor your choice.

I know that Ryker is different. He's not like the others who've only cared about their own desires, their own amusement. In this small moment, it dawns on me that he might actually care about me. About how I feel. The realization rocks me to my core, shaking the very foundations of everything I've ever known.

A slither of relief slides between us—but it's from his side.

"Wait. Why are you relieved?"

He curses under his breath. "I'd hoped you'd miss that."

"Ryker."

"It's dangerous."

I shrug. "Everything here is dangerous. Including you."

His eyes darken. "Especially me." He steps closer, deliberately invading my space. "But you're not afraid of me anymore, are you, little wolf?"

"Should I be?"

"Always." His voice drops to that rumbling register that does things to my insides I refuse to acknowledge. "But that doesn't stop you from wanting to touch, does it?"

I lift my chin, refusing to back down this time. "You're being terribly arrogant."

"And yet you want me."

I open my mouth to deny it but decide to change the subject instead. "Answer my question."

He sighs, running a hand through his hair. "Pack law requires me to ask all those who can help to do so. But I don't want you within spitting distance of this cesspit."

"Why?"

"This place can destroy you. It happened to our last seer. She became so enamored with the visions that she never surfaced. Her body slowly wasted away."

I grimace. "And you think that would happen to me?"

"I don't know. But I'd rather not risk it."

I glance over at the pool, watching the light dance across the water. "What happens if I want to, though?"

He stills. "But you don't, so let's not have this conversation."

"Humor me."

Ryker growls under his breath. "The mechanics are simple, you float in the water. When your gift connects with the Vision Well, you'll go into a trance. Once in that state, you don't just see—you *search*. Your mind moves like a shadow through the world, slipping through cracks, chasing threads."

"So I'm not just seeing what's shown to me," I murmur. "I'm able to look for something specific."

He nods. "Exactly. Intentions, plans, memories, secrets. You scry until something catches."

I move to the edge of the pool, watching the water ripple gently in the soft breeze. "That's a powerful gift."

"It's also a dangerous one."

My wolf scratches her neck, yawning. *We could do it. The last seer didn't have a mate.*

I frown. "Did the last seer have a mate?"

Ryker shakes his head. "No. He was killed before the claiming could be completed."

*She became lost in memories. Her love kept her tethered. Yours will free you.*

I frown at my wolf.

*I'm not in love with Ryker.*

She huffs, then curls into a ball, turning her back to me.

"I'll do it," I say, surprising all of us.

"What?"

I glance at Ryker. "I'll do it. I'll scry."

"No."

I roll my eyes. "Yes. You said it was my choice. I'm making it. I want to help the pack."

"Kitara, no. I won't let you—"

I lay a hand on his chest, halting him.

"Ryker, trust that I can do this. Unlike Cheyenne, I have a mate to keep me tethered to this reality. If anyone can save me, it will be you."

A muscle in his jaw pulses as if he's fighting to stop the

words he wants to say. Finally, he speaks. "I did my duty by asking this of you. I'm regretting that decision."

I grin, knowing I've won. "You can regret it if it fails."

He mumbles something under this breath that sounds a lot like "stubborn mate," then drops his hand to my waist.

"We'll do this if you'll allow me to guide you through it." His gaze meets mine, serious and intent. "If I say we need to end it, we end it. No questions, no protests. You understand?"

I nod.

"Fucking hell." He runs a hand through his hair once more. "I can't believe I'm letting this happen. God damn it."

I lean into him. "It'll be fine, Ryker. You watch."

"It better be." He huffs out a sigh. "Kitara, before you do this, there's something you should know about Thaddeus. About why his hatred for me runs so deep."

I wait, sensing the importance of whatever he's about to reveal.

"Thaddeus Solomon is my father."

# THIRTEEN

The words hang in the air between us, heavy with implication. I stare at him, searching his face for signs of deception and finding none.

"Your father?" I echo, struggling to process the revelation. "Thaddeus is your—but—"

"Why does he want me dead?" Ryker's laugh holds no humor. "He doesn't know."

He turns back to the Vision Well, his reflection fractured by ripples that seem to form without cause.

"My mother was an alpha, born to the Grayback Pack. Thaddeus was already Grand Alpha when he met her during territory negotiations." Ryker's voice takes on a distant quality, as if reciting a story told many times. "He became obsessed with her, convinced that combining her blood with his alpha line would create offspring of unprecedented power."

My heart aches, already sensing where this story leads.

"He took advantage of her innocence, and installed her as his mistress, hiding her away from his official mate in the Grand Pack." Bitterness edges his words. "For two years, she lived in seclusion, a prized possession rather than a wolf. It was only when she discovered he already had a mate that she left. But by that stage it was too late—I'd already taken root."

Ryker's hands clench at his sides. "I was born with these eyes." He gestures to his mismatched gaze—one gold, one blood-red. "The mark of what the ancient texts call 'shadow blood.' My mother saw it as punishment for her indiscretion."

I hesitate only a heartbeat. Then I step closer.

He doesn't move. Doesn't reach for me. Doesn't draw me in like he usually would.

I gather my courage and reach for him.

My hand lifts, fingers trembling slightly, and I gently brush beneath his left eye—the brilliant gold. Then the right —deep crimson, the color of blood and dusk and power.

My touch is featherlight. Reverent. As if I can erase the years of shame stitched into his skin with nothing more than a caress.

"They're beautiful," I whisper. "You're beautiful."

His gaze burns into mine.

"What happened?" I ask, still stroking his cheek, though I fear I already know.

"My mother feared Thaddeus finding out so fled with me to the mountains where she found sanctuary with a small, struggling pack. This pack was the beginning of what would eventually become Shadowmist." His expression hardens. "We survived. Grew stronger. She taught me everything about our kind's history, about the prophecies surrounding shadow blood. And about Thaddeus's greatest fear."

"Which is?"

"That he would die by his son's hand." Ryker's smile is razor-sharp. "A vision that came to the last seer before her death. The same vision you saw when Thaddeus forced you to look."

Realization dawns, cold and clarifying. "That's why he reacted so strongly. He recognized it."

"Yes." Ryker's hand finds mine again, his touch

anchoring. "When my mother left, I swore I'd fulfill that prophecy. Partly for vengeance, but mostly because he needs to be removed. Our kind have suffered under him. The packs are fragmented, fighting between each other. They've forgotten the old ways, becoming more human with every year that passes."

"And your prophecy?"

He swallows. "That shadow blood will heal the fractures Thaddeus created between the packs."

The weight of his revelation settles. This isn't merely a territorial dispute or injured pride—it's a blood oath born of lies and hate.

"And me?" I ask quietly. "Where do I fit in this prophecy?"

His gaze softens as he meets my eyes. "You weren't part of what Cheyenne saw. You're the variable no one predicted." His hand comes up to cup my face. "Which makes you the most valuable piece on the board."

The responsibility of that position should terrify me, but instead, I find myself standing taller. If I'm unpredicted, I'm also unconstrained by prophecy's rigid paths.

"What happened to your mother?"

His lips quirk into a smile. "She met her true mate—a wolf in the Fallow Pack—a few years after the Blood War. She moved there to be with him. She and he live there under the leadership of their son—my brother."

I cock an eyebrow. "Are you saying I have a mother, father, and brother-in-law, and my brother-in-law is another alpha?"

"Is that a problem?"

I throw my hands up, spinning away. "Is that a problem? Ryker! When were you going to tell me?"

"I—"

I hold my hand up to him, halting his excuses. "I don't want to hear it. I'm to be surrounded by dominant badasses."

Quick as a flash, he has me back in his arms, holding me tight. "Is that so bad, little wolf?"

His words are teasing, but his eyes are anything but. His mouth slants over mine with a growl, one hand fisting in my hair while the other cradles my jaw like I'm something precious. His lips are hot, demanding, tasting me like I'm the only thing in this world that could satisfy his hunger. I melt into him for a moment—heat sparking along every nerve, blood thundering.

With an almighty shove, I push him back. "Stop."

He does, immediately. "Are you okay?"

I wave a hand, dismissing his concerns. "I'm fine. I just don't want to be distracted before I scry. We can do… umm… that, later."

His lips curling into a self-satisfied grin. "That, hmm?"

I roll my eyes. "Stop making out with me and let's get this show on the road. Show me how to use the Well."

Ryker sighs heavily. "You sure I can't talk you out of it?"

"Positive."

He studies me for a moment, pride and concern radiating from him before he sighs again. "Fine. Come here."

He guides me to the pool's edge, himself behind me.

"Close your eyes," he instructs, his voice dropping to the low register that vibrates through my bones. "Reach for our bond first. Anchor yourself in it."

I do as he says, finding the connection between us instantly.

"Good," he murmurs, his breath warm against my ear. "Now, keeping that anchor, extend your awareness to the water. Don't look at it yet. Feel it."

With eyes still closed, I reach out with my senses. The air above the pool feels different—cool but charged and alive with potential. I imagine my gift extending toward it, like fingers stretching to touch something just beyond reach.

"The Well responds to intention," Ryker continues, his

hands settling on my shoulders. "Focus on Thaddeus. On his plans for us."

I form the image in my mind—the Grand Alpha as I last saw him at the Claiming ceremony, white hair gleaming in torchlight, face lined with cold authority. I think of his rage when Ryker claimed me, of his determination to reclaim what he considers his property.

"Open your eyes," Ryker commands softly. "And look."

I obey, staring as the pool's surface transforms before me. The still water swirls, colors bleeding through its depths like ink dropped in clear glass. Images form and dissolve—too fast at first, then slowing as my focus sharpens.

"Now, step into it."

I do as directed, the water closing over my head. For a brief moment I'm sucked down and into the deep pit where all air and life is cut off. Then I begin to float up, bursting to the surface with a short gasp.

"Okay?" Ryker asks, crouching beside the pool.

I nod, sweeping back my wet hair as I tread water. "I should have taken my clothes off first though."

His gaze drops down to my chest. "Yes, you should have."

I splash him, laughing before kicking my feet up until I'm on my back. Holding my head up, I ask, "What now?"

"Now lay back, close your eyes, and find what you're looking for."

I do as told; my eyes open as I stare up at the deep blue sky. For a while, nothing happens. I just float in the coolish water, watching as clouds slowly float by.

In the heartbeat between one moment and the next, it happens. The world tilts, and I'm sucked into a vision, a moment, a future, a present, so deeply that I cannot escape it.

*Thaddeus appears, seated at a massive table surrounded by wolves I don't recognize. Maps are spread before them, territories marked in blood-red ink. His finger traces a path through what must be Shadowmist lands, his expression cold and calculating.*

"*... must strike during the new moon." His voice ripples through the vision, distorted but understandable. "When their powers are weakest."*

*Another wolf leans forward—a female who's shadowed from my view. "And the seer? She'll see us coming."*

*"Not if we use silver dust in our approach," Thaddeus answers. "It clouds their sight. And with the new moon's influence, her gift will be at its lowest ebb."*

*The vision shifts, showing warriors gathering. Hundreds of them, from multiple packs, their fur marked with different territorial signifiers. An army being assembled, armed with silver weapons specially forged for wolf killing.*

*"The Shadowmist alpha dies," Thaddeus declares to the gathered forces. "The seer returns to us for a proper cleansing. Any who resist are to be eliminated."*

*Cold dread washes through me, but I force myself to keep watching, to see every detail of their planned assault. I try to memorize the routes mapped through our territory, their strategies for overcoming our defenses.*

*The vision blurs again, colors swirling together before resolving into a new scene. This one feels different—sharper, more immediate, as if it's happening in real time rather than the future.*

*Thaddeus stands alone in an ornate chamber, staring at his reflection in a mirror much like Ryker's scrying bowl. But it's what I see behind him that makes my breath catch—a shadow that should not be there, moving independently of its caster.*

*The shadow forms into a shape—a massive wolf with eyes that glow even in the darkness. As I watch, paralyzed, the shadow-wolf lunges forward, passing through Thaddeus like smoke. But the Grand Alpha doubles over as if struck by physical force, blood trickling from his nose.*

*"No," he gasps, staring at his reflection with sudden fear. "Not yet. I'm not ready."*

*The mirror cracks, a jagged line splitting his reflection in two. And in that fractured glass, for just an instant, I see something else*

*—Ryker standing over Thaddeus's body, blood dripping from his hands, his mismatched eyes blazing with triumph and sorrow.*

The vision slams shut with jarring force, throwing me up and out of the Well. I flail in midair, caught between the end of the vision and reality. Strong arms catch me, steadying me against a solid chest.

"I've got you."

I cling to Ryker, blinking up at him, shivering. His heartbeat thunders beneath my cheek, faster than I've ever felt it. His voice is steady, but his arms are tight around me, too tight.

"How long?"

He glances at the sky through the open ceiling. "Hours."

I swallow, squirming to be let go, but he ignores my weak struggles and pulls me from the pool to lower us both to the floor. Ignoring my protests, he settles me in his lap as if I weigh nothing. His hands tremble—barely—but I feel it.

His hair is mussed, like he's been running his fingers through it over and over, the way someone does when they're trying not to panic. There's tension in his jaw, and a faint crease between his brows.

He's trying to look calm.

But I know better.

He was scared.

"What did you see?" he asks, voice soft—too soft for Ryker.

I'm shaking, the images still burning behind my eyes. "He's planning an attack during the new moon. They'll use silver dust to try and cloud our detection. He's amassing an army of hundreds from multiple packs." I take a steadying breath. "And there's something else. Something I don't understand."

His arms retighten around me. "Tell me."

"I saw you standing over his body," I whisper. "I saw you kill him."

Ryker goes utterly still behind me. Through our bond, I feel a complex surge of emotions—satisfaction, vindication, but also unease.

"The prophecy," he says finally.

I turn in his arms, needing to see his face. "Yes and no. There was a shadow wolf that moved independently. It struck him, weakened him somehow."

"Shadow-walking. It's an ancient ability of those with shadow blood." His hand comes up to touch my cheek, his expression intense.

"You have that?"

He shakes his head. "But it could be a metaphor for being stealth-like. Or it could be something else entirely."

I nod slowly. "I guess that makes sense. It wasn't clear." The trembling in my limbs increases as reaction sets in. "There was so much blood, Ryker. So much death coming for us."

His expression hardens with determination. "Then we prepare. The new moon is fourteen days away. We have time."

"Against hundreds? From multiple packs?" Fear makes my voice sharp. "Even the Shadowmist can't stand against those numbers."

"We won't face them alone." His thumb brushes my lower lip. "We'll unite the other packs and use your visions to anticipate their movements. Set traps. Fight in the shadows where we have the advantage."

The confidence in his voice steadies me slightly. "And if it's not enough?"

"It will be." He presses his forehead to mine, our breath mingling. "You and I together—sight and shadow. We're what Thaddeus fears most."

Through our bond, his certainty flows into me, pushing back the panic that had begun to take hold. This isn't the reckless bravado of an alpha who's never known defeat—it's the calculated assessment of a strategist who's survived against impossible odds before.

"Come on," he says, lifting me in his arms as he climbs to his feet. "Let's get you washed and rested before tonight's ceremony."

*Fuck.*

A different kind of nervousness replaces my fear. Tonight, I'll be presented to the pack as Alpha Female—officially acknowledged as Ryker's mate before all the Shadowmist wolves.

And I've never felt less prepared for anything in my life.

# CHAPTER
# FOURTEEN

Darkness falls quickly in the mountains, the last rays of sunset giving way to deep purple twilight as we make our way to the Moonstone Clearing. Ryker walks beside me, a steady presence radiating power and purpose. Unlike the others, who wear minimal clothing for easy shifting, he's dressed in formal attire—black pants, a sleeveless shirt that displays the painted runes marking his left shoulder, and a cloak fastened with a gold clasp shaped like a crescent moon embracing a star.

I'm similarly adorned, though my outfit was clearly designed with my human form in mind. The dress Lithia brought to our chambers is midnight blue, its fabric light enough for movement but warm enough for the mountain air. Gold embroidery traces patterns along its edges—the same runes that mark Ryker's shoulder, symbols of the Shadowmist's ancient lineage.

The path to the clearing winds through old-growth forest; solar powered lights illuminate our way at regular intervals. Around us, pack members move in anticipation, voices hushed. I catch glimpses of Zella among them, her encouraging smile easing some of my tension.

"Remember," Ryker murmurs as we near our destination, "you are my equal. No hesitation. No submission."

I nod, drawing strength from his confidence and the claiming bond humming between us. Days ago, I might have faltered under the weight of such expectations. Now, after seeing the truth of what we face, what's coming for us, my resolve is hardening.

The mark at my throat pulses, and I'm hyperaware of Ryker's body as we walk. His scent wraps around me, a deep ache igniting in my belly.

My wolf stirs, restless beneath my skin. She too is watching him with sharp interest.

His shoulder brushes mine and my breath catches. My skin feels too tight, every hair on my body vibrating with awareness of him.

I glance at him from the corner of my eye. The sharp line of his jaw. The way his fingers flex like he's readying for a fight.

Or a touch.

I shouldn't be thinking about touch right now. But I am.

He catches me staring. "Okay?"

I flush, turning to look ahead. "Yes."

*No,* my wolf growls. *We want. We ache. We need.*

I ignore her as the trees open into the Moonstone Clearing—a vast natural amphitheater nestled in the mountainside. At its center stands a circle of standing stones, each twice the height of a man, their surfaces covered in the same runes that decorate our clothing. Moonlight bathes the entire clearing in silver, lending an otherworldly quality to the gathering.

Hundreds of wolves have already assembled, creating a living ring around the stone circle. They part silently as we approach, bowing their heads in respect to their alpha. I recognize faces from the den, Elias and his hunting unit including Zella, who offers a small wave; Lyra standing with other elders, Levi watching with the same unreadable expression I've come to expect from him.

Lithia awaits us at the circle's entrance, formally dressed in silver and black. She bows deeply as we reach her.

"Alpha. Alpha Female." Her acknowledgment of my title carries no trace of the hostility from our first meeting. "The pack is gathered. The moon rises full."

"Let it begin," Ryker commands.

A howl rises from somewhere in the forest—a signal that echoes across the clearing before being taken up by voice after voice until the night vibrates with their combined call. The sound resonates in my bones, awakening something primal.

Ryker leads me into the center of the stone circle, where a raised platform of polished granite awaits. We climb the shallow steps together, turning to face the gathered pack. From this vantage, I can see every face turned toward us, expectation heavy in the air.

"Wolves of the Shadowmist," Ryker's low, rumbling voice carries effortlessly across the clearing, the gravelly tone stroking a heated path across my skin. "Tonight we gather under the full moon's blessing as we have for generations. Tonight we honor our ancestors, our traditions, our pack bonds."

He places his hand at the small of my back, a public claim of possession and protection.

"Tonight I present my mate, Kitara, before the moon and the pack. Marked and claimed as Alpha Female of the Shadowmist."

A murmur runs through the gathered wolves, not hostile but not entirely welcoming either. I stand taller, refusing to shrink under their scrutiny.

"Some question my choice," Ryker continues, his tone hardening slightly. "Some see only her human form and not the gift she carries. Let me be clear—my mate is the first true seer to join our pack in a generation. Her visions have already saved Shadowmist lives. Her gift will help us face the storms that gather against us."

His hand moves to my shoulder, squeezing gently. "Step forward, Kitara. Let the pack see their Alpha Female."

Heart pounding, I move to the edge of the platform. The moonlight seems to intensify as I reach the edge, bathing me in silver radiance that makes the embroidery on my dress shimmer like liquid metal.

"I come before you as I am," I say, my voice steadier than I expected. "Just as the Moon Goddess shaped me. I cannot run with you as wolf, but I will see for you as seer. I cannot fight with claws, but I will protect with visions."

The words feel right, flowing from some deep well of certainty I didn't know I possessed.

"I am Kitara, mate to your Alpha, claimed and marked." I touch the claiming mark at my throat, feeling Ryker's power pulse in response. "And I pledge my gift, my loyalty, my life to the Shadowmist Pack."

Silence falls over the clearing, heavy with judgment and decision. For a heartbeat that stretches into eternity, I wait—exposed, vulnerable, wondering if my words will be enough to bridge the gap between what they expected and what I am.

Then, from the edge of the circle, a howl rises—Lyra, the elder, her song carries the unmistakable cadence of acceptance. Another joins her—Elias, then Zella, then more voices I can't identify until the clearing rings with their acknowledgment.

Not universal, not complete—I can see faces that remain silent, eyes that watch with reservation. But enough. Enough to begin.

The pack shed their clothing then Ryker steps forward again, standing naked beside me as the howls gradually subside. Pride flows through our bond, warming me from within.

"Tonight we run under the full moon's blessing," he

announces. "Tonight we hunt as one pack, one blood, one purpose."

He turns to me, his mismatched eyes gleaming in the moonlight. "Are you ready?"

I nod, knowing what comes next. We've discussed it, planned it, but the reality still makes my heart race with equal parts nervousness and anticipation.

In one fluid motion, Ryker shifts. Where the alpha stood a moment before, now towers his massive wolf form—midnight-black fur rippling with silver highlights, shoulders level with my own despite my standing on the raised platform. His mismatched eyes—gold and blood-red—fix on mine as he moves to position himself beside me.

The gasps and murmurs from the gathered pack confirm what I already knew—this is unprecedented. The Alpha will carry his mate who cannot shift, rather than leaving her behind.

With practiced movements, I gather my dress and slide onto Ryker's back. My fingers tangle in his thick fur, securing my position as he adjusts to my weight. Through our bond, I feel his satisfaction, his pleasure at this public display of our connection.

*Mine*, his thoughts reach me, clearer than they've ever been before. *My mate. My queen.*

He turns to face the pack, presenting us together—Alpha and Alpha Female, unified despite my inability to shift. Then, without warning, he leaps from the platform, landing with effortless grace despite my added weight.

The pack parts before us as Ryker pads to the edge of the stone circle. At some unspoken signal, the gathered wolves begin to shift—a wave of transformation rippling through the clearing until hundreds of wolves stand where humans had been moments before.

Lithia approaches in her wolf form—silver-gray with striking white markings around her eyes, the same scar that marks her human face visible as a line of white fur down her muzzle. She bows her head to us before taking position at Ryker's right flank.

Elias joins her, his russet fur gleaming in the moonlight, followed by the rest of his hunting unit. Zella's wolf form is sleek and lithe, with unusual markings that remind me of dappled sunlight through leaves. She nods to me as she takes her place, eyes bright with excitement.

Ryker throws back his head and howls—a sound so powerful it seems to shake the very stones beneath us. The pack answers, hundreds of voices joining in a primal chorus that vibrates through my chest and echoes across the mountains.

Then we run.

Ryker leads the charge from the clearing into the forest beyond, the pack flowing around us like a living river of fur and fang. I cling to his back, the wind whipping through my hair as we race through the darkness. His powerful muscles bunch and release beneath me, carrying us effortlessly over fallen logs and rocky outcroppings.

I've never experienced anything like this—the speed, the freedom, the belonging. Through our bond, I feel Ryker's wild joy, his wolf exulting in the run, in the night, in the pack that follows him. And beneath that, pride that his mate rides with him, that he can share this most sacred ritual with me despite my human form.

*Ride me, my queen.*

I lean down, pressing myself against him.

*Like this?*

He lifts his head to howl his approval.

We race along hidden paths, climbing higher into the mountains until we reach a ridge overlooking a vast valley. The pack gathers around us, breathing hard but vibrating with energy. Below, in the moonlit basin, a herd of elk grazes, unaware of the predators watching from above.

Ryker turns his head, meeting my gaze with those mismatched eyes. Through our bond, I understand what he's asking.

*Watch. See. Guide us.*

I close my eyes, reaching for my gift with the practiced control I've been developing. The vision comes easily—smoother, clearer than before—showing me the herd's movements, the strongest prey, the best approach.

I lean forward, whispering in Ryker's ear though I know the bond would have carried my thoughts. "The large bull at the northern edge. He'll break right when startled."

Ryker's satisfaction pulses through our connection. He turns to the gathered wolves, communicating my directions. The pack divides, groups moving into strategic positions around the valley.

The hunt that follows is a dance of perfect coordination—wolves moving as a single entity, guided by Ryker's commands and my visions. When the bull elk attempts to escape, Lithia's group is already there to cut off his retreat. The takedown is swift, merciful, executed with the precision of predators born to hunt.

As the pack feeds, Ryker carries me down to join them. In Silvercrest, I would never have been permitted to participate in a ceremonial hunt, much less share in its bounty. Here, wolves move aside respectfully as Ryker approaches the fallen elk, allowing me access to choose portions despite my inability to participate in the actual kill.

The ceremony that follows blends primal ritual with surprising sophistication. Blood from the hunt is used to mark each wolf's forehead—Lyra performing this duty for me with gentle hands, her eyes knowing as they meet mine.

"The blood binds us," she explains. "One pack, one purpose, regardless of form."

After the ritual markings, the pack settles into what can only be described as celebration. Some wolves shift back to human form, while others remain as wolves, all mingling in the moonlight. Music begins, drums and flutes, creating rhythms that call to something deep and instinctive.

Ryker shifts back to human form beside me, unconcerned with his nudity in a way that speaks to wolf-kind's comfort with their dual nature. Someone brings him clothing, simple pants that he pulls on with fluid grace before turning to me.

"You did well," he says, his voice pitched for my ears alone.

"I barely did anything," I demur.

His fingers trace the blood mark on my forehead. "You saw. You shared. You participated." His smile is rare and precious. "You were part of the pack tonight, Kitara. Not just as my mate, but as yourself."

The simple truth of his words settles into me, filling cracks I didn't realize still existed in my sense of self-worth. For the first time in my life, my gift has been celebrated rather than exploited. My difference acknowledged without becoming a barrier.

As the celebration continues around us, Ryker pulls me close, his arms encircling my waist. "Let them see," he murmurs against my hair. "Let them understand what you are to me."

The possessiveness in his touch is balanced by something I'm only beginning to recognize, respect, perhaps. Or an emotion far deeper that neither of us is ready to name.

In the distance, I spot Zella watching us, her expression unreadable before she turns away. Levi observes from the shadows, his gaze calculating but no longer openly hostile. Lithia converses with Elias, both occasionally glancing our way with what might be cautious approval.

The pack is adjusting to their Alpha's unusual mate. Not all are convinced, not all are pleased, but the first steps have been taken. Tonight, I rode with the Alpha. Tonight, I hunted with the pack. Tonight, I belonged.

The fire crackles behind me, casting golden light across our gathered wolves—laughing, dancing, eating, teasing. I smile with them, laugh with them. But inside me, something else is stirring. Stronger. Deeper.

Hotter.

I can feel him at my back, always near, always watching. Ryker. My mate. The man I once feared touching me now haunts my every thought with the hope that he will.

Desire has been building in me for days, a slow, simmering ache I didn't know how to name. I used to flinch when someone reached for me. Now I ache to be reached for. By him.

His presence doesn't overwhelm me anymore. It intoxicates. The low rumble of his voice. The heat in his eyes when he looks at me. The restraint that simmers just beneath his skin. He hasn't pushed, but gods, I want him to.

And tonight? Tonight, I stop waiting.

I turn toward him, heart pounding. He's standing just beyond the circle of firelight, arms crossed, mouth tilted in that faint, knowing smirk.

I reach for him.

The moment our hands touch, desire crackles through me. His palm is rough with calluses, but it only makes my skin feel softer, more sensitive in contrast. Heat pours from him, chasing up my arm and settling low in my belly. My fingers curl around his, imagining how those same hands might feel gripping my hips, pinning me down, pulling me closer.

I lift my gaze to his.

And gods help me, I want.

Ryker lets me pull him toward the trees, his steps easy but his grip firm, controlled.

"Where are you taking me, mate?"

I grin, ignoring his teasing gruffness. "Come, wolf. Let me show you."

# FIFTEEN



We barely make it through the door of our rooms. The second it clicks shut behind us, I lose the leash I had on my control.

Her surrender tastes sweet, but her desire tastes like fucking heaven.

Kitara's mine, and every part of me—both wolf and man—howls to claim her. But this isn't about me. This is about giving her the kind of pleasure that will ruin her for anyone else.

Not that she'll need anyone else. Ever.

I crowd her back against the wall, hands braced on either side of her head. She's panting, pupils wide, chest rising in quick little bursts that have the scent of her arousal spiking. My cock aches.

*Gods, I want her.*

Her scent has been changing over the past few days—growing richer, more complex. My wolf had paced restlessly, recognizing what was coming even if she hadn't. He wants to take her now—fast, rough, mark her with teeth and knot until she forgets her own name. He wants to come in her, fill her up, come on her breasts, her back, her face. He wants his scent rubbed into her skin and our pup planted in her belly.

Unlike my wolf, I'm not prepared to rush. I want her trembling, begging, shaking with need. I want her thick thighs wrapped around my head and her cunt pressed to my mouth as I taste her sweet surrender.

"Take it off," I growl, tugging at her dress.

She fumbles with it, but she's shaking, clumsy. I step in, helping my mate.

"Let me."

I fist the fabric in my hands and with one tug, rip it apart. The sound is satisfying, primal. Kitara gasps, bare now to my gaze. Her skin gleams, soft and perfect, every inch of her mine to explore.

"You're so fucking beautiful," I murmur, kissing her shoulder, her neck, the tender spot behind her ear. She shivers arching into me. "Let me take my time with you."

Her fingers curl in my hair. "Yes."

With a curse, I lift her into my arms, carrying her easily across to our bed—where I've spent the last few weeks hard as a rock, fighting my wolf as she sleeps peacefully beside me.

I'd woken early each morning, thick and hard, aching to touch her, to taste her, to give her pleasure. Instead, I'd slung out of our fucking room to crawl into an ice cold shower while I jerked off to fantasies of Kitara.

Not one of those imaginings stands up to the reality of her. Kitara far exceeds any fantasy I might have entertained.

Now on the bed, I stretch over her body, settling my weight on her. Her hands come to grip my hips, the thin material of my pants barely a barrier between us.

I kiss her slowly this time—deep and lingering. A kiss made for claiming, made for unraveling. My hands find her waist, thumbs stroking her ample hips, then slide up. I palm her heavy breasts, lifting them, thumbs brushing over her nipples until they pebble beneath my touch.

She gasps my name, arching into me, and I smile against her mouth.

"Sensitive?"

She nods, breath catching.

"Good."

I lower my mouth to her breast, taking one nipple between my lips and sucking slowly. I use my tongue, teasing her areola before sucking until she moans. I roll the other between my fingers, teasing it to the same peak. I switch sides, lavishing attention on each breast until she's trembling, panting, clinging to me.

I learn that she likes gentle teasing from my fingers but strong, wet suction from my mouth. I alternate over and over, lost in her taste and texture, relishing the way she grips my hair.

"Ryker," she groans. "That—gods, Ryker. That feels... so good."

I pause, lips still on her breast. "You like that, little wolf?"

She whimpers, nodding.

"Good girl."

Her throaty moan goes straight to my cock. I'm already hard as fuck, desperate to bury myself in her hot, tight pussy.

*Patience. Good things come to those who wait.*

"You make the prettiest sounds when you're praised," I tell her. "Gods, I could spend all night making you sing for me."

She groans again, and it hits me—that sound, the way she clutches at me, the flush blooming over her chest.

*She has a praise kink.*

Her fingers tighten in my hair as if hearing my thoughts.

"You love being worshipped. Don't you, Kitara?" I nuzzle her breast, laying gentle kisses on her rib cage. "You love being praised."

Her breath catches. "Yes."

I nip her gently. "Then let me praise every inch of you. Let me show you how perfect you are."

I keep my focus there—licking, sucking, gently biting—until she's practically writhing beneath me. Her hands knot in my hair, trying to guide me lower, but I'm not done worshipping.

Only when she's gasping, skin flushed and damp, do I kiss my way down. Her belly quivers under my mouth; her hips twitch as I move lower.

My hands slide down her body to dig into her thighs, encouraging them apart. She's soaked, her cunt slick with evidence of her desperate desires. My fingers slide through her slick folds, and she arches into my touch with a whimper.

"You're ready for me," I murmur against her belly. "Let me show you."

I slide my thumb gently over her clit, circling it with slow, deliberate pressure, watching how her hips buck, how her breath catches.

"There?" I murmur.

She moans, her head thrashing on the bed.

"That's it, good girl," I whisper, continuing the movement until she's panting, her body practically vibrating with need.

"Please," she whispers.

I hum in approval and slip a finger inside her, slow and careful. She gasps, clutching at my arms.

"Relax. You're doing so well. Gods, look at how perfectly you're taking me."

I watch my finger curl into her, working her, determined to teach her pleasure while stretching her in preparation for me.

"You're so tight, Kitara. You're such a good girl. *My* good girl."

"Ryker!" Her cunt clenches around my fingers,

"Fuck yes, good girl. That's it, baby. Work my fingers. You're mine, Kitara. Take it."

She moans in agreement, her head tipping back, her body open and needy. I keep stroking, slow and steady, one finger on her G-spot, my thumb circling her clit. I add another finger, stretching her until she starts to tense, her moans high and breathless.

Her hips begin to pulse, and I can feel the flutter of her orgasm around my fingers. Just before she tips over, I stop.

"What?! Ryker—!"

I hush her with a kiss. She looks at me, dazed and desperate, and I give her a wicked grin.

"Not yet. I want you coming on my tongue first."

She doesn't get the chance to argue. I drop to my knees at the edge of the bed and drag her to me, spreading her thighs wide. One long lick up her slit and she's sobbing.

"Fuck, Ryker—"

I wrap my arms under her thighs and pull her closer, my mouth working over her. Her fingers tangle in my hair, tugging, grounding. She's close again, I can feel it. Her whole body is vibrating.

Her sweet, slick heat coats my tongue and makes me growl with need. She's so wet, her arousal clings to my lips and soaks my face. I'm ravenous, devouring her like a starving man.

I suck her clit, just once, hard.

She explodes.

Her cries echo off the walls, her thighs clenching around my head, her entire body going taut and then slack as the orgasm crashes through her. Her cream coats my mouth, my tongue, my cheeks and I can't get enough. I keep licking, though gentler now, easing her down.

But I'm not done worshipping her. Not by a long shot.

I turn to kiss the insides of her thighs, nipping at the sensitive skin until she squirms. Then I begin my slow ascent —up her abdomen, her hips, her belly, her ribs, the underside of her breasts. I take one nipple in my mouth, sucking gently while my hand cradles the other, thumb teasing the peak until it stiffens under my touch.

She moans, her back arching, hands clutching at my shoulders.

"More," she whispers.

"Everything," I vow, trailing kisses up her sternum, over the hollow of her throat. My teeth scrape her pulse point, and she shivers.

When I reach her mouth again, I kiss her deeply, letting her taste herself on my tongue. Her fingers dig into my back, pulling me tighter against her. Our bodies align perfectly— her softness to my hardness, her heat dragging the last threads of control from my grip.

Still, I go slow.

"You're everything to me," I whisper. "And tonight, I'm going to show you."

Her eyes are heavy-lidded, her lips parted. She's flushed and sweaty, and there's a glow I've never seen on her face.

It's addictive.

I rise, shedding my clothes as I go, baring myself fully to her gaze.

She stares at me with wide eyes, then down to where I'm thick, hard, and leaking.

"That's not going to fit."

I chuckle darkly. "Oh, it will. Slowly. Gently. I'm going to worship every inch of you while I make it fit."

I crawl up her body, kissing her knees, her thighs, her hips, her breasts—biting lightly at her nipple until she moans. When I reach her lips, I pause.

"Still want this?"

She nods.

"Say it."

"I need you, Ryker."

I guide my cock to her and slide in slowly, inch by inch. She gasps, body tensing.

"Easy, baby. I've got you. Just feel."

She's wet and tight, and the heat of her surrounds me, dragging a groan from my chest. She's the best fucking thing I've ever felt.

*Fuck.*

For a beat, I have to fight for control, battling with every ounce of willpower I have to keep from rutting on her like an untested pup.

I still, letting her adjust, kissing her throat, her cheeks, whispering praise. When she's adjusted and begins squirming, that's when I start to move.

Slow thrusts at first, dragging out our pleasure. Then deeper. Harder. Her nails score my back, her legs wrapping around me, pulling me closer. She's keening now, her body slick and needy beneath mine.

"Good girl," I pant into her ear. "You're taking me so fucking well."

She groans, back arching. "Please, Ryker."

I grin against her neck. "You're perfect, Kitara. So sweet. So tight. Your cunt was made for me—for my cock, for my knot."

She clenches at the words, her moan guttural.

"You love that, don't you? Love knowing I'm going to fill you up. Fuck you so full you'll feel me for days."

She's panting now, almost there.

"Going to make you come so hard, you'll still be shaking when I knot you. Gonna pump you full, baby. Fill you until you drip."

I reach between us, thumbing her clit.

Her orgasm builds fast. I feel it coming, and when it hits, I let go too.

My knot begins to swell, readying to lock deep inside her.

Her eyes fly open, lips parted in a shocked gasp.

Among wolves, the knot is more than simple anatomy—it's a symbol of a true claiming. A physical bond that only forms with a true mate. The thick swell at the base of my cock grows, catching inside her, anchoring me in the hot clutch of her body. It keeps us joined and my cum locked inside her—and fuck if that doesn't drive me wild.

My cock pulses, the knot vibrating against her inner walls, adding to her pleasure. Kitara writhes against me, gasping as the sensation floods her—stretching, claiming, filling.

"Oh—gods—Ryker!"

"That's it," I groan. "Take it, little wolf. You're mine. Let me breed you. Let me fill you until you're round with our pup."

The thought of her filled makes my teeth ache. I want to bite her, mark her.

The knot finally locks in place, vibrating, and we both come apart. She screams, her entire body pulsing around me as I empty into her with a groan loud enough to be heard a territory over.

I collapse, careful not to crush her, and then roll us to the side, still joined, still panting.

She presses her face into my neck, sighing. "You've ruined me."

I grin. "Good. You'll never forget who you belong to."

She surprises me by nipping at my throat. "Neither will you."

Heat flares beneath my skin—not just arousal, though gods, there's that too—but mostly satisfaction. She's claimed me as surely as I have her.

I tip my head back, offering more of my neck without even thinking, baring it to Kitara's teeth like some lovesick fool. My chest tightens with a wild ache. She could ask anything of me right now, and I'd give it. Hell, I'd fall to my knees and thank her for the privilege.

A rough laugh escapes me, low and full of wonder. "Fuck, you're perfect."

Her cheeks flush with pleasure and her fingers curl against my chest.

We lie like that, tangled and sated, the bond between us thrumming like a drumbeat beneath our skin. Her fingers stroke lazily over my chest. I can feel her heart still racing against mine.

"This is real," she murmurs, her words barely audible. "All my life I thought..." She pauses, her fingers tracing a particularly deep scar across my ribs. "I was seven when my gift first manifested. I saw death coming for our hunters, warned them. After that, I was just a tool. My father wouldn't even look me in the eyes. Just ordered me to 'see' whenever he wanted."

I stay silent, listening as she opens up.

"I've never had anyone touch me the way you do," she confesses, her voice small. "My mother used to flinch when I'd reach for her."

Rage flickers at the thought of a child reaching for comfort and finding only rejection.

Kitara's fingers find another scar, this one jagged across my shoulder. "What caused this?"

I allow her a retreat. "Fae hunters. I was twelve. My mother and I were separated. They caught me, used silver to keep me from shifting." The memory still burns. "When she found me, she and the other wolves tore them apart."

She presses her lips to the scar, a benediction I don't deserve. "I feel silly telling you about my issues when I have no scars."

I roll us until she's under me. "Just because my scars bled on the outside doesn't mean yours cut any less deep."

Her hands come up to frame my face. "I don't understand you at all, Ryker Ashmere."

I press my forehead to hers. "All you need to know is that our bond cannot be broken, Kitara." I brush my thumb over the mark that decorates her neck.

We stay there, breathing each other in. I trace lazy patterns on her skin. There's a peace in this moment I've rarely known —a quieting of the constant vigilance that leadership demands.

"What happens now?" she asks, her head pillowed on my chest.

Dropping a kiss to her collarbone, I begin to move down her body. "Now, I need to taste you again." I rub my cheeks across her breasts. "And you get to lay back and enjoy."

She giggles, the sound a delicious rasp. "I might be able to do that."

# SIXTEEN

I wake to fire beneath my skin.

Every inch of me burns, a fever with no source, a thirst with no remedy. The furs feel like sandpaper against my hypersensitive skin. I kick them away, gasping as cool air hits my overheated body.

"What's happening to me?"

My wolf stirs, restless and hungry in a way I've never experienced. *Mate,* she whines. *Need mate.*

The claiming mark on my throat pulses in time with my racing heart. Each throb sends waves of heat cascading through my body, pooling low in my belly and between my thighs. I press my legs together, seeking relief that doesn't come.

Instead, the pressure only intensifies the ache.

I've heard whispers about this—wolves in my old pack discussing heats in hushed tones. But I never imagined I would experience one. How could I? I can't shift.

Yet here I am, burning from the inside out.

Burning for Ryker.

His name forms in my mind and my body responds instantly, a fresh wave of desire making me arch against the empty bed. Through our bond, I sense him—distant but approaching, his presence growing stronger with each passing moment.

He knows.

The door to our chambers opens, and Ryker steps inside. Even in the dim light, I can see his eyes glowing—one amber, one crimson—fixed on me with an intensity that should terrify me but only makes the ache worse.

"Kitara." My name in his voice is a physical caress.

I bite my lip to hold back a moan. "Something's wrong with me."

He approaches slowly, like a predator stalking wounded prey. His nostrils flare as he scents the air, and a growl rumbles deep in his chest.

"Nothing's wrong," he says, voice rough with restraint. "It's your heat."

"But I can't shift," I protest weakly, even as my body betrays me by arching toward him.

"The claiming triggered it." He stops at the edge of the bed, not touching me though I can see how much it costs him. "Your wolf may be trapped inside, but she's still there. Still part of you." His hands clench at his sides. "Still calling for her mate."

A whimper escapes me. "Make it stop. Please."

His expression darkens. "I can ease it." His voice drops lower. "But only if you're certain."

Despite the haze of need clouding my thoughts, I recognize what he's offering—and what he's asking. Permission. Choice. Even now, with both our wolves howling for completion, he waits for my consent.

"I need you." The words pour out before I can stop them. "I don't understand what's happening, but I know I need you."

Something in him breaks at my admission. In one fluid movement, he's on the bed, his powerful body caging mine.

His scent—earth and stone and wild places—surrounds me, intensifying the ache to an almost unbearable degree.

"This will be different," he warns, his voice strained as he fights for control. "The heat changes things. Makes it more... intense."

I reach up, touching his face, feeling the tension in his jaw. "I'm not afraid of you."

His eyes flash. "Maybe you should be."

With that, his mouth claims mine in a kiss nothing like the ones we've shared before. This is possession, pure and raw. His tongue slides against mine, demanding surrender, and I give it willingly, melting beneath him as heat sizzles along every nerve.

His hands are everywhere—tangling in my hair, cupping my breast, sliding down my side to grip my hip with bruising intensity. I should feel trapped beneath his massive frame, but instead, I feel sheltered, safe despite the storm raging inside me.

"You're burning up," he murmurs against my throat, his lips finding the claiming mark and sending a jolt of pleasure so intense I cry out.

"Yes," I gasp, my hands clawing at his shoulders as he sucks at the mark. "Ryker, please—"

He pulls back, eyes wild as he studies my face. "Tell me what you need."

"I don't know," I admit, frustrated tears pricking my eyes. "Everything hurts but feels good at the same time. I just need... more."

Understanding flashes across his face. With deliberate slowness, he drags his hand down my body until his fingers brush the slick heat between my thighs.

"Here?" he asks, circling my entrance with maddening restraint.

"Yes," I hiss, hips bucking against his hand.

He slips one thick finger inside me, and I nearly come

undone from that alone. A second finger joins the first, stretching me, preparing me, his thumb finding the bundle of nerves that makes me see stars.

"So wet," he growls, his control visibly slipping as he works me with his hand. "So ready for me."

I reach for him, desperate to touch, to taste, to have all of him. My fingers fumble with the fastening of his pants until he catches my wrist.

"Not yet," he says, voice tight. "You first. Need to make sure you're ready."

Before I can protest, he moves down my body, replacing his fingers with his mouth. The first touch of his tongue against my core sends lightning through my veins. He devours me like a starving man, his powerful shoulders keeping my thighs spread wide as he tastes every inch of me.

The pleasure builds, a tidal wave I can't escape and don't want to. When it crashes over me, I scream his name, my body arching off the bed as the first orgasm of my heat washes through me.

But instead of satisfaction, it only feeds the flames. The relief is momentary, the need returning stronger than before.

"More," I beg, reaching for him. "Please, I need more."

Ryker rises above me, his eyes glowing with primal intensity. He sheds his clothing in quick, efficient movements, revealing his powerful body—all sculpted muscle and battle scars. My mouth goes dry at the sight of him, thick and hard and ready.

He positions himself between my thighs, the blunt head of his cock nudging my entrance. Through our bond, I feel his struggle for control, the wolf in him demanding he take, claim, breed, while the man fights to be gentle.

"It's alright," I whisper, framing his face with my hands. "I won't break."

His smile is feral. "No, you won't." He pushes forward

slowly, inch by exquisite inch, stretching me around his considerable girth.

"Perfect," I finish for him, lifting my hips to take him deeper. "And it will be. Because it's with you."

His expression softens even as his body remains taut with restraint. He leans down, capturing my lips in a kiss more tender than I expected given the circumstances.

When he's fully seated within me, he pauses, letting me adjust to the intrusion. The feeling of fullness is overwhelming—physically, emotionally, spiritually. Through our bond, I feel his pleasure mirroring my own, the connection between us strengthening with each shared heartbeat.

"Mine," he growls against my lips, the word both possession and promise.

"Yours," I agree, wrapping my legs around his waist to draw him even deeper.

That simple action breaks his control. With a sound more wolf than man, he begins to move, his powerful body driving into mine with a rhythm that speaks to something primal inside me. Each thrust sends waves of pleasure radiating from where we're joined, the heat in my veins turning molten.

His pace increases, driven by the dual needs of our wolves, recognizing their other half even as our human sides are still learning each other. The bond between us flares with each movement, carrying sensations back and forth until I can't tell where my pleasure ends and his begins.

I feel the change in him first—the subtle swelling at the base of his cock that signals his approaching climax. The knot I'd felt once before but still wasn't prepared for.

"Ryker," I gasp, both warning and plea.

"I know," he grits out, his movements becoming more urgent. "Can you take it? All of me?"

"Yes," I answer without hesitation, instinctively tilting my hips to receive him fully. "Give me everything."

With a final powerful thrust, his knot locks inside me, stretching me to the edge of pain before tipping over into blinding pleasure. The pressure against sensitive nerves triggers another orgasm, more powerful than the first, tearing a cry from my throat that echoes off the stone walls.

Ryker follows immediately, his release hot and copious inside me, his massive body shuddering with the force of it. Through our bond, I feel his satisfaction, his wonder, his fierce joy at claiming me so completely.

We remain locked together, his weight supported on his forearms as he presses his forehead to mine. Our breath mingles, our heartbeats gradually slowing to match each other's rhythm.

"Better?" he asks, voice rough with exertion.

I nod, the burning fever temporarily banked though not entirely gone. "How long will this last?"

"The heat? Three days, maybe four." His hand strokes my hair back from my face with surprising tenderness. "We'll weather it together."

"And this?" I shift slightly, gasping as the movement tugs on where we're still joined.

His smile is pure male satisfaction. "About half an hour, give or take." His lips brush mine. "Long enough for you to rest before the next wave hits."

As if summoned by his words, I feel the heat beginning to build again, slower this time but no less demanding. My body tightens around his still-hard length, drawing a groan from him.

"Already?" he asks, a mix of surprise and anticipation in his tone.

I smile, feeling strangely powerful despite my vulnerable position. "Disappointed?"

His laugh is dark and promising. "Not even slightly." He shifts his weight, somehow managing to flip our positions without breaking the intimate lock between us so that I straddle his lap, his knot still firmly seated inside me.

The new angle sends sparks of pleasure shooting through me, making me gasp.

"This time," he says, his hands settling on my hips, "you set the pace."

I rock my hips slowly, experimentally, relishing the way Ryker groans beneath me, the way his hands grip my thighs, letting me move but not guiding.

I move again, deeper this time, the motion sending delicious friction through my core. I can feel every inch of him, the stretch, the pressure, the sheer fullness.

His breath shudders. "Kitara…"

I set the pace, slow and devastating, grinding my hips in steady circles that keep us locked together and send sparks dancing along my nerves. His eyes never leave mine—those mismatched flames burning with devotion and something older, something wild.

The tension coils tight, heat and hunger sharpening with each pass, and then—

It happens.

The world shifts.

I'm still riding him, but it's like I've fallen inward.

The stone walls melt away, replaced by moonlight and trees. A forest. Wild. Free.

I see *him* there—Ryker. But not Ryker. His wolf. Massive. Silver-streaked and scarred and magnificent.

And beside him—me.

My wolf.

She's real. Solid. No longer trapped. She's running, howling, fur brushing his as we race through the night. I cry out, not in fear, but in release.

"Ryker—"

I lean forward, instinct screaming, and sink my teeth into the curve where his neck meets shoulder.

His roar echoes through both worlds—real and vision.

I feel his knot swell again inside me, locking us in place. His hands tighten, his mouth finding my breast, his hips buck once, twice—and he breaks, spilling into me with a cursed growl.

Around us, the dream-forest bursts into silver flame, and our wolves howl in unison. A chorus of belonging.

His blood touches my tongue, and I realize what I've done.

I've completed our mate bond.

I collapse against his chest, trembling and gasping. His hands are in my hair, on my back, his heart a thunder beneath my cheek.

"You saw it," I whisper. "The forest. Our wolves."

"I did." His voice is hoarse, reverent. "She's beautiful, Kitara. Just as you are."

I close my eyes, a single tear slipping free. "We're not broken."

"No." He kisses my temple. "You just needed to be seen."

The heated ache is gone, replaced with a fierce and molten need. Satisfaction curls through me, and I have a bone-deep certainty that he is mine.

I shift slightly, and his hands slide instinctively to hold my hips. His breathing is ragged, lips parted, eyes half-lidded but glowing.

"You bit me," he murmurs.

"I did." I'm shockingly unapologetic. "I marked you back."

A low, reverent laugh escapes him. "I fucking loved it."

I drag my fingers through the sweat-damp hair at his nape. "You're mine, Ryker. All of you."

He looks at me like I've become the sun. "Say it again."

I lean down, lips brushing his. "Mine."

The bond flares again, bright and burning and whole. His

blood still lingers on my tongue, metallic and alive, and my wolf stretches in triumph.

I feel full. Not just from his knot, still locked inside me, but from the rightness of it all.

He strokes my spine, voice rough with awe. "You feel it too."

"Everything." I rest my forehead to his.

"Good." His voice is all gravel and affection. "Want to bite me again?"

I smile.

CHAPTER

# SEVENTEEN

I wake wrapped in Ryker's arms, a cocoon of warmth and gentle possession. I should be satisfied, but the ache —that raw, ravenous hunger—still thrums through me, wild and untamed.

My heat hasn't burned out.

It's smoldering.

Every inhale drags Ryker deeper into my lungs—earth and storm and sex and sweat. My muscles clench greedily, and I'm once again desperate to have his thick knot pulsing inside me.

I shift against him, the movement making me hiss. Gods, I'm so sensitive—but I'm wet again. Aching again. The bond thrums between us, stirring my wolf and setting every nerve on edge.

*More*, she growls. *Want our mate.*

"Still with me, little wolf?" he murmurs, voice hoarse, eyes half-lidded but blazing with heat.

"Barely." I roll my hips and whimper.

He brushes his fingers over my cheek, then down to my lips, thumb teasing until I open for him. I suck it into my mouth slowly, deliberately, dragging my tongue along the pad, then bite down hard enough to make his eyes flash.

He groans. "Fuck, you're perfect." He shifts until he can cup my breasts. "You're flushed," he murmurs, dragging kisses down my throat.

"You think?"

His fingers trail down my stomach, and my thighs fall open for him.

*Gods, I want.*

"You're so hot, Kitara. Just pure, filthy heat."

My wolf howls in agreement.

"I need you," I whisper, desperation riding me hard.

His gaze locks with mine. "Say it again."

"And say what?" I arch up, grinding my pussy against his thigh. "That I want you so deep inside me I forget where I end and you begin? That I want to ride you until I'm crying and shaking, until you knot me again and again and—"

His mouth crashes to mine, all tongue and teeth and desperation.

I roll him to his back, straddling him with slick thighs around his hips. I grab his cock, thick and hot and already leaking, and rub the tip through my folds, coating him.

He hisses through his teeth. "Kitara."

"Let me." I lower myself slowly, inch by inch, moaning as he stretches me open again.

His hands grip my thighs, his jaw clenched tight. "Fuck, you feel like heaven. Tight. Hot. Mine."

"Yours," I breathe, rocking my hips.

I ride him slowly, grinding in tight, punishing circles that make us both shake. His hands drift up to my breasts, fingers pinching and rolling my nipples until I'm gasping.

"You like this?" he growls.

"Yes... gods, yes..."

He jerks up, greedily sucking one nipple deep while

thumbing the other. I ride him harder, thighs trembling, slick pouring down his cock and soaking his lap.

"Fuck," he groans around my nipple. "These tits—gods, Kitara, look at them. Full, heavy, fuckable. I could die a happy wolf right now."

I flush, arching as I push closer, encouraging him to suck harder.

"You're going to come for me again, little wolf. I want to feel you squeeze me while I fill you up. Want to knot you so deep you choke screaming my name."

I'm already there. My orgasm crashes over me, brutal and overwhelming. I shatter in his arms, crying out as I clench around him.

He flips us, driving into me with deep, punishing thrusts. I barely have time to catch my breath before I'm flying again, another orgasm building fast.

"You're taking me so well, pretty girl," he groans. "So tight. So fucking wet."

His knot swells again, stretching me wide, locking us together as his cock pulses deep inside. I scream as the pressure sets off another orgasm, white-hot and all-consuming.

We collapse together, still joined, his knot anchoring him deep inside my soaked, twitching cunt.

He kisses my temple. "Still want more?"

I laugh breathlessly. "You have no idea."

We rest for a while, tangled in sweat-slicked limbs, breath syncing slowly. I trace his scars with lazy fingers, my wolf purring beneath my skin.

He brushes my hair back, fingers gentle. "I feel it building again."

"It's not stopping," I whisper. "It's... simmering."

A knock at the door. Sharp. Persistent.

Ryker growls. "No!"

"Alpha," Elias calls through the wood, voice hesitant. "Scouts have returned. There's movement on the southern ridge."

Ryker snarls. "Deal with it. I'm occupied."

"They said it could be Thaddeus's people."

Ryker sighs, planting one last kiss to my shoulder before carefully withdrawing from me. I whimper at the loss.

He grabs a sheet and drapes it around me. "Don't move. I'll be five minutes. Ten if someone bleeds."

He vanishes out the door, growling, naked except for the blood-warm fury rolling off him.

I curl into the furs, body still humming. But it doesn't take long before the ache returns. Fiercer. Deeper.

By the time Ryker returns, I'm slick and writhing, fingers tangled in the sheets, teeth clenched against the building wave.

His eyes flash the second he sees me. "Kitara."

"Please," I gasp. "It's worse."

He drops to his knees, crawling up the bed. "I've got you, little wolf."

This time he worships me. He eases inside slowly, holding eye contact, breathing with me as our bodies align.

We move in perfect rhythm, not just fucking—but claiming. Again.

Again.

And again.

Until the sun rises and sets and rises again. Until the ache becomes a memory.

Until the bond glows, golden and wild, between us, and the burning heat cools.

I doze, exhausted in the hazy aftermath, sweat cooling on our skin, the scent of sex and satisfaction thick in the air. My body aches in the best way.

The heat has apparently been satisfied.

He kisses the curve of my shoulder and murmurs, "You're mine."

I fall asleep smiling.

# EIGHTEEN

awn breaks cold and clear over the Shadowmist territory, the first rays of sunlight painting the mountain peaks gold against the fading night. I stand at the entrance to the pack's den, wrapped in Ryker's coat, watching as patrol groups return from their night shifts and day teams prepare to take their place.

Ryker rolled out of bed an hour ago and I followed, wanting to be close.

"Be careful," I'd whispered, tilting my head back for a kiss. He'd chuckled, taking his time tasting my mouth, ignoring the wolves around us who teased and catcalled the mark on his neck as they'd wandered by.

"Be good," he'd whispered against my lips before shifting and bounding outside.

"You should be resting." Zella appears at my side, interrupting my thoughts. She's looking surprisingly alert despite the late night. "How are you feeling?"

"Fine."

Zella bumps me with her hip, wiggling her eyebrows suggestively. "Fine, hmm?"

I flush, hiding a smile. "How about you?"

She sighs dramatically. "The single wolves in this pack, I tell you, they're all bite and no play. And the biting isn't even the good kind."

I chuckle, then turn back to stare out at the sunrise.

"Talk to me, Kitara."

I sigh, shaking my head. "I can't stop thinking about what's coming," I admit, keeping my voice low though we stand alone.

She nods. "Ryker told the council about your vision."

This surprises me. "He shared it already?"

"Before the ceremony. The senior wolves needed to know." She touches my arm gently. "Your gift is our advantage, Kitara. It's the only reason we have a chance."

The responsibility settles heavier on my shoulders. In Silvercrest, my visions were weapons to be used against other packs. Here, they've become shields to protect my new family.

"I'm not sure it's enough," I confess. "There were so many wolves, Zella. And from multiple packs."

"Numbers aren't everything in warfare," Zella says with quiet confidence. "The Shadowmist has survived against worse odds before." Her smile turns encouraging. "Besides, we have something they don't."

"What's that?"

"Allies. Ryker's working hard to bring them into our circle. We won't be alone." She squeezes my hand. "That makes all the difference."

Her faith warms me despite the morning chill. Over the past days, Zella has proven a steady friend—always appearing when I need guidance, offering insights into pack customs and personalities, she's made me feel less alone in this new world.

"The Alpha called a war council," she continues. "Midday in the Strategy Chamber. As Alpha Female, your presence is expected."

A nervous flutter rises in my stomach. "I've never participated in military planning before."

"Then it's time you learned," Elias says from behind us.

I turn to find him fully dressed—fitted black clothing that allows for quick movement, the gold symbol of the Shadowmist Pack gleaming at his throat.

Zella immediately bows her head, exposing her neck in a show of submission. "Elias. I was just informing the Alpha Female about the council."

"So I heard." His gaze moves briefly to her before returning to me. "Thank you, Zella. You're dismissed."

She nods, squeezing my hand once more before departing with that silent grace all shifted wolves seem to possess.

When we're alone, Elias gestures at me to walk with him. I fall into step as we begin to stroll down toward the river that laps the mountain.

"The pack speaks of nothing but you this morning."

Anxiety spikes through me. "Because of how I participated? Riding Ryker?"

"Because of how you contributed," he corrects. "Your vision guided the hunt to the strongest prey."

We walk on for a time in companionable silence before he breaks it. "Something's troubling you," he observes. "Beyond the obvious threat."

I consider deflecting but decide on honesty. "The vision from the Well. I saw Ryker doing something he can never take back."

A look flickers across his face, old pain, quickly mastered. "We all do terrible things when we have no other option."

I hesitate, searching for words. "Doesn't it weigh on you?"

"Every day," he admits, surprising me with his frankness. "But not in the way you might think." He stops at the river, bending to pick up a smooth stone. "To be alpha is a hard job. It's to fight and draw blood, to destroy and protect. All in an effort to create something better in its place.

"It's a heavy burden to bear." He tosses the rock, watching as it skims across the water. "Thaddeus has ruled through fear for generations. He's convinced the packs that only strict hierarchy and separation can ensure our survival. But it's a lie, one that serves only to maintain his power."

"And you think killing him will change that overnight?"

His laugh holds no humor. "Nothing changes overnight. But it begins with removing the obstacle that prevents all progress." He shrugs. "Ryker believes it will change the way we proceed."

"And you? What do you believe?"

He sighs. "That without Thaddeus corrupting the packs we can finally live as we have always meant to."

I consider his words, remembering the celebration after the hunt, the joy of inclusion and connection.

"First, we have to survive what's coming," I remind him.

"Yes." His expression hardens with resolve. "Which is why you need to rest before the council. You will be crucial in the days ahead." He turns to me, his gaze serious. "Don't underestimate your power, Kitara. You may have the sight, but it is your influence over Ryker that will be tested. You are his greatest strength—and weakness. Not because you can't shift," he says, interrupting my protest. "But because you are his mate. He's bound to you. You are his and he is yours. There is no beginning or end in a mate bond, there only is the bond."

He pats me on my shoulder. "Come, let's get you some breakfast."

As I follow him silently back to our den, I know he speaks true. Which worries me far more than any vision I've ever had.

INSIDE THE SMALL Strategy Chamber sits a massive stone table that dominates the space. Its surface is carved into a topographical representation of the region. Small markers in various colors indicate pack boundaries, patrol routes, and defensive positions.

When Ryker and I enter, the chamber is already filled with wolves of various ranks. I recognize Lithia and Elias at the head of the table, along with Elder Lyra and several others whose names I'm still learning. Zella stands among a group that's off to one side, observing rather than participating in the discussion.

Conversations halt as we approach, all eyes turning to us. To my surprise, the wolves bow not just to Ryker but to me as well—acknowledgment of my position.

"Let's begin," Ryker commands as we take our places at the head of the table.

Lithia nods, stepping forward. "Border patrols have been doubled, focusing on the three most likely approach vectors based on the Alpha Female's vision." Her silver eyes meet mine. "We've installed early warning systems with scent markers that will trigger if crossed."

"The tunnel network?" Ryker asks.

"Secured," Elias confirms. "We've collapsed all secondary entrances, leaving only the main passages. They're rigged for controlled detonation if needed."

I listen carefully, trying to absorb the military terminology and strategic concepts being discussed. Through our bond, I sense Ryker's focus, his careful consideration of each aspect being presented.

"What of our allies?" Ryker asks, directing the question to a lean wolf I don't recognize.

"The Ghost River Pack confirms support," the wolf replies. "They can provide thirty fighters. The Mountain Striders another twenty. Both will arrive within three days."

"Not enough," Lithia states flatly. "Thaddeus brings hundreds."

"Quality over quantity," Ryker counters. "These are wolves who've fought alongside us before. They understand what's at stake." He turns back to the lean wolf. "And the other packs?"

"We're still working on them, Alpha."

Ryker nods once. "Keep discussions moving forward, Thomas. Whatever you need, you can have it."

The discussion continues, discussing supplies, weapons, evacuation plans for the youngest and oldest members of the pack. I'm struck by the thoroughness of their preparations—clearly, the Shadowmist wolves have faced existential threats before.

"And what of the Alpha Female's gift?" Elder Lyra asks, her weathered face turning toward me. "What role will it play in our defense?"

All eyes shift to me, expectant. I straighten my spine, forcing myself not to shrink under their collective gaze.

"I can monitor Thaddeus's planning," I say, my voice steadier than I expected. "See adjustments to his strategy as they form. And during the battle itself, I can try to anticipate movements, provide real-time intelligence."

"Try?" Levi challenges from farther down the table. "Our lives will depend on more than possibilities."

Before Ryker can intervene, I meet Levi's gaze directly. "My gift has been growing stronger since the claiming. But yes, there are still limitations—silver dust clouds my sight, as does the new moon's phase." I lift my chin. "I won't promise what I can't deliver with certainty."

A murmur runs through the gathered wolves—not disapproval, I realize, but something closer to respect for my honesty.

"Well said." Elder Lyra nods. "Better truth than false comfort."

"Kitara will continue training with me," Ryker states, his tone making it clear the matter is settled. "Her gift, combined with our territorial knowledge and fighting skills, gives us the edge we need."

Lithia clears her throat. "With respect, Alpha, we should discuss worst-case scenarios. If we're overrun—"

"We won't be," Ryker cuts her off.

"But if we are," she persists, her scarred face set with determination, "protocols must be established. Particularly for the Alpha Female."

I tense, understanding the subtext. In wolf society, the alpha pair represents the pack's future. If defeat seems inevitable, the Alpha Female would traditionally be evacuated to ensure the bloodline continues.

"I'm not leaving," I say before Ryker can respond, drawing startled looks from around the table. "If the pack fights, I fight. If the pack falls, I fall with it."

Through our bond, I feel Ryker's warring emotions— pride versus protective instinct, approval alongside concern.

*All will be well*, I tell him silently.

*I can't risk you*, he responds. *I'm sorry, Kitara.*

*What? No!*

"We'll establish a guard for Kitara," Ryker says, despite my silent protests. "If the worst comes, they will take her to the European packs. She should be safe there."

"As you wish," Lithia acknowledges after a moment, inclining her head.

I sit silently, seething as the council continues to discuss specific tactical decisions. I listen intently, occasionally offering insights based on what I've seen in my visions. The senior wolves consider my contributions seriously, integrating them into their planning without hesitation.

Their confidence makes Ryker's decision even more infuriating.

By the time the meeting concludes, the hour is late. My

head throbs with information, even if my heart is sick at Ryker's lack of faith.

We have a plan. We have allies. We have a chance.

If only Ryker could trust in me.

As the council disperses, my mate keeps me at his side, his hand a warm presence at the small of my back. Zella approaches, bowing.

"Alpha Female," she addresses me formally. "I've been assigned to your security detail during the preparations. If you're willing, I'd like to begin training you in basic defense techniques."

"I need a security detail?"

She grins. "Not when I'm done with you. But in the meantime, we'll work together on how to protect yourself in human form," she counters. "You don't need claws to be dangerous."

"When do we start?"

"Now, if you're not too tired," Zella suggests. "The training hall should be relatively empty at this hour."

I can feel Ryker's desire to keep me near, but my anger at him overrides any wish I have to be near him right now.

"Let's do it."

As Zella leads me through the corridors toward the training hall, I'm struck by how different I feel from the wolf I was just days ago. In Silvercrest, I would never have been included in war councils, never offered combat training, never treated as an equal.

"Something amusing?" Zella asks, noticing my smile.

"Just reflecting on how quickly life can change," I reply honestly.

Her answering smile is warm. "For the better, I hope?"

"Definitely." The certainty in my voice surprises even me. Even in my anger, I know that Ryker is only doing what he thinks is best.

*I forgive you*, I tell him.

*It doesn't feel like it*, he responds, his tone wry.

*Well, you've yet to apologize for being an ass.*

His chuckle is warm in my mind. *I won't apologize for protecting you, Kitara. I love my pack, but I cannot live without you.*

His response douses some of the heat from my anger.

*Next time, speak to me before making decisions about my future. I might not convince you of a different path, but surely we can come to some kind of compromise?*

*That I can promise to do.*

The tension between us eases, and I follow Zella into the training room with a lighter step.

"We'll start with the basics," she says, moving to the center of the floor. "Stance, balance, leverage. You don't have a wolf's strength, but you have other advantages."

"Like what?" I ask skeptically.

"You're smaller, potentially faster if trained properly. Your center of gravity is lower." She circles me, assessing. "And your sight is an advantage, as Lithia and Dane can attest."

I grin. My lessons in predicting their movements have come along in leaps and bounds, so much so Lithia hasn't managed to land a hand on me in two days.

Zella takes a fighting stance. "Now, let's see what you're working with. Try to hit me."

The next hour passes in a blur of instruction, correction, and repetition. Zella proves a patient but demanding teacher, showing me how to use an opponent's size and strength against them, how to target vulnerable points, how to fall without injury when thrown.

To my surprise, I find myself enjoying the physical exertion after days of mental training. There's something liberating about learning to defend myself actively rather than always relying on my visions.

"You're a quick study," Zella comments as we take a water break. "Most beginners struggle more with the basic forms."

I wipe sweat from my brow, pleasantly exhausted. "I've spent a lifetime observing how wolves move. Maybe some of it rubbed off."

Her head tilts thoughtfully. "Maybe."

Before I can respond, the training hall door opens to admit a group of younger wolves—perhaps only six or seven years old by the look of them, led by an older male I recognize from the council meeting.

"Alpha Female," they greet me with varying degrees of awkwardness and respect.

The instructor inclines his head. "We didn't mean to interrupt your training."

"We were just finishing," Zella assures him, then turns to me with a smile. "Same time tomorrow?"

I nod, grateful for both the session and her friendship. As we leave the training hall, I notice the young wolves watching me with undisguised curiosity.

On impulse, I cross to them, smiling at their instructor. "May I be introduced?"

For the next few minutes, the bubbly pups surround me, asking questions and chatting about their lessons. They're enthusiastic and adorable bundles of arms and legs.

"They'll be talking about this for days," Zella comments as we walk toward the bathing chambers.

"About what?" I ask, still learning the intricacies of pack protocol.

"Meeting you. In most packs it's unheard of for youngsters to meet an alpha. Wasn't it like that in your pack?"

I shrug. "I wouldn't know. I wasn't exactly integrated into the pack hierarchy."

Zella nods. "Well, let me tell you, it's very unusual."

"How long have you been with the pack?" I ask as we enter the bathing chamber, the mineral-rich pools steaming invitingly.

"Five years," she answers, stripping efficiently and sliding into the water. "They took me in when no one else would."

I follow her example, easing my sore muscles into the heated pool with a grateful sigh. "What happened?"

A shadow crosses her face. "My original pack was... traditional. Females were expected to know their place and to submit to the strongest males regardless of preference." Her fingers trace patterns in the water's surface. "I refused a claiming. Fought back when forced. They cast me out—damaged goods, as they said."

My heart aches for her. "I'm sorry."

She shrugs, the gesture deliberately casual though pain lingers in her eyes. "Ryker found me half dead from silver poisoning. Brought me back to the Shadowmist, healed me, offered me a place." Her smile returns. "Here, I'm valued for my tracking skills, not my breeding potential. It's a nice change."

It's no wonder we've connected so quickly—our journeys, while different, share common threads of pain and a desire to belong.

"That's why you're so loyal to him," I observe.

"To him. To the pack." She meets my gaze directly. "And now to you."

The simple declaration warms me. In Zella, I've found not just an instructor but a true friend—something I've never had in the Silvercrest Pack, where I was kept isolated and apart.

We finish our bath, dress in clean clothes, and part ways at the corridor junction that leads to the alpha's chambers.

"Tomorrow," Zella reminds me. "Don't be late. I won't go easy on you just because you're sore."

I laugh, enjoying her teasing. "I wouldn't expect you to."

When I reach our chambers, I find Ryker already there, studying maps spread across the table. He looks up at my entrance, his mismatched eyes taking in my damp hair and relaxed posture.

"Training went well?" he asks.

"Better than expected," I admit, moving to examine the maps over his shoulder. "Zella's a good teacher."

"She's one of our best." His hand finds my waist, drawing me against his side. "How are you feeling after the council? Do I need to apologize in person?"

I consider his question. "Yes to apologizing. As for the rest, I'm overwhelmed. Nervous. But... ready, I think."

"The senior wolves were impressed by your contributions. Even Lithia commented."

"Really?" I can't hide my surprise. Lithia's respect feels like a significant achievement given her initial hostility.

Ryker's thumb traces small circles at my waist, a casual intimacy that has lazy warmth spreading through me. "You're proving yourself to them. Earning your place not just as my mate, but as a leader in your own right."

The assessment makes me uncomfortable, though I'm not sure why. "I'm just trying to help."

He lifts me, carrying me across to sit me on his desk before stepping between my legs. "That's what makes you a true leader. Many in positions of power take, but true leaders serve. They don't do this for power or influence—they accept this mantle because it's the best way to serve our people."

I think of the Silvercrest Pack, where Alpha Varick led through fear and dominance, taking whatever he wanted without consideration for his pack's wellbeing. Ryker's approach couldn't be more different—his power tempered by responsibility, his strength used to shield rather than subjugate.

"Tomorrow we begin strategizing," he says, changing the subject. "Combining your visions with tactical response."

"More work in the East Chamber?" I ask, thinking of our previous sessions.

"No. The Vision Well."

I tense, remembering the overwhelming intensity of my last experience there. "I see."

"If you're uncomfortable we don't have to do it."

"No, I want to. It's just... different to anything I've experienced before."

His hand comes up to cup my face. "I won't push you beyond your limits. I'll be there with you every time. And if you say you don't want to, then that's fine. We'll find another way."

"I know." I press a kiss to his cheek. "But promise you'll pull me out if it becomes too much."

"Always."

As we share a quiet dinner in our rooms, discussing strategy and training plans, I realize how quickly I've adapted to this new life. Now I'm contributing to war councils, being treated as a true Alpha Female.

The woman I was in the Silvercrest Pack wouldn't recognize the woman I'm becoming here.

The thought pleases my wolf.

*See? You are more here. A mate cannot harm.*

Later, as darkness falls over the mountains and the pack settles into their night routines, Ryker pulls me close in our bed. His arms encircle me from behind, his chest a solid wall of heat against my back. The claiming bond hums between us, stronger and more defined with each passing day.

"Rest," he murmurs against my hair. "Tomorrow will demand much from both of us."

The gentle touch of desire whispers along my skin, but he's right. I'm far too tired to give him my full attention. Instead, I nestle closer, drawing comfort from his presence.

In ten days, the new moon will rise. Thaddeus and his army will come. Blood will be spilled and fates decided.

But tonight, in the arms of the Shadowmist alpha, I'm safe.

Over the past seven days, a rhythm has formed—a brutal, relentless cadence to our lives that echoes the coming war. Mornings begin with Kitara submerged in the Vision Well, afternoons bring bruises and sweat in training with Zella, and evenings are spent in dim war rooms with my senior wolves, poring over maps and planning defenses.

The den pulses with tension. Everyone can feel the storm building.

But me? I watch Kitara.

Every morning, I escort her to the Well. Every morning, I steel myself against the instinct to demand she stop using her gift—to protect her from the toll it takes—but I know what it means to her. To the pack.

Today marks her seventh dive. She's changed. Stronger. Calmer. Her control deepens with every session. I can feel it in the bond that hums like live wire between us.

"You're sure you want to go again?" I ask, keeping my voice steady despite the worry that prowls beneath my skin whenever I look at her. Her skin gleams in the morning light, the claiming mark at her throat visible just above the surface. Gods, she's breathtaking.

"Tell me what to look for."

I sigh, pushing aside my unease to trust my mate to know her limits. "Focus on their approach vectors. I want to know where they'll strike."

She closes her eyes, and I feel it—her magic unfurling. The moment she reaches for me through the bond and anchors herself in my presence, it hits like a goddamn blow to the chest.

The power of it stirs my wolf, makes him pace restlessly within me. He wants to protect her, to shield her from the strain this puts on her mind and body—but we both know there's no other way. What comes for us will require everything we have. Everything she is.

A flicker passes across her face, and I know she's found what we seek. Thaddeus's forces are gathering, and we need to know how they plan to approach our territory.

"They've adjusted again," she reports, her voice sounding distant, as if it's coming from somewhere beyond her physical form. "They're planning a three-pronged attack. A primary force will come through the southern pass. A smaller unit circling from the north. And..." She squints, a small furrow appearing between her brows as she struggles to bring something into focus. "There's another, but I can't make it out."

I move closer to the edge of the Well, instinctively wanting to ground her. "What can you see?"

She concentrates, and I feel the increased strain through our bond. It takes everything in me not to pull her back, to protect her from the pain I know is building behind her eyes. But I trust her strength, her determination.

"The old mining shaft," she says after a moment. "The one we collapsed after the first attack."

A growl of frustration rumbles through my chest before I

can stop it. "Why would they be looking there? The pass is destroyed."

She tries to push deeper, and I feel her reaching for more —but then I sense something pushing back, a resistance that shouldn't be there. Pain spikes through our bond, and I know she's reaching her limit.

"There's... I can see...." She strains, her body tensing in the water. "Someone helping them. A shadow I can't quite..." She winces, and I feel the sharp pain behind her eyes as if it were my own. "I can't see who."

"Enough," I say, my voice cutting through the vision's grip. I won't allow her to hurt herself, not even for information we desperately need. "Come back now."

She withdraws her consciousness from the Well, and I can feel the effort it takes—like pulling herself from quicksand, one painstaking inch at a time.

I'm already there, hands around her waist, pulling her from the Well. Her body sags against mine. She's trembling. But fuck me—she's brilliant.

"Better," I murmur, holding her close. "You maintained the vision longer. How do you feel?"

She nods, a small smile touching her lips despite the exhaustion evident in the shadows beneath her eyes. "Exhausted, but I can feel it becoming easier. It's less like diving into frigid water."

I reach for a cloth, then begin to towel the water from her skin, taking more time than is strictly necessary. My wolf purrs at the contact, at this simple act of caring for our mate. Each sweep of the cloth across her arms, her shoulders, her back, is both practical and possessive—drying her and marking her with my scent in one motion.

"I'm sorry I couldn't identify the other wolf," she says, the frustration clear in her voice. "Someone's helping them, Ryker. Someone who knows our defenses, but I can't see who."

Frustration rises in my throat, sharp and bitter, but I swallow it down before it touches my voice. She's done more than enough. Pushed herself further than I would've dared ask. But gods, knowing someone within our walls is feeding information to Thaddeus... it curdles my blood.

"I've suspected we might have a mole in our midst. Your visions are showing adjustments based on our plans each day. If I didn't know better, I'd think Thaddeus had his own seer."

"Do you think so?" The question is hesitant, worried.

I shake my head. "We'd know about it if he did. It's more likely to be a rat."

"Do you have suspects?" she asks, leaning against me slightly.

The subtle weight of her, the trust in that simple gesture, tugs at a primitive part of me. I want to wrap her in my arms, carry her to our den, and keep her safe from all of this. Instead, I continue my careful ministrations, considering how much to share.

"Several," I finally admit, my jaw tightening at the thought. "But without proof, accusations only create division when we need unity most."

I crouch beside Kitara, dragging the towel lower to dry her calves, lingering just a moment too long at the delicate skin behind her knees. She leans into me, her body pliant, trusting. That trust is a blade to the chest.

I reach up, run my hand down her spine in slow, grounding strokes. "You've done well. You see more than any of us could. This isn't your burden to carry alone."

The war is coming. I can feel it in the air, see it in the increased preparations throughout our den. My wolves are readying themselves, weapons being forged, defenses reinforced, evacuation plans finalized for those too young or old to fight. The weight of their lives and safety rests on my shoulders—a familiar burden, but one that's grown heavier since claiming Kitara.

Before, I had only myself to risk. Now, I have everything to lose.

"Let me try once more," she suggests, turning back toward the Well. "Maybe if I focus specifically on the traitor—"

"No." My refusal is gentle but firm. I catch her elbow, turning her away from the temptation of the pool. "You're near your limit. Pushing further risks your health."

I can see she wants to argue, but then she nods, accepting my decision. This, too, is new—this trust between us that allows her to yield when necessary, just as I've learned to give ground when she pushes back.

"You are not failing," I say more firmly, cupping her chin so she looks at me. Her eyes are glassy, dark with exhaustion and self-doubt. I lean closer, lowering my forehead to hers.

She swallows hard, a small nod the only answer she can give. I press a kiss to her brow and capture her hand, entwining our fingers.

"I'll reassign the tunnel patrols," I say as we walk back toward the main dens. "Double them, using only wolves I've known since they were pups. And I'll have Lithia personally inspect the old mining shaft."

"You trust her that much?"

"With my life." The answer comes without hesitation. "She's certainly saved it often."

I see recognition in Kitara's eyes—she's likely remembering the vision she had of Lithia during their first confrontation on the stairs, where she saw how my second took a silver blade meant for me, earning the scar that marks her face.

"She's loyal to you above all else," Kitara observes.

"To the pack," I correct, because the distinction matters. "As Alpha, I embody the pack's interests, but Lithia's ultimate loyalty is to our people. If she ever believed I was acting against their welfare..." I shrug. "She would challenge me without hesitation."

This truth doesn't trouble me. In fact, it's one of the reasons I trust Lithia so deeply. She serves the pack first, me second. As it should be.

"What about the others?" Kitara asks. "Elias, Kaden, Dane, and Levi?"

I consider each member of my inner circle, weighing what I know of them against the possibility of betrayal. "Elias follows the chain of command. His loyalty is structural—to the position of Alpha rather than to me personally." I pause, thinking. "Dane is like his sister. Kaden's loyalty is earned through fairness and strength. He follows because I've proven worthy of following. Levi..."

I hesitate, choosing my words carefully. "Levi tolerates my leadership because challenging me would cost more than he's willing to pay. But he has ambitions of his own."

"He has alpha tendencies," Kitara notes perceptively.

I nod, acknowledging the truth of her observation. "In any other pack, he'd be alpha."

"Could he be the traitor?" she asks, voicing the thought that's crossed my mind more than once.

"Possibly," I admit. "But betraying the pack to Thaddeus doesn't serve his ambitions. If I fall, Levi wants to be the one who caused it—not because he's become the Grand Alpha's puppet."

The assessment is cold but necessary. Wolf politics have always been about power—who has it, who wants it, who's willing to do what to get it. I've navigated these waters my entire life, calculating risks and rewards, reading the motivations that drive others.

I glance over at her, the flush on her cheeks still high, her body humming with the aftermath of her magic. I should be thinking about the traitor. About war.

But all I can see is her.

"You did well today," I murmur, keeping my voice low and intimate. "Fucking impressive how fast you've progressed." I lean down until my mouth brushes the shell of her ear. "Such a good girl."

Her reaction is instant. Her breath catches. Her pulse kicks. And through the bond, I feel the flood of arousal that hits her. My cock twitches in my pants, thick and eager.

Her scent sharpens—sweet and slick and fucking mine.

Whatever plans I had for tonight? Gone. Erased by the way she shifts just slightly toward me, like her body's already answering mine.

"I have a good teacher," she replies, and there's a new confidence in the way she holds my gaze that makes my wolf surge with approval.

"And I have a dedicated student." I let my gaze hold hers with an intensity I no longer try to temper. "I think you deserve a reward."

I can almost taste her arousal in the air between us—the sweet musk of it calling to the predator in me, urging me to chase, to claim, to take. We've had so little time together since the training began. Each day filled with preparations for war, each night collapsing into exhausted sleep. But right now, she's here and alive and *mine*.

"Zella will be expecting me," she says weakly, but her body betrays her, leaning into my space rather than toward the door.

"Zella can wait." My hand comes up to cup her face, thumb brushing her lower lip in a gesture that's become achingly familiar. The softness of her skin, the slight tremble beneath my touch—it drives my wolf wild. "There are other forms of training equally as important."

"What kind of training?" she asks, and there's a new tease in her tone that makes my cock stiffen painfully against the constraint of my pants.

I don't answer with words. Instead, my fingers trail from

her face down the elegant line of her throat to the claiming mark, sending a surge of power through the bond. Her gasp and the way her pupils blow wide with desire tell me she feels it too—this connection that grows stronger each day, demanding completion.

My wolf is frantic with need by now, pawing at the boundaries of my control. It's been too long since I've properly claimed her, since I've reminded her—reminded us both—who she belongs to. Who I belong to.

My arm slides around her waist, pulling her flush against me with a suddenness that makes her gasp. "Come, little wolf," I murmur, letting the hunger show plainly in my voice. "It's time for you to teach me all the ways in which to please you."

Her scent spikes with arousal as I claim her mouth, my lips demanding, my tongue seeking entrance. She yields beautifully, melting against me with a soft moan that vibrates through my chest. Heat floods through our bond, and I feel her desire mirroring mine, amplifying it until it becomes impossible to tell where my need ends and hers begins.

She responds instinctively, arms winding around my neck, body arching into mine. Through our bond, her surrender pulses—rich and heady—encouraging me to take more, claim deeper.

*You own me,* her thoughts brush against mine, an intimate confession that makes my control fray further.

*And you me,* I respond, the truth of it resonating through my bones.

I've had countless females in my long life—temporary distractions, fleeting pleasures that meant nothing once the night ended. None of them prepared me for this—this bone-deep need to possess and be possessed, to mark and be marked. To belong.

I lift her effortlessly, carrying her toward our bed with strides made long by impatience. Her weight is nothing in my arms, her curves fitting perfectly against my harder planes. She belongs here, against me, with me. Every instinct I possess screams it.

Setting her down with more gentleness than my trembling muscles want to allow, I stand back to look at her—really look at her. Those eyes that see too much, both with her gift and without it. The face that's gradually losing the haunted, hunted look it wore when she first came to me. The body that was always meant to fit against mine.

"Tell me what you want, Kitara," I say, needing to hear it from her lips.

Instead of answering with words, she reaches for the hem of her shirt, pulling it over her head and tossing it aside with newfound confidence. The sight of her—skin flushed with desire, breasts heavy and perfect—drives the air from my lungs. My cock throbs painfully, demanding release.

She cups her breasts, offering them to me like some pagan sacrifice, and it takes everything in me not to fall to my knees before her.

"I want you to touch me again," she says, voice husky with need. "Like before. I want to feel..." Her breath hitches deliciously. "I want to feel you inside me."

The growl that tears from my throat is barely human. "You say things like that and expect me to go slow?"

"No," she admits, lifting her chin with that defiance that makes my wolf howl. "I want you to lose control."

"Kitara, I—" I start to warn her that she doesn't know what she's asking for, that the beast she's provoking has teeth and claws and no mercy—but she cuts me off, moving toward me with purpose.

Her hands brush mine aside, fingers finding the clasp of my belt, dragging it slowly from the loops. Each movement is deliberate, exploratory—as if she's learning how to be bold, how to take what she wants instead of waiting for it to be given.

She leans forward, pressing those soft lips to the hard plane of my stomach, just above the waistband of my pants. The touch is fire, sending jolts of electricity straight to my already aching cock. I exhale through my nose, fighting for control that's slipping with every second.

"I've been patient," she murmurs, each word a hot breath against my skin as she kisses lower, her fingers teasing at my waistband. "We've both been exhausted, but you can't promise me something then not deliver, Ryker." She looks up at me, and the sight of her like this—on her knees, eyes dark with want—nearly undoes me. "Make love to me."

"Kitara—" I try once more to warn her, to give her an out before the beast breaks its chains—but then she's tugging my fly down, and my cock springs free, hard and aching and so ready for her it's nearly purple with need.

The moan she makes at the sight of me is enough to shatter what's left of my restraint.

"Can I taste?" she asks, her small hand wrapping around my length, and gods help me, but the image of those perfect lips stretched around my cock makes my head spin.

"You can do whatever the fuck you want to me," I tell her through gritted teeth, knowing it's the absolute truth. There's nothing I would deny her, nothing I wouldn't give if she asked. "But know you're playing a dangerous game, little wolf."

"Good," she whispers, her hand giving my length a slow, experimental pump that has me seeing stars.

My control snaps at her response, at the teasing smile playing at the corners of her mouth. I fist one hand in her hair, dragging her head back so our eyes meet. I need her to see what she's unleashed, what's coming for her.

"You want to act like a little tease?" I growl, nostrils flaring as I inhale the rich scent of her arousal. "Fine. But you're not getting out of this bed until I've knotted you so deep you forget your own damn name."

A devil dances in her eyes as she meets my gaze. "Promise?"

The challenge in that single word is the final straw. With a snarl that's pure alpha, I yank her up to me, claiming her mouth in a kiss that's all teeth and tongue and primal need. There's no gentleness in it, no restraint, just raw hunger that's been building since the moment I first scented her in that clearing.

She meets me with equal fervor, clawing at my shirt, biting my bottom lip in a way that makes my cock throb with anticipation. I push her back onto the bed, pinning her with my weight, reveling in the way she yields and challenges all at once.

"You think you're in charge?" I rasp against her mouth as my hands shred what's left of her clothes, needing her bare beneath me now. "You think you can just touch me and I won't lose control?"

She gasps as I press one thick thigh between her legs, forcing her to grind against the hard muscle. The heat of her, the slick evidence of her desire, makes my mouth water with the need to taste her again.

"I was trying to be polite," she pants, rubbing herself shamelessly against my thigh. "But if you want to throw me down and fuck me—gods, Ryker, please—"

I grab her thighs, my hands digging into their fleshy fullness with a strength that will leave marks tomorrow—marks that satisfy some primitive part of me. "Oh, I'm going to ruin you."

"You already did," she pants, the words half challenge, half surrender as she licks up to my jaw. "And I want more."

I'm panting like a beast in rut as I leave her to drop down between those soft thighs, one broad palm splaying over her belly to hold her in place. The scent of her arousal is intoxicating—sweet musk and heat that calls to my wolf.

"I need to taste you," I tell her, my voice barely

recognizable even to my own ears. "Need to see how wet you've been for me, how aching and unsatisfied."

I force her legs open wider and dive in without preamble, my tongue flicking over her clit once, twice, before I begin to feast like a starving man. The taste of her—gods, the taste—is better than anything I've ever known. Rich and complex and addictive. I could spend hours worshipping her like this, learning every fold and secret place, cataloging each sound she makes as I draw her pleasure higher.

She arches off the bed, thighs trembling on either side of my head, her moans a symphony that drives me wild. I suck and lick, teasing her clit with slow, deliberate circles that have her writhing beneath my mouth.

"You're soaked," I groan, pulling back just enough to look at her—spread and glistening and perfect. My mouth is wet with her essence, and something about the way her eyes darken at the sight makes me even harder. "You need this. You need me."

"Yes," she gasps, clawing at my arms with desperate hands. "Please, Ryker. Fuck me. Knot me. I want to feel you claim me."

The words are like gasoline on a fire, burning through what little control I have left. I rise over her, cock thick and aching between us, ready to give her exactly what she's begging for.

"Turn over," I command, wanting to take her from behind, to mount her properly the way my wolf is howling for.

"No," she refuses, wrapping those soft thighs around my waist and pulling me closer. "I want to see your face when you lose control."

The defiance in her eyes makes my wolf snarl with equal parts frustration and desire. Even now, yielding to me, she's challenging me. Making this her choice, her surrender rather than my conquest.

It drives me fucking wild.

"You think you're in charge?" I growl, positioning myself at her entrance, the head of my cock sliding through her slick folds, teasing us both.

"No," she whispers, dragging her nails down my back in a way that makes my hips buck involuntarily. "But I want to be taken."

The balance of surrender and demand in her words snaps the last thread of my restraint. I thrust forward in one savage stroke, burying myself to the hilt in her tight heat. The sensation is so intense, so overwhelming, that for a moment I can't breathe, can't think, can only feel.

She's so tight, so perfect around me, her inner walls clenching and fluttering as she adjusts to my size. I have to fight not to come immediately like some untested pup, the pleasure so acute it borders on pain.

"Fuck, Kitara—" I groan, trembling with the effort of holding still, giving her time to adjust. "You're so fucking tight."

She can't speak—head thrown back, eyes squeezed shut— as she takes all of me. I can feel her working through the stretch, the initial burn giving way to pleasure as her body adapts. The bond between us thrums like a live wire, each sensation amplified and shared until it's impossible to tell where her pleasure ends and mine begins.

I pull out slowly, watching with fascination as her body clings to mine—reluctant to let me go—then slam back in, harder this time, driven by the need to claim every inch of her.

"Is this what you wanted?" I growl, establishing a rhythm that's just shy of brutal. "You aching for it, little mate? You begging to be knotted like a good girl?"

"Yes," she gasps, her legs wrapping tighter around me, heels digging into my back to pull me deeper. "Don't stop. Please, don't stop—"

I have no intention of stopping. Not now, not when she's

finally, properly mine. I fuck her like I've wanted to since the moment I first caught her scent—deep, hard, possessive. Each thrust is a claim, each withdrawal a promise to return.

My hands grip her hips, pulling her into every punishing thrust. My mouth finds her skin, biting, marking, tasting the salt of her sweat and the sweet flavor that's uniquely her. My cock drives into her with a rhythm that builds and builds, chasing our shared release.

"You're mine," I snarl, needing to hear her say it, needing her to acknowledge what we both know is truth. "Say it."

"I'm yours," she gasps, her eyes holding mine with an honesty that makes my chest ache.

"Again," I demand, needing more, always more from her.

"Yours, Ryker. Always yours."

Something breaks inside me—not just the thin veneer of civilization I've maintained, but a wall I didn't know existed until her simple declaration brought it down. A rumble tears from my chest, a sound almost broken with the weight of emotion behind it.

My thrusts grow faster, harder, more punishing as I feel my release building, my knot beginning to swell at the base of my cock. The pressure builds with each stroke, my body preparing to lock with hers, to seal us together in the most primal way possible.

She feels it too, her eyes widening as the growing knot catches at her entrance with each thrust. "You're close—" she gasps, her body trembling beneath mine.

"So are you," I growl, fucking her faster, chasing that last edge that will send us both over. I can feel her tightening around me, the telltale flutter of her inner walls signaling her approaching climax. "Come for me, Kitara. Fuck my cock. Show me you're mine."

And gods, she does. Her body locks around me, back arching off the bed as she screams my name, her release triggering my own. With one final, powerful thrust, my knot swells to its full size, locking us together as I spill inside her in pulsing waves that seem endless.

I roar as I come, the sound tearing from somewhere deeper than my chest, somewhere primal and ancient that recognizes this moment for what it is—not just physical release but something transcendent, something that binds us together more completely than even the claiming mark.

She feels it too, I know she does. The bond between us explodes with white-hot magic, crackling through our veins like lightning finding ground. Through it, I feel everything— her pleasure, her awe, her surrender and triumph all at once.

And beneath it all lays a fear that sits cold and heavy in my gut despite the heat of our joined bodies. The terror of loss. The knowledge that what we've found together is both perfect and fragile, a flame that could be extinguished by the coming storm.

She reaches up, pulling me down to kiss her, long and slow and soft—a promise sealed with gasping breath and trembling limbs. *I'm not going anywhere*, the kiss seems to say. *This is just the beginning.*

We lie there, fused together by my knot, the aftershocks still rippling through us. Her body softens beneath mine, tension melting away as she relaxes into the aftermath. I shift my weight to avoid crushing her, though I remain buried deep inside her, unable to separate even if I wanted to.

"I didn't mean to be rough," I murmur against her neck, suddenly aware of how wild I'd been, how completely I'd lost control. "Did I hurt you?"

"Never," she whispers back, and the trust in that single word undoes me all over again. "And also... that was really hot."

A laugh breaks free, the sound rusty but genuine. "You've ruined me, little wolf."

Her smile is wicked, satisfied in a way I've never seen

before. "I'll ruin you again. Just give me five minutes and a glass of water."

My chest shakes with laughter, joy and relief and a hundred other emotions I can't name washing through me. "Deal."

As my knot slowly begins to recede, I hold her close, memorizing every detail of this moment—the way her body fits perfectly against mine, the weight of her in my arms, the scent of us mingled on her skin.

The war is coming. Thaddeus gathers his forces. A traitor moves among us. But right here, right now, none of that matters.

She is mine. I am hers. And woe be to anyone who tries to separate us.

# TWENTY

As the days tick down toward the new moon, the atmosphere in the Shadowmist den shifts. Where before there was tension and preparation, now there's grim determination, an almost palpable sense of imminent confrontation. The new moon is just two days away, and every pack member old enough to fight has been assigned to defensive positions.

"You're certain about the timing?" Ryker asks as we review the latest intelligence in our chambers. Maps cover every surface, marked with defensive positions and enemy approach vectors based on my visions.

"Yes," I confirm, tracing the southern approach with my finger. "Thaddeus will lead the main force himself. They'll reach the outer perimeter just before midnight on the new moon." I indicate another position on the map. "The east force will move an hour earlier, hoping to emerge behind our lines during the initial engagement."

Ryker studies the markings, his expression thoughtful. We've prepared for this attack from every angle—traps laid along approach routes, and ambush points established.

There's nothing more we can do but keep adjusting as we gain new information.

I should feel confident in our preparations, but unease lingers at the edges of my awareness.

It makes me nervous.

A sharp knock interrupts my thoughts. Lithia enters without waiting for permission, her scarred face tense with urgency.

"Forgive the intrusion, Alpha, but a messenger has arrived at our borders. From the Grand Alpha himself."

Ryker straightens, immediately alert. "Carrying what message?"

"A truce offer." Lithia's expression reflects her skepticism. "Thaddeus requests a summit. Neutral territory. Tomorrow at midday."

The timing is too convenient to be coincidence—just one day before their planned attack.

"Who delivered this request?"

"One of his personal guards. Alone, unarmed, carrying the white flag of parley." Lithia's voice carries grudging respect for the messenger. "It bears Thaddeus's seal."

Ryker turns to me, his mismatched gaze questioning. "What do you see, little mate?"

I close my eyes, reaching not for a full vision but for the intuitive sense my gift provides even without the Well's amplification.

But something catches.

A thread. A pull.

I frown, focusing.

The world tilts.

My breath catches as I'm dragged under—not gently, not like the warm pull of the Vision Well, but like claws yanking me into freezing water.

*Darkness.*

*Then firelight.*

*I stand on the edge of a wide plateau, the night sky above me pulsing red with embers. Below, wolves gather. Hundreds of them. Their eyes glow like coals in the dark. And in the center, elevated on a rise of stone, Thaddeus.*

*He's different to when I've seen him in past visions. Gaunt. Haggard. Yet his presence burns brighter. Stronger.*

*Desperation can be a kind of power.*

*He raises his hand and silence falls. "This is not war," he says, voice carrying unnaturally. "This is correction. Shadowmist has forgotten its place. Ryker has broken the order. I will restore it."*

*The wolves howl in reply—some loyal, some bound by blood, others too afraid to defy him.*

*But not all.*

*Behind him, a figure shifts. Cloaked. Female.*

*She turns her head, and for a moment, her face flickers—between identities, between masks. A blur where there should be certainty.*

*I try to focus on her, to see—but her presence resists me, slippery as oil. The vision fractures around her edges.*

*Then the sky splits.*

*A second figure descends from the cliffs—Ryker.*

*His eyes meet mine.*

*Not the vision's me—me. The real me.*

*His voice rips through the dreamspace like thunder. "Kitara. Get out!"*

Pain lances behind my eyes. My legs give out.

Reality rushes in, jagged and sharp, and I find myself crumpled in Ryker's arms, shaking, cold sweat coating my skin.

"Kitara—fuck, what happened?"

I shake my head, battling to make sense of what I saw.

"I... I don't now. Thaddeus is rallying his wolves. But there's someone else, someone behind him. A woman. She's cloaked, I couldn't get a fix."

Without a word, he rises, carrying me through our rooms

to our bed. Gently, he lays me down, calling for a cup of water.

His profile is sharp, the scar across his eye catching the sun, casting a faint glow along its edge.

Lithia enters, handing me the cup.

"What happens if we refuse?" I ask her, handing back the empty vessel.

"He'll claim we rejected peaceful resolution and use it to justify greater force against us. Perhaps sway neutral packs to his cause." She shakes her head. "Politically, refusing makes us appear the aggressors despite the reality."

"And if we accept?" I ask

"It's almost certainly a trap," Ryker replies. "But one we enter with eyes open, on our terms."

Through our bond, I feel Ryker's thoughts churning—weighing options, calculating risks, considering angles. His strategic mind, so different from mine and yet complementary to it, works through the scenarios.

"Bring the council," he decides. "We'll discuss this together."

The council chamber fills quickly, all senior wolves responding to the urgent summons. Elias arrives with his hunting unit, including Zella who offers me a reassuring smile as she takes her place. Elder Lyra enters last, her silver-streaked hair gleaming in the torch light.

"A summit," Levi says once Lithia has explained the situation. His tone drips with suspicion. "Conveniently timed."

"Could they know we're aware of their plans?" Elias asks. "Perhaps this is an adjustment to our foreknowledge."

I consider this possibility. "I don't think so. The messenger would have been dispatched before my most recent visions of their movements."

"Then it's definitely a trap," Kaden concludes, unusually

serious. "The question is, what kind, and is it one worth walking into?"

Ryker stands at the head of the table, power radiating from his massive frame. "Opinions. Starting with Lithia."

His second straightens. "I advise caution but engagement. Attend with a strong escort. Use the meeting to gather intelligence on their forces. At minimum, it delays their attack while giving us additional preparation time."

"Elias?"

The security chief frowns. "Too risky. Thaddeus wouldn't offer truce unless he believed it served his advantage. I recommend declining with diplomatic language that doesn't close the door entirely."

"Zella?"

She glances at me before addressing Ryker. "I suggest a compromise. Accept the summit but send representatives rather than attending yourself. The Alpha is too valuable to risk in what's likely a trap."

Murmurs of agreement follow her suggestion, but I feel Ryker's immediate rejection through our bond. He doesn't send others into danger he himself won't face.

"Elder Lyra?" Ryker turns to the oldest wolf present.

The elder studies him with knowing eyes. "You must go," she says simply. "But not alone, and not unprotected. Take a small force of your most trusted. Leave the majority here to prepare for what follows, regardless of the summit's outcome."

Ryker nods, and I know her assessment aligns with his own instincts. "Kitara?" he asks, looking to me. "What do you advise?"

"I believe we should accept," I say after careful consideration. "But I should accompany you."

Immediate protest erupts, voices overlapping in objection. Ryker raises a hand, silencing them with the simple gesture.

"Explain," he prompts me.

"My gift could prove invaluable during negotiations. I might sense deception, see intentions hidden behind diplomatic words." I meet his gaze steadily. "And more importantly, Thaddeus wants me. My presence may distract him, make him less cautious. If he breaks the truce, then no wolf will stand with him—the laws are what binds the wolves."

"It will make you a target," Lithia counters.

"I already am a target," I remind her. "But one who now has means to protect herself."

"If I may," Zella interjects, her expression earnest. "I've been training with the Alpha Female. Her progress is remarkable, but a battlefield or diplomatic confrontation is different from controlled practice." She looks to me with apologetic eyes. "I recommend against placing her in unnecessary danger."

Before I can respond, Levi speaks.

"For once, I agree with the Alpha Female," he says, surprising everyone. "Thaddeus's obsession with seers is well-documented. Her presence changes the dynamic in ways that could benefit our position."

The debate continues, perspectives shifting as various scenarios are explored. Through it all, Ryker remains silent, absorbing every viewpoint while his own decision forms. I feel it taking shape—certainty crystallizing from the chaos of possibilities.

"Enough," he finally says, commanding immediate silence. "We will accept Thaddeus's offer. I will attend, along with a small escort of elite fighters." His eyes meet mine. "And yes, the Alpha Female will accompany me."

I want to sink with relief, grateful he won't leave me behind.

*Thank you.*

He shakes his head silently. *I don't want to put you in harm's way, but you're right. You can help more there, than here.*

I know what it costs him to admit that—and to put me in danger. Under the table, my hand finds his, squeezing.

The others accept his decision in varying degrees, though I notice Zella's lingering concern as the council disperses to prepare for the summit.

"You're certain about this?" she asks, catching me in the corridor afterward. "Thaddeus is dangerous, especially to someone with your gift."

"I'm certain I belong at Ryker's side," I reply. "Whatever comes."

Her expression softens. "Then allow me to accompany you as personal guard. I've been training you—I know your capabilities and limitations better than anyone except the Alpha."

I'm touched by her offer. "I'll speak to Ryker about it," I promise.

She nods, seemingly satisfied, and moves to join the other wolves preparing for tomorrow's summit. Over her shoulder, I see Lithia watching me. Her gaze is steel as she stares, her face blank. That vague unease returns, a whisper of knowledge that I'm missing something.

Forcing myself to turn away, I go in search of my alpha.

NIGHT FINDS RYKER and me in our chambers, finalizing preparations for the summit. He's selected five wolves to accompany us—Lithia, naturally, along with Elias and three elite fighters I've come to know during training sessions. Zella has been added as a last-minute addition to the party at my request, assigned specifically as my personal guard.

"I still don't like this," Ryker admits as we prepare for bed. "Taking you into potential danger goes against every instinct I possess."

"Yet you agreed," I observe, watching him pace like his wolf form would, powerful and predatory even in human skin.

"Because your reasoning is sound." He stops, turning to face me fully. "And because our bond is stronger together than apart. If anything happens, if Thaddeus tries something unexpected..."

"We'll face it together," I finish for him, approaching to place my hands on his chest.

His arms encircle me, drawing me against the solid wall of his body.

"You should try to seek a vision tonight," he suggests, his voice rumbling through his chest against my ear. "See what you can of tomorrow's summit. Any advantage we can gain..."

I nod, though fatigue pulls at my limbs after a day of preparation and planning. "Will you anchor me?"

"Always." The single word carries layers of meaning between us.

We move to the bed, arranging ourselves—Ryker seated with his back against the headboard, me nestled between his legs, my back to his chest, his arms encircling me.

"Ready?" he asks, his lips at my temple.

I nod, closing my eyes and reaching for our bond. It responds instantly, his power flowing into me through the claiming mark. Anchored in his strength, I extend my gift outward, seeking glimpses of what awaits us at tomorrow's summit.

*The vision comes slowly, fragmented at first, less clear than if I was within the Well. It's a clearing in neutral territory, wolves from multiple packs are gathered. I push deeper, trying to see beneath the diplomatic veneer to the Grand Alpha's true intentions.*

*Images flash faster—Thaddeus's eyes fixed not on Ryker but on me. I push harder, seeking clarity, trying to see if there's a moment when diplomacy will give way to violence. The vision blurs, resistance pushing back against my probe as if something or someone is actively shielding these particular futures from my sight.*

*Pain spikes behind my eyes, the familiar warning that I'm reaching my limits despite Ryker's anchoring presence. I try to withdraw gently, but the vision clings to me with unusual tenacity, dragging me deeper despite my resistance.*

*A new scene forms—unfamiliar stone walls, silver chains, a small chamber lit by torchlight. I see myself, bound and isolated, cut off from the bond by silver's deadly influence. The image is so vivid, so immediate that it feels less like possibility and more like inevitability.*

*Then, strangely, the vision shifts once more—but instead of seeing, I hear. A woman's voice, familiar yet distorted by the vision's haze, speaking words I can't quite grasp.*

*"It ends here."*

With a gasp, I wrench myself free, returning to the present with jarring suddenness. Ryker's arms tighten around me as I tremble with the aftermath of forced withdrawal.

"Kitara?" he asks, concern evident in his voice.

"I'm okay." I fold forward, breathing deep. "Just tired."

He rubs my back gently as I try to calm.

"It's a trap," I manage through ragged breaths. "The summit is definitely a trap. Thaddeus wants me, not peace."

Ryker's growl vibrates through his chest against my back. "Then we don't go."

"No." I turn in his arms, needing to see his face. "We must. There's something else happening, something I couldn't quite see. If we don't go tomorrow, we won't end this."

His gaze searches mine. "You truly believe this is important enough to risk your safety?"

"I think so." I struggle to articulate the certainty I feel despite the vision's fragmentation. "The prophecy, Ryker. Tomorrow might be when you confront Thaddeus."

His expression hardens, determination replacing concern.

"Then we prepare accordingly. Double guards, additional precautions."

The image of myself in chains flashes through my mind again, disturbingly vivid. "If we're separated?"

"We won't be," he says with absolute conviction. "No matter what happens, I will find you. I will always find you."

The certainty in his voice should comfort me, but the lingering impression of that final vision—me alone, bound in silver, cut off from our bond—haunts me as we prepare for sleep.

As Ryker's breathing deepens beside me, sleep eludes me. I stare into the darkness, turning over fragments of the vision like puzzle pieces that refuse to form a coherent whole. The woman's voice in that final moment nags at my memory—familiar yet strangely distorted, speaking of duty and necessity.

Whose voice? What duty? What ending?

The questions circle without resolution until exhaustion finally claims me, dragging me into uneasy dreams of silver chains and severed bonds.

DAWN BREAKS clear and cold over the Shadowmist territory, the mountain peaks catching first light while the valleys remain shrouded in shadow. Our preparations begin early—weapons checked and secured, final strategies confirmed.

Ryker stands before me in his full alpha regalia—black clothing of the finest materials, gold symbols of the Shadowmist Pack gleaming at his throat and wrists. Power radiates from him in almost visible waves, his authority absolute and unquestioned.

"Here," he says, presenting me with a bundle wrapped in soft leather. "For you."

I unwrap it to find a dagger unlike any I've seen before. Its blade seems to shift between silver and shadow depending on how light falls across its surface, its hilt carved with the same runes that mark Ryker's shoulder.

"Shadow silver," he explains as I examine it with reverent fingers. "Extremely rare. Lethal to wolf-kind when in our blood stream but doesn't cause the burning reaction of pure silver when touching our skin."

"It's beautiful," I murmur, testing its balance in my hand.

"And deadly, in the right hands." His fingers close over mine around the wooden hilt. "Zella tells me you've become quite skilled with blade work during your training."

Pride warms me at his acknowledgment of my progress. I've thrown myself into combat training with single-minded determination, driven by the knowledge that I cannot rely solely on others for protection in the coming conflict.

I'm not the best, but I can hold my own if required.

"Keep it concealed but accessible," he instructs. "Use it only if absolutely necessary, but without hesitation if that moment comes."

I nod, understanding both the gift and the responsibility it represents. The dagger disappears into a specially designed sheath at my waist, hidden by the folds of my dress but ready to hand if needed.

The clothing chosen for me makes its own statement—a fitted dress in the Shadowmist colors of black and silver, but cut to allow freedom of movement unlike the restrictive garments typically worn by Alpha Females. The claiming mark at my throat remains deliberately visible, a clear declaration of my status and protection.

"Ready?" Ryker asks as our final preparations conclude.

I reach for our bond, drawing strength from his unwavering presence. "Yes."

But neither of us moves right away.

He steps in close, hands finding my waist as his forehead

lowers to mine. We stand there for a long moment, breathing in sync, hearts aligned. His thumbs trace soft circles through the fabric at my hips, grounding me with his touch.

Then he kisses me.

It's not rushed, hungry, or desperate. This is no goodbye kiss. It's a promise, a reminder that I'm not facing this alone, and neither is he.

When we part, his forehead finds mine again. We don't speak. We don't need to.

We descend to the den's main entrance where our escort awaits—Lithia and Elias in formal attire that doesn't quite conceal the weapons they carry. The three elite fighters—Thorn, Vex, and Ash—and Zella, are dressed more practically in clothing designed for quick movement rather than ceremonial impression. More wolves follow—our extra guards.

"Alpha Female," Zella greets me with a respectful nod. "I'll be at your side throughout the summit. Just signal if you need anything."

Our journey to the neutral meeting ground takes several hours, moving through territories that border multiple packs. The location—an ancient clearing marked by standing stones —has historically served as meeting ground for pack negotiations and treaties.

As we approach, the scents of other wolves reach us— Moonclaw, Red River, Grayback, and others I don't recognize, all mingling in the clearing ahead. Ryker's posture shifts subtly, his entire being radiating the controlled power that makes him such a formidable alpha.

"Stay close to me," he murmurs, his hand finding mine for a brief, reassuring squeeze. "Watch everything. Trust no one except our own."

The clearing opens before us, revealing a scene much like my fragmented vision—wolves from multiple packs arranged in careful formation, tension vibrating in the air despite the ostensible peaceful purpose of our gathering. At the center stands Thaddeus, his white hair gleaming in the midday sun, power rolling off him in waves matching Ryker's own.

Our arrival causes a ripple through the assembled wolves, conversations faltering as attention shifts to the Shadowmist alpha and his unusual mate. I feel the weight of countless stares—some curious, some hostile, some calculating in ways that make my skin crawl.

"Ryker Ashmere." Thaddeus's voice carries across the clearing, powerful despite his advanced age. "You honor us with your presence."

"Grand Alpha." Ryker's acknowledgment is minimal, his tone revealing nothing of his true feelings toward his father.

Thaddeus's gaze shifts to me, his silver eyes cold with assessment. "And the seer. How... interesting to see you participating in pack politics so soon after your claiming."

The subtle barb doesn't escape me—the implication that my presence is somehow inappropriate, that a female so newly claimed should be sheltered rather than involved in diplomatic affairs. Before Ryker can respond, I step forward.

"I go where my Alpha goes," I reply, my voice steady despite the nervous flutter in my stomach. "As is proper for the Alpha Female of the Shadowmist Pack."

A murmur runs through the gathered wolves at my boldness. Through our bond, I feel Ryker's approval. Thaddeus's expression remains impassive, but something flickers in his eyes—calculation, perhaps, or reassessment.

"Indeed." He gestures toward a circular arrangement of seats at the clearing's center. "Shall we begin? There is much to discuss."

As we move forward, our escort falls into practiced formation around us. I notice Zella positioning herself at my right shoulder, slightly closer than strictly necessary. Her presence is reassuring, despite my unease at our situation.

The summit proceeds with formal declarations from each

pack represented—grievances aired, positions stated, alliances affirmed. Throughout it all, I observe Thaddeus closely, searching for hints of his true intentions beneath the diplomatic facade. Through our bond, I sense Ryker doing the same.

When Thaddeus finally addresses the central issue—his accusation that Ryker "stole" a valuable seer from the collective packs—I feel tension spike through our escort. Hands move subtly closer to concealed weapons, bodies shift into more defensible positions.

"The claiming was legitimate under pack law," Ryker states, his voice carrying just enough edge to remind everyone of his reputation. "My mate ran in the ceremony, she bears my mark willingly, and even now a pup may be growing within her. The matter is settled."

"Is it?" Thaddeus's smile doesn't reach his eyes. "A seer of such power should belong to all wolf-kind, not sequestered with a single pack—particularly one with such... unconventional views on our traditions."

"She is not property," Ryker counters, his control admirable despite the provocation. "She is my mate, my Alpha Female. Her gift is hers to do with as she wishes."

Thaddeus leans forward, his attention shifting fully to me. "And what do you choose, little seer? Do you truly wish to remain bound to the shadow wolves, cut off from your proper place among civilized packs?"

The direct address catches me by surprise. In traditional pack dynamics, alphas speak to alphas—not to their mates. Ryker tenses beside me, but I place a calming hand on his arm.

"I choose to honor the pack that values me," I reply, meeting Thaddeus's gaze directly. "And to be with the alpha who sees me as partner rather than tool." I lift my chin slightly. "I choose the Shadowmist freely and without reservation."

Something dangerous flashes in Thaddeus's eyes. "Bold words from one who spent her life serving the Silvercrest."

"Servitude and choice are different matters," I respond. "As you well know."

Thaddeus's expression hardens, power crackling around him like static electricity. "Enough pleasantries," he declares, rising to his full height. "I extended this invitation hoping reason might prevail, but I see the shadow wolf's influence has already corrupted you beyond salvation."

Ryker stands as well, his massive frame dwarfing even Thaddeus's considerable presence. "If you have a proposal, make it. If not, we're finished here."

"Oh, I have a proposal." Thaddeus's smile turns predatory. "Surrender the seer to a proper cleansing, rescind your claim, and return to your mountains. Do this, and the allied packs will allow the Shadowmist to continue its existence unmolested."

"And if I refuse?" Ryker's voice drops to a dangerous rumble.

"Then what follows will be on your head alone." Thaddeus's gaze sweeps our small group. "You are outnumbered, outmatched, and surrounded. Even now, forces gather at your borders, waiting for my signal."

The threat hangs in the air, clear and unambiguous. I feel Ryker's calculation—not fear, never fear, but he's struggling to see a way forward that doesn't end in bloodshed.

"We came here in good faith. You would break truce to own another's mate?"

"I break no truce," Thaddeus snarls. "You have broken sanctity with us, long ago."

"The Shadowmist has never lost sight of our true lore—that of the wolf. We will not start now."

"Then war it is." Thaddeus's declaration carries finality. "Beginning here, beginning now."

The words act as a signal—wolves from multiple packs

shifting stance from diplomatic to aggressive, hands moving to concealed weapons, bodies tensing for combat. Our escort responds instantly, forming a protective circle around Ryker and me.

Adrenaline spikes, a sharp tang on my tongue. I don't move—can't—but every nerve is lit up, my senses on fire. The thud of my heartbeat echoes through my chest, each beat a warning drum. Still, I force myself to stay upright, rooted, watching. Observing every shift in posture, every flicker of movement.

Then, instinctively, my hand drifts to my waist, fingers brushing the hidden sheath beneath my dress. The dagger Ryker gave me waits.

"This violates our sacred truce," Ryker growls, though he sounds unsurprised. "Even for you, Thaddeus, breaking parley is low."

"Nothing is sacred when the future of our kind hangs in the balance." Thaddeus makes a subtle gesture, and his personal guards step forward. "One last chance, shadow wolf. Surrender the seer."

"Never."

The single word carries absolute conviction. I can feel Ryker's unwavering resolve, his willingness to fight and die rather than yield me to Thaddeus's "cleansing"—a process I know would destroy not just my freedom but my sanity.

Time seems to slow as tension crests toward inevitable violence. I reach for Ryker's hand, our fingers intertwining in silent solidarity. Whatever comes, we face it together.

"As you wish." Thaddeus steps back, and chaos erupts.

Wolves from all sides surge forward, weapons appearing as if by magic. Our escort meets them in a violent clash—Lithia engages three attackers at once, Elias back-to-back with Thorn take on a group of Moonclaw enforcers, while Vex and Ash create a defensive perimeter around us alongside the remaining escort.

Ryker pulls me behind him as he shifts, his massive black wolf manifesting in an eyeblink. He shakes off the remnants of his shredded clothes, baring his teeth. The transformation sends attackers stumbling back, even hardened warriors hesitating before the legendary Shadowmist alpha.

Then the battlefield erupts.

All around me, wolves clash in a frenzy of fur and steel. Snarls split the air, a guttural, violent chorus that drowns out rational thought. The coppery tang of blood invades my nostrils, thick and metallic, mingling with the scent of sweat, fear, and fury. Blades flash under the moonlight—silver arcing through shadows— met with claws and teeth bared in feral rage.

A wolf from our escort lunges toward a rival, jaws locking onto the other's throat. They tumble to the ground in a blur, limbs tangled, snarls deafening as they roll through the dirt. Another warrior screams—human, not shifted—the sound abruptly cut off as he falls to his knees, crimson gushing from a wound in his side.

I recognize him—Oliver, one of the youngest fighters from the eastern flank. His sword slips from his hand as he's tackled by two larger wolves, one of them sinking teeth into his shoulder.

My breath catches and everything slows for half a second. *This is real.*

Zella appears at my side, her hand clamping down on my arm. "Stay with me," she urges, tugging me toward what looks like a thinning in the fight—a narrow corridor of potential escape that's rapidly closing.

"We can't leave him—" I protest, my eyes tracking Ryker. He's a force of destruction, all primal fury and lethal grace. Every movement is purposeful, deadly—fangs flashing, claws raking down flesh, blood spraying as he sends enemy after enemy to the ground. He's holding nothing back.

Instinct rebels at the idea of running. Our bond thrums like a struck chord, vibrating through my bones with protest.

*Don't leave. Stay. Fight.*

"He ordered me to protect you at all costs," Zella says fiercely, yanking again. "Trust me, Kitara. Please."

The battlefield shifts again—our defenders pushed back by sheer numbers. A feral scream cuts through the melee, followed by the unmistakable sound of metal meeting bone.

"This way!" Zella growls, dragging me now. "Quickly, before they surround us completely!"

My body finally responds. Decision made, I follow her, trusting her instincts more than my own. We race toward the tree line, her body half shielding mine from the chaos behind.

Through our bond, I feel Ryker's sharp flare of alarm at our movement—then reluctant approval.

*Get clear. I'll find you after.*

The words settle me, a balm in the storm.

We break into the forest just as the sounds of battle begin to dim behind us—though they never truly fade.

"Where are we going?" I ask between ragged breaths, dodging branches as we run.

"Secondary rendezvous point," she replies, never slowing. "Established during planning. The others will meet us there if separated."

The explanation makes sense, though I don't recall this specific detail from our preparation discussions. Before I can question further, sounds of pursuit reach us—crashing underbrush and voices calling commands.

"They're following," I warn, though Zella has clearly heard as well.

Her expression hardens with determination. "Then we need to move faster." She grasps my hand more firmly. "Stay with me. Don't look back."

We run deeper into unfamiliar forest, the sounds of the summit battle fading only to be replaced by the more immediate concern of pursuit. Zella navigates the uneven terrain with supernatural grace, adjusting our pace to my human limitations while still maintaining distance from our hunters.

After what feels like miles, she pulls me into a small ravine, the steep sides providing momentary concealment.

"Wait here," she instructs, her breathing barely elevated despite our sprint. "I'll draw them off, then circle back for you."

Alarm spikes through me. "No! We should stay together."

"They're too close. I can move faster alone, create a false trail they'll follow. You'll be safer hidden."

"Zella, I don't think—"

"Trust me," she interrupts, her green eyes pleading. "I won't fail you."

Before I can respond, she's gone, scaling the ravine with effortless grace and disappearing into the forest.

Left alone, I press myself against the earth wall, controlling my breathing as I strain to hear our pursuers.

Footsteps approach from above—multiple wolves moving with the controlled quiet of trained hunters. I remain motionless, hoping the ravine's shadows conceal me from casual inspection.

"Anything?" a male voice asks.

"Trail splits here," another replies. "One heading east, probably the tracker female. The other..." A pause, followed by a sound of satisfaction. "Down there. The seer's scent is clear."

My heart freezes. They shouldn't be able to track me so easily, not with Zella's expert misdirection. Unless...

Understanding crashes over me with sickening clarity just as figures appear at the ravine's edge, looking down at my hiding place with predatory satisfaction. The woman's voice from my vision—familiar yet distorted—suddenly makes horrifying sense.

"Today is about duty, about necessity, about the greater good."

A familiar figure joins them at the ridge, her chestnut hair gleaming in dappled sunlight filtering through the trees. Zella looks down at me, her expression no longer warm or friendly but coolly detached.

"Well done," one of the males tells her. "The Grand Alpha will be pleased."

"Just fulfilling my duty," she replies, her voice carrying easily to my shocked ears. "As I've done since he placed me in their den."

The betrayal hits like physical pain, stealing my breath more effectively than any blow. Zella—my friend, my trainer, my confidante—has been Thaddeus's agent all along.

The shadow silver dagger seems to burn against my side, reminding me of its presence. I consider fighting—the ravine provides certain defensive advantages—but the number of wolves above makes success unlikely.

Instead, I reach for the claiming bond, pushing as much information as possible toward Ryker.

The images flow between us with desperate intensity, his answering rage immediate and overwhelming, followed by a promise that needs no words—he is coming for me.

I close my eyes, knowing he won't make it in time.

"Take her," Zella instructs the others. "Carefully. Silver restraints only—she's more dangerous than she appears."

As they descend toward me, I straighten my spine, refusing to cower despite the odds against me. Whatever happens next, I will face it as Alpha Female of the Shadowmist Pack—with dignity intact and resistance unbroken.

My hand slips to the dagger at my side.

"I trusted you," I tell Zella as the wolves surround me.

Her expression reveals nothing. "That was the point."

Silver chains appear in their hands—the same ones from

my vision, designed to bind not just my body but my gift as well.

I can feel Ryker's fury and determination racing toward me like fire. He may be fighting like hell, but he won't make it in time.

"He will come for me," I warn them, the certainty absolute in my voice.

Zella's smile holds no warmth. "We're counting on it."

The words make my blood run cold—this isn't just a kidnapping. They're going to use me as bait for a larger trap. They want Ryker.

As the silver chains close around my wrists, pain lances through me—not just physical burning, but deeper agony as the metal begins to interfere with the claiming bond. Our connection weakens, Ryker's presence in my mind growing fainter despite his desperate attempt to maintain contact.

The last sensation I feel through our bond before silver severs it completely is his absolute, unwavering vow—a promise that transcends words, that resonates with primal certainty.

*I will find you, Kitara. I will reclaim you. And those responsible will pay with their lives.*

A cloth is slotted over my hair and strong hands lift me from the ravine, carrying me toward whatever fate Thaddeus has planned for me.

The prophecy unfolds, inevitable as the sunset, unstoppable as the tide. And I am now its unwilling catalyst.

# CHAPTER
# TWENTY-ONE

Pain.

Silver against skin, burning cold despite the cloth wrapped beneath to prevent direct contact. The chains bind my wrists and ankles, heavy links rattling with every jolt of movement as I'm carried deeper into unknown territory. The hood over my head blocks all light, leaving me in suffocating darkness punctuated by the sounds of my captors—footsteps, occasional murmured orders, Zella's voice directing their movements with the same calm efficiency she'd shown during our training sessions.

Worst of all is the silence in my mind where Ryker's presence should be. I reach for him repeatedly, straining against the metal's suppression, catching only fragments of his rage and determination before the silver pulls me back into isolation.

Time becomes meaningless in this sensory-deprived state. Minutes or hours could have passed since my capture—I have no way to tell. My body registers the information my eyes cannot, an initial uphill climb from the ravine, then level ground for what feels like days, and finally a descent into cooler air that carries the damp mineral scent of underground spaces.

The group stops abruptly. I'm set down, not gently but not with deliberate roughness either. Professional, that's the word for their treatment. Like handling dangerous cargo that must be delivered intact.

"Remove the hood," Zella orders. "We're secure here."

The covering is ripped away and light assaults my eyes forcing me to blink rapidly as I adjust. We're in what appears to be an ancient mining tunnel, support beams weathered with age framing a passage that disappears into darkness. Torches provide limited illumination, their flames casting dancing shadows across rough-hewn walls.

Five wolves surround me, all wearing the distinctive markings of the Grand Alpha. Currently in human form, they watch me with wary attention, hands never far from weapons. Zella stands slightly apart, her familiar face now a mask of cool detachment rather than the warmth I've grown accustomed to.

A commotion from farther down the tunnel draws my attention. Two more guards appear, dragging a struggling figure between them. My breath catches as I recognize the silver-blonde hair, the scarred face now twisted in fury.

*Lithia.*

They throw her down beside me, her body hitting the ground with a heavy thud. Blood stains her temple and her breathing comes in pained gasps, but her eyes when they meet mine are clear and filled with cold rage.

"Lithia," Zella greets. "You'll make a valuable addition to our prizes."

"Should've killed me when you had the chance, traitor," Lithia spits, her voice raw but strong despite her injuries.

Zella smiles thinly. "The Grand Alpha has specific plans for you. As the Shadowmist's enforcer, you hold valuable intelligence. And I've no doubt you'll share it, once you're properly persuaded."

I watch in helpless rage as they secure Lithia with silver chains similar to my own. Unlike me, she fights despite the futility, earning a backhanded blow that splits her lip. Only when they've finished binding her does she still, her silver eyes finding mine in silent communication.

"Ryker lives. He'll come for us." A guard backhands her, silencing her once more.

"Why are you doing this?" I ask Zella.

She studies me coldly. "You were never meant to be claimed by the Shadowmist alpha. Your gift is too valuable to waste on a pack of outcasts."

"Waste?" Anger flares through me, momentarily overwhelming the pain of the silver. "They respected my gift. Taught me to control it without breaking. They treated me as a person rather than a tool. I'm stronger because of them."

Her laugh holds no humor. "Don't mistake Ryker's intentions for love, Kitara. He claimed you for an advantage in his feud with Thaddeus. He's using you, just as surely as the rest of us will."

"If that's true," Lithia interjects, her voice cold with contempt, "he wouldn't have trained her. He would have used her exactly as Silvercrest did—draining her dry whenever convenient."

Zella's expression tightens at the interruption. "Tell me, Lithia, did you enjoy playing nursemaid to a wolf who can't shift? Does it please Ryker to have his fiercest fighter reduced to babysitting?"

"I serve my Alpha," Lithia replies with quiet dignity despite her chains. "And his mate. Kitara serves our pack. I am proud to call her Alpha Female."

"How touching." Zella turns away dismissively. "Separate them. Different transport routes, different final destinations.

The Grand Alpha wants no chance of coordinated escape attempts."

"No!" I struggle against my restraints as guards move toward Lithia. "We stay together!"

My protest earns no response beyond an impassive glance from Zella. The guards haul Lithia to her feet, ignoring her pained grimace as the silver chains grind against her wounds.

"Stay strong, Kitara," Lithia calls as they drag her toward a branching tunnel. "Remember who you are, what we've taught you. And know that our Alpha will not rest until—"

A guard's fist cuts her off midsentence. The crack of the blow rings through the chamber like a gunshot. My stomach twists as her body crumples, silver-blonde hair fanning like a halo as she's hauled unconscious into the dark.

My wolf surges, howling for blood and retribution. Rage boils under my skin.

"You'll regret separating us," I tell Zella, forcing my voice to sound steadier than I feel. "Ryker will come for us, and I'll be right there beside him when he exacts his revenge."

"We're ready," she replies, her expression unreadable in the torchlight.

I'm silent for a moment as I glare at her, trying to control my fury.

I shake my head. "Why are you doing this?"

"For the greater good."

I lean forward despite the chains' weight. "How does any of this serve the greater good?"

She dismisses my question. "The Grand Alpha has a careful rehabilitation program planned. You'll be treated with dignity, your gift properly managed by experienced handlers."

"Handlers." I put every ounce of contempt I possess into the word. "At least have the courage to say what you mean. I'll be a prisoner, my visions forced from me whenever convenient, my body used to breed more seers your Grand Alpha can control."

Zella's jaw tightens. "It's necessary. The packs need seers to survive in these times. Your gift is too rare to risk."

"My gift. My choice." I meet her gaze directly. "And I chose the Shadowmist."

She turns away from me. "Get some rest. Our journey isn't finished yet."

We emerge from the tunnels hours later, and I'm loaded into a jeep, sandwiched between two enforcers. The silver chains remain, though they've been adjusted to allow minimal movement within the confined space.

I catch no further glimpse of Lithia, though I strain to spot any sign of where they might have taken her. *Different routes*, Zella had said. *Different destinations*. The strategic value of separating us is obvious—dividing Ryker's attention, forcing him to choose which of us to pursue first.

The car begins moving, each jolt sending fresh pain through my silver-burned skin. The windows are heavily tinted, but I glimpse forest giving way to rolling hills, the landscape unfamiliar after our circuitous journey. We're heading east, away from Shadowmist territory, though I can't determine our precise destination.

My thoughts turn constantly to Lithia—fierce, loyal Lithia. Her capture is my fault, a direct result of her determination to protect her pack. What will Thaddeus do to her? What "specific plans" does he have for Ryker's most trusted enforcer?

The questions haunt me as miles pass, as day fades to evening and then full night. The sedative they administered before the journey gradually wears off, allowing clearer thought but also heightening the constant burning of silver against my skin.

I use the growing clarity to reach repeatedly for our bond,

pushing against the silver's suppression with desperate determination.

*Lithia taken too*, I project, hoping against hope that Ryker might sense at least fragments of my message. *Separated. East for me. Unknown for her.*

No answering presence reaches me, but I continue trying throughout the journey, refusing to surrender to despair. Ryker will come. I know this with bone-deep certainty. The question is when.

As moonlight filters through the windows of the jeep, I close my eyes and make a silent vow—not just to survive, but to escape. Not just to endure, but to find Lithia. Not just to wait for rescue, but to prove myself worthy of being Alpha Female to the most feared wolf in five territories.

Silver may suppress the bond, may weaken my visions, may restrict my movement. But it cannot touch the determination that now flows through me like iron.

I am Kitara, Alpha Female of the Shadowmist Pack. And I am no one's prisoner.

# TWENTY-TWO

## RYKER

Blood.

It coats my muzzle, splashes across my chest, and drips from my claws as I stand over what remains of a scout. The fourth I've found since beginning the hunt, each one carrying Kitara's scent on their hands—proof of their participation in her abduction.

They lived long enough to tell me where she'd been taken, but no more.

The clearing where the so-called summit took place lies miles behind me now, the trap having sprung exactly as Thaddeus planned. While I engaged his personal guard in direct combat, specialized teams had targeted Kitara, separating her from our main force with expert precision.

And Zella—trusted, trained, seemingly loyal Zella—delivered my mate directly into enemy hands.

But that isn't the full extent of their treachery. Lithia too has disappeared in the chaos, her scent trail abruptly ending at a ravine not far from where Kitara was last seen. My second, my most trusted enforcer, taken alongside my mate—a coordinated strike designed to cripple both my heart and my right hand.

The betrayal burns colder than any silver weapon could, fueling a rage I've never before felt. Zella had been with us for five years, rescued from apparent persecution by her former pack, given shelter and position within the Shadowmist. All that time, she'd been Thaddeus's agent, planted to await the perfect opportunity.

My wolf howls with the need to tear her apart limb by limb, to make her suffering legendary among wolf-kind. But vengeance must wait—finding Kitara and Lithia takes precedence over all else.

I lift my head, scenting the air as I seek any trace of either of them. The claiming bond, which should guide me directly to Kitara, has gone ominously silent—a clear indication they're using silver to suppress her gift and our connection. The absence leaves a cold void in my consciousness, a constant reminder of how thoroughly Thaddeus planned this abduction.

Movement to my left alerts me to approaching wolves. I tense, ready for further combat, then relax marginally as familiar scents reach me—Elias, Dane, and several elite enforcers who managed to regroup after the ambush. They approach cautiously, respecting the dangerous mood I'm in.

Dane shifts to human form first, his face grim. His sister's capture has affected him deeply—the bond between twins leaving him hollow-eyed with worry.

"We've found something," he says without preamble. "Traces of two separate transports leaving the ambush site."

I shift as well, the transformation providing momentary distraction from my rage. "Two distinct trails?"

"Yes," Elias confirms, also shifting. "One heading southeast toward Moonclaw territory. The other east, possibly toward the Grand Alpha's primary den."

The implications are clear and strategically devastating. They've deliberately separated my mate and my second, forcing impossible choices about which to pursue first. "They want to divide our forces," I growl, the words barely human despite my shifted form.

"It's worse than that," Dane adds, his voice tight with controlled fury. "We've captured one of their messengers. Under questioning, he revealed they plan to use Lithia as leverage against you—threatening her life to ensure your compliance regarding the seer."

The trap grows more complex with each revelation. Thaddeus anticipates not just my pursuit but my priorities, using my loyalty to my pack against me. The calculation reminds me why he has remained Grand Alpha for so many decades despite widespread resentment of his rule.

"What would you have us do, Alpha?" Elias asks, his tone carefully neutral while his eyes reflect the impossible position we face.

I study both wolves, weighing options I never wanted to consider. Dane waits with visible tension—duty to his alpha warring with his instinctive need to pursue his captured sister. Elias maintains professional distance, though his loyalty to Lithia as his direct superior is evident in his rigid posture.

"We split our forces," I decide after a moment of brutal calculation. "Dane, take half our fighters and track Lithia's trail. Elias, your best trackers remain with me to pursue Kitara."

Dane's eyes widen with surprise. "You want me to lead the rescue for Lithia? Not you?"

"You're her brother," I reply simply. "Your bond will guide you where normal tracking might fail. And there's no wolf I trust more to bring her home safely."

Relief and determination cross his features, the responsibility clearly weighing heavily but welcome nonetheless. "I won't fail you. Or her."

"And the Alpha Female?" Elias asks, his voice carefully neutral.

"Her trail runs cold at the ravine," I admit, frustration evident in my tone. "They used silver to mask her scent."

Elias's expression darkens. "She's strong," he says, offering rare words of encouragement. "Stronger than they realize."

The assessment would mean more if I could feel Kitara through our bond, could know with certainty that she remains unharmed. The silence where her presence should be feels like a physical wound, raw and bleeding.

"We need to move quickly," I decide, strategic necessity finally asserting itself over the wolf's demand that I hunt alone. "Dane, gather your team and head southeast. Track Lithia as if your life depends on it—because hers might."

He nods, already turning to organize his hunters. "We'll find her, Alpha. And when we do, those responsible will learn why the Shadowmist is feared."

"Elias, you're with me," I continue, turning to the security chief. "Your best trackers, focused on Kitara's trail. We head east, following every trace no matter how faint."

"If they're smart, they'll have switched directions multiple times, and used water to mask scent trails, possibly even underground passages," he points out.

"Then we check every false trail, every water crossing, every tunnel entrance between here and Thaddeus's den," I reply, my voice leaving no room for doubt. "I will find her."

As our teams prepare to separate, I pull Dane aside for a final word. "If you find Lithia first," I tell him quietly, "get her to safety, then send word. Don't wait for us."

He studies me with surprising perception. "And if you find the Alpha Female first?"

"Then Thaddeus finally faces the prophecy he's spent decades trying to escape." My voice drops to a growl despite my human form. "And no wolf will forget what happens to those who take what belongs to the Shadowmist alpha."

Dane nods. "Hunt well, Alpha."

"And you."

As he departs with his team, heading southeast toward Moonclaw territory, Elias approaches with our own unit. "Ready when you are, Alpha."

I close my eyes, focusing all my concentration on the claiming bond. If any mated pair could overcome such suppression, it would be us.

*Kitara*, I project with all the force of my will. *I'm coming for you. Hold on.*

For a moment, nothing. Then—faint but unmistakable—a whisper of her consciousness touches mine. Not words, not even coherent emotion, just the barest sense of her presence, like a distant light glimpsed through heavy fog.

She lives. She endures. She waits for me.

It's enough to focus the rage into something colder, more controlled, more deadly. I shift back to wolf form, my massive body rippling with barely contained violence as I scent the air once more.

The hunt begins.

DAYS PASS IN GRUELING PURSUIT, each second increasing the distance between captives and rescuers. Elias and his tracking team prove their worth repeatedly, identifying the faintest traces of Kitara's scent despite Thaddeus's people using every technique to mask their trail.

On the fourth day, we find confirmation of our direction— a fragment of cloth caught on a thornbush, bearing both Kitara's scent and traces of her blood. The discovery sends my wolf into a frenzy of protective rage, though the rational part of me recognizes it as potentially deliberate—a breadcrumb left to ensure we follow the path Thaddeus has prepared.

Trap or not, we have no choice but to pursue. The cloth fragment proves our quarry passed this way within the last twenty-four hours, narrowing the gap between hunters and prey.

By nightfall, we reach the outer territories surrounding Thaddeus's primary stronghold—ancient lands that have belonged to the Grand Alphas for generations, heavily patrolled and warded against intruders. Pausing at the border, I gather our diminished forces, now reduced to Elias and seven of our most elite trackers.

"They've taken her directly to Thaddeus," Elias confirms, crouching over a claw-marked root where a faint trace of Kitara's scent still lingers. "No more diversions or false paths. They want us to follow."

"Of course they do," I mutter, eyes scanning the valley below. The Grand Alpha's den sprawls across the rockface like a festering wound—defensible, elevated, and crawling with guards. "The trap was always meant to end here—at his seat of power, surrounded by his forces, on his terms."

"We're outnumbered at least ten to one," Elias observes, not panicked, just stating fact. "Even with your strength, a direct assault would be suicide."

He's right.

Thaddeus's elite fighters are no joke—fanatically loyal, trained for blood, and bolstered by pack alliances that have survived generations through fear, power, and political marriage. Add to that his war seers and ancient wards, and we're walking into a death trap if we go loud.

But I've never played by the Grand Alpha's rules.

"We won't charge the gates," I say. "We cut the legs out from under them."

Elias lifts his head. "Guerrilla tactics?"

I nod. "Skirmishes. Strikes on supply lines. Eliminate patrols. Pick off his forces one by one. Quietly."

The others gather close as I continue, voice low but resolute.

"Thaddeus is counting on our desperation. On my rage. He wants me reckless. Instead, we'll make him bleed from a thousand small cuts. Thin his ranks. Sow fear and doubt. And when the cracks appear—when his command structure starts to crumble—that's when we slip in."

"Won't that take time?" one of the trackers asks.

"Not as much as you think," Elias answers for me, eyes gleaming. "You've never seen what Shadowmist wolves can do with a week and a grudge."

I offer a grim smile. "And we've got both."

There's a quiet moment—a breath shared between wolves, instinctive, electric.

We're outnumbered. Outarmed. But we're not outmatched.

"I want two-man teams," I continue. "Fast, smart, silent. Strike only when you can do so without being seen. Disappear before they can track you. Collapse bridges, sabotage food stores, disable weapon caches. I want Thaddeus questioning his own shadows."

"What about Kitara?" Elias asks. "If we delay too long—"

"We won't delay," I cut in. "We're buying ourselves a window. A clean one. When it opens, we go in—and we get her out."

No one argues because they understand what's at stake. They know what Kitara means to me. To the pack.

War fought in daylight belongs to tyrants like Thaddeus. But war fought in the dark? That's where we thrive.

"Let the battle begin."

# CHAPTER
# TWENTY-THREE

I force my eyes open despite the throbbing at my temples and the dull ache radiating from every limb. The room is small, windowless, stone-walled, and silent. I lie on a narrow cot with a threadbare blanket that smells faintly of mildew and blood, neither of which are mine but both make my stomach churn.

A single chair sits near the wall. A camp torch flickers in a bracket overhead, casting long, shifting shadows that creep across the cracked floor like ghosts. The air is heavy with age and dust, and thick with the scent of wolf-kind. There's no breeze, no sunlight, and no sounds beyond those made by the wolves holding me prisoner.

My clothes have been changed. My dress has been replaced with coarse leggings and a too-thin shirt. My boots and socks are gone. The shadow silver dagger Ryker gave me? Vanished. My feet press against the frigid stone floor as I roll off the bed to stand, and I grit my teeth against the cold.

My chains rattle as I move. They're long enough to let me take three small steps in either direction—far enough to reach the chair, or touch the wall, or pace like an animal—but no farther. I test them with a sharp jerk. They don't even creak.

My wolf growls inside me, feral with rage. *We don't stay in a cage.*

Her anger pulses beneath my skin, wild and snarling. But there's calculation there too. She's hunting for options, not just blood.

*No pack scent,* I tell her, heart sinking. *Wherever they've taken Lithia, it's not here.*

Her tone turns razor-sharp. *They've cut us off.* She lowers her head, ears flat, teeth bared. *But we are not helpless.*

I examine the wall, letting the chain pool at my feet. The stone is cool, smooth, and ancient. I search for cracks, loose mortar, anything that I might be able to use. Nothing gives.

*The stone's old but solid. No weak points. The chain's silver-threaded and burns when I pull too hard.* My wrists already bear the angry marks of failed attempts.

*We wait.* My wolf paces behind my ribs.

I close my eyes. *We wait,* I agree.

*We endure. And when the moment comes, we bury our teeth in their throats.*

The sound of approaching footsteps warns me a beat before the door to my cell swings open. I straighten my spine, determined to face them head-on.

The open door admits four figures—three guards in Thaddeus's personal colors flanking a fourth wolf I recognize immediately despite never having met him officially. Xavier Drake, alpha of the Moonclaw Pack, regards me with clinical interest from the doorway.

He's tall, lean, and immaculately dressed in a tailored slate-gray coat that gleams faintly under the torchlight. His silver-tipped hair is swept back from his angular face, not a strand out of place.

But it's his eyes that pin me—pale, glacial blue. There's nothing warm in them, just a predator's stillness, with the kind of cruel intelligence that enjoys torture.

My wolf bares her teeth in warning.

"You're awake," he observes, his voice calm and precise, the syllables clipped like surgical incisions. "Good. I was hoping to speak with you before the next sedative."

I remain silent, spine straight despite the chains. I won't cower before him. I won't give the bastard the satisfaction.

Xavier tilts his head slightly, studying me the way one might study a weapon on display—assessing for flaws, for weaknesses, for sharp edges worth respecting.

I meet his gaze steadily, refusing to respond to being discussed as if I were an interesting specimen rather than a person. The silence stretches until he finally dismisses me as a threat.

*Good, let him underestimate me.*

"Do you know where you are?" he asks, stepping fully into the chamber while the guards remain at the threshold.

"In a cell," I reply evenly. "Presumably within Moonclaw territory, given your presence."

A small smile touches his lips, neither kind nor cruel but merely acknowledging my reasoning. "Not quite, You're in the holding chambers beneath the Grand Alpha's central den. These rooms were designed specifically to contain seers and other wolves with gifts who might be useful to our cause."

The information is offered freely, suggesting either confidence that I cannot use it or an attempt to establish rapport. I decide to test which.

"Why are you here rather than Thaddeus?"

Xavier clasps his hands behind his back. "The Grand Alpha is busy dealing with your mutt of a mate. My pack has been entrusted with your care until his return."

"You're my guard."

His expression doesn't change. "I prefer carer. Seers require particular care—their gifts can be unpredictable, they are a danger to themselves and others if not properly managed."

I hold up my hands, shaking the chains. "I'm sorry a little sight has you so spooked."

There's a look in his eyes—not guilt, exactly, but perhaps recognition of the moral ambiguity in his position. "Times are changing," he says after a moment. "We'll take good care of you here, don't worry. The crude extraction techniques used by packs like Silvercrest to harness your gift will be replaced with more humane approaches."

"Humane." I repeat the word with all the contempt it deserves. "Like keeping me in silver chains? Drugging me? Planning to breed me for more seers to exploit?"

"You misunderstand the Grand Alpha's intentions," Xavier replies. "You'll be treated with the respect your gift deserves. The silver is merely a precaution during initial transition, and the sedation was necessary for safe transport."

"And what of separating me from my mate?"

Xavier's jaw ticks. "That is not my concern, nor should it be yours any longer. The claiming will be officially severed once the ceremony can be arranged."

Cold fury washes through me at his casual dismissal of a bond that has become the center of my existence. "The claiming cannot be broken except by death," I remind him. "Wolf law is clear on this matter."

"Exceptions exist for claims made under duress or improper circumstances," he counters smoothly. "The Grand Alpha will deal with it."

The clinical way he discusses severing my bond with Ryker—as if it were as simple as filing paperwork rather than the tearing apart of two souls—makes my hands clench into fists.

"My claiming was willing and proper," I state, each word precise and firm. "No ceremony can undo what has been done. I am Kitara, Alpha Female of the Shadowmist Pack, mate to Ryker, alpha of the Shadowmist. You cannot change that."

"Your loyalty is honorable, if misplaced. The shadow wolf claimed you for your gift, nothing more. Once you understand that—"

"You know nothing of our bond," I interrupt. "Nothing of what exists between us."

"I know more than you might think." His expression hardens. "I know the shadow wolf's history. He's a bastard pup plucked from obscurity to lead a rogue pack. His vendetta against the Grand Alpha is well known, as is his willingness to use any weapon to advance his pursuit—including you."

The words are clearly meant to hurt, to plant seeds of doubt about Ryker's motives. Weeks ago, they might have succeeded. Now, having experienced the depth of our connection, having felt Ryker's mind joined with mine, his respect and regard flowing unfiltered through our bond, they merely reveal Xavier's ignorance.

But it's his words that reveal a crucial piece of information —they don't know Ryker is Thaddeus's son.

"Is that all you see when you look at me?" I ask softly. "A weapon to be wielded? A tool to be used? A broken wolf whose only value lies in forced visions?"

He doesn't answer immediately, his hesitation more revealing than any words could be. "What I see," he finally says, "is a gift too valuable to waste."

I lean forward slightly, chains rattling with the movement. "Tell me, Alpha Drake, do you truly believe Thaddeus acts for the good of wolf-kind? Or merely for his own good?"

"Your questions are irrelevant. What matters is stability, continuity, the preservation of our ways against forces that would tear apart centuries of tradition."

"Even when those traditions cause unnecessary suffering?" I challenge. "Even when they waste potential and crush spirits under the guise of necessary order?"

Before he can respond, a commotion erupts outside the chamber—raised voices, hurried footsteps.

One of the guards leans in, speaking to Xavier in a tone too quiet for me to hear. Whatever message he delivers causes Xavier's expression to shift.

"Secure the prisoner," he orders sharply. "Double the silver, no exceptions. And send for a team immediately. We need to move her. Now."

As the guards hurry to comply with his commands, I feel a surge of hope. Only one thing would cause such alarm, such urgent reinforcement of my captivity.

Ryker is coming.

Xavier turns back to me, all pretense of civility abandoned. "It seems your mate has arrived. It's inconvenient timing, we had hoped for more time to complete preparations."

"How unfortunate for you," I reply, unable to suppress a smile despite the guards approaching with additional silver chains. "The Shadowmist alpha doesn't surrender what belongs to him. Especially not his mate."

"We'll see." Xavier steps back as the guards begin securing the additional restraints around my existing chains. "The Grand Alpha has prepared for this contingency."

As they layer more silver against my skin, I reach desperately for our bond, fighting the increased suppression with everything I have. For a moment, nothing. Then, like a thunderclap in my mind, Ryker's presence breaks through—distant still, but unmistakable in its fierce determination.

*I'm coming, Kitara.*

A pin prick to my shoulder has darkness rushing in.

# TWENTY-FOUR

## RYKER

Fury.

It builds with each passing hour, each false trail, each moment my mate remains beyond my reach.

"Alpha." Elias approaches where I stand observing the entrance of the Grand Alpha's den from a concealed position in the forest. "Scouts confirm heavy guard presence. At least thirty wolves patrolling the outer perimeter, with more inside."

I nod, unsurprised. Thaddeus would have anticipated my pursuit and reinforced it with willing sacrifices. "And the underground entrances?"

"Two identified so far. Both heavily watched." He hesitates before adding, "They're using silver dust around all entry points. They know you're coming."

Of course they do. This entire operation was designed not just to capture Kitara but to lure me into confrontation on their terms, in their territory, surrounded by their forces.

"Have they detected our presence yet?" I ask, my voice unnaturally calm despite the rage burning beneath the surface.

"Not that we can tell. We've kept beyond scenting range, used the methods you taught us for masking our approach."

Good. Surprise remains our greatest advantage against superior numbers. That, and the fact that they expect me to be driven purely by rage, by the wolf's need to reclaim its mate.

They forget I've survived decades of warfare precisely by thinking beyond the immediate, by turning apparent disadvantage into opportunity.

"What of our reinforcements?" I ask.

"In position south of the ridge line. Twenty from Ghost River, fifteen Mountain Striders." Elias's voice drops slightly. "Dane also reports thirty of our own have insisted on joining, despite your orders to maintain den defense."

A smile touches my lips briefly. My pack's loyalty runs deeper than blind obedience. They know what Kitara represents—not just to me, but to all of us.

"Signal them to maintain position until my mark," I instruct. "No movement without direct order."

Elias nods, then hesitates again, concern evident in his posture. "The silver dust will significantly impact your strength if you attempt direct entry. And if the Alpha Female is being held with silver restraints, as seems likely..."

He doesn't finish the thought. Silver weakens all wolf-kind, but those with shadow blood suffer more acutely than most. A direct assault through silver-treated defenses would leave me vulnerable in ways Thaddeus is undoubtedly counting on.

"Prepare the diversion as planned. When their attention fixes on the eastern approach, I'll enter from below."

He bows his head in acknowledgment. "And once inside?"

"I find my mate." The words emerge as a growl, my control slipping briefly. "I eliminate anyone who stands between us. And I bring her home."

Elias bows his head. "For your lips to the Goddess's ears."

"Begin the first phase," I order. "Pick them off—slowly, silently. I want their numbers thinned before we make our main move."

Elias nods. "How many nights?"

"Two. No more. On the third night, we strike."

As Elias departs to organize our forces, I move deeper into the forest, finding a vantage point that overlooks the sprawling stronghold below. Thaddeus's den is carved into a mountainside, stone buildings extending outward from the natural caverns within. Guards patrol in patterns, their movements disciplined but predictable to my experienced eye.

I settle in to wait, to observe, to plan. Every detail matters —shift changes, patrol routes, weak points in their perimeter. And with each passing moment, I reach for our bond, sending my determination across the silver-clouded connection.

*I'm coming, Kitara.*

The first night begins with silence.

Two of our best hunters—Vex and Ash—slip through the outer perimeter as darkness falls. Their mission is simple but crucial, eliminate the scouts positioned farthest from the main compound without raising an alarm.

From my vantage point, I watch through a night-vision scope as they move through the underbrush. They take down the first pair of Thaddeus's wolves with brutal efficiency— one moment the guards are scanning the forest edge, the next they're on the ground, throats torn out before they can howl a warning.

Vex and Ash drag the bodies into dense undergrowth, carefully obscuring any blood trail. Four more guards fall similarly before they return to our position, their fur barely stained despite the carnage they've inflicted.

"Southern perimeter scouts eliminated," Vex reports upon shifting back to human form. "No alarms raised."

I nod approval. "Rest. You'll lead the eastern team tomorrow."

As night deepens, another team strikes—this time targeting a supply line. Three trucks carrying provisions and, more importantly, additional silver weapons are ambushed on the narrow mountain road. The attack is swift, surgical—drivers and guards neutralized, vehicles disabled, supplies taken or destroyed.

By dawn, Thaddeus's forces have lost twelve wolves and critical resources without realizing they're under attack. It's only when they wake they'd realize.

The second night proves even more productive—despite the additional guards.

Elias leads a team that infiltrates the water supply system, introducing a mild sedative that won't be detected until its effects manifest during the third night's assault. Another team sabotages communication equipment, ensuring that when the attack comes, coordination between Thaddeus's forces will be compromised.

I personally lead a strike against their silver weapon storage—a small, heavily guarded outbuilding near the main compound. The five guards posted there die quickly, their bodies concealed as we empty the building of its lethal contents. What we can't take, we destroy, ensuring the defensive advantage silver provides them is significantly diminished.

One guard manages a partial shift before I silence him, his claws raking across my shoulder in a desperate last attack. The wounds sting but heal quickly—minor damage compared to what I'll willingly endure to reclaim my mate.

"We've reduced their fighting force by nearly a third," Elias reports as we regroup before dawn. He hands me some jerky from his ration pack. "Their supply lines are cut, communications compromised, and silver defenses weakened."

"And our casualties?" I ask, chewing.

"None, Alpha. Three minor injuries, all healing."

The knowledge satisfies but doesn't surprise me. My wolves are trained for this.

"Tomorrow night, we bring her home," I tell them, feeling their anticipation rise like a physical force. "Rest. Prepare. What comes will test us all."

As the others withdraw to their assigned positions, I remain alone, watching the compound below where dawn patrols are discovering the first signs that something is wrong. Confusion ripples through their ranks, and along with it… dissent.

I can smell it on the air, see it in the way the guards whisper together, their heads bent conspiratorially.

*Hold on, little mate. Tomorrow, I come for you.*

CHAPTER

# TWENTY-FIVE

Darkness recedes slowly, consciousness returning in fragments that refuse to align properly. My head throbs with the aftereffects of whatever sedative they administered, my vision blurring and clearing in nauseating waves.

I'm no longer in the stone cell where Xavier visited me. This room is larger, circular, with smooth white walls. I'm lying on a low slab that masquerades as a bed. No blanket, no pillow—just cold stone beneath my back, radiating a chill that sinks into my bones. My wrists are cuffed and chained to the edges of the platform, enough give to move but not escape. My ankles, too.

"She's awake," a voice announces from somewhere beyond my field of vision.

Footsteps approach, and a figure comes into view—not Xavier or Zella, but an older woman with steel-gray hair pulled back in a severe knot. Her eyes, a peculiar amber-gold, study me with clinical detachment.

"Can you hear me, seer?" she asks, her voice carrying the distinctive accent of the northern packs.

I manage a nod, unwilling to reveal how disoriented I still feel.

"Good." She makes a note on a tablet she carries.

"Where am I?" I ask, my voice rougher than intended.

"Somewhere safe. For everyone concerned." She sets aside the tablet and approaches, examining the silver chains with a disapproving frown. "These are crude. Effective, but unnecessarily harsh. Once the ceremony is complete, we'll replace them with more humane restraints."

"Ceremony?"

I catch a look of pity in her expression. "The severance of your claiming bond, of course. It's scheduled for tomorrow night."

"Who are you?" I demand, trying to sound stronger than I feel.

"Dr. Amara Reed. I specialize in wolf-kind genetics and psychic bonding patterns." She picks up her tablet again. "I've studied seers for decades. Your case is particularly fascinating—a seer who cannot shift, yet maintains a functional bond with an alpha of exceptional power. The data we'll gather from severing that connection will advance our understanding considerably."

The clinical way she discusses destroying something so fundamental to my being makes my wolf rise with fury. She snarls and snaps behind my ribs, her rage amplifying my own.

"You speak like I'm a scientific experiment," I say, unable to keep the disgust from my voice.

She regards me with mild surprise. "That's precisely what you are. All advancement requires careful study and, occasionally, sacrifice." Her head tilts slightly. "Your discomfort is understandable but unnecessary. Once the bond is broken, you'll be integrated into a program designed specifically for seers."

"And what of my choice in this? My consent?"

Her smile is thin. "Your previous pack conditioned you to believe your worth was tied to a male wolf's possession. We're offering freedom from that limitation."

"Freedom?" I laugh, the sound bitter even to my own ears. I rattle my chains pointedly. "Is that what you call this?"

Dr. Reed sighs, apparently disappointed by my reaction. "The restraints are temporary. Your cooperation will determine how quickly they become unnecessary." She makes another note before continuing. "I understand transitional periods are difficult. But I assure you, once the process is complete, you'll recognize the benefits of your new situation."

I stare at her, understanding dawning with sickening clarity. "You truly believe you're helping me."

"I know I am." Her conviction seems genuine, which somehow makes it worse. "The shadow wolf claimed you for power, nothing more. Once freed from his influence, your true potential can emerge."

The argument is disturbingly similar to what Zella said—a coordinated narrative designed to make me doubt Ryker's motives, to question our bond, to accept their violation as liberation.

"You're wrong," I tell her simply.

Annoyance flickers in her eyes. Before she can respond, a commotion erupts outside the chamber—raised voices, hurried footsteps.

A guard bursts in without ceremony, his expression tense. "Doctor, we need to move. Now."

"What's happened?"

"Perimeter breaches. Multiple locations. Missing patrols. The commander believes it's the Shadowmist alpha." The guard glances at me, his expression hardening. "He's coming for her."

A fierce joy surges through me despite my circumstances. Ryker is here.

Dr. Reed curses under her breath. "We can't move her. The bond hasn't been severed."

"Those are the commander's orders," the guard insists. "We secure the seer in the inner sanctum until the Grand Alpha returns."

A small smile touches my lips as Dr. Reed and the guard turn their attention back to me.

"What's amusing?" Dr. Reed asks, her tone sharpening with suspicion.

"You've made a grave miscalculation," I reply calmly. "You believe you're facing a wolf coming for his property. But what's coming for you is something far worse."

The guard's hand moves to his weapon nervously.

"And what might that be?" Dr. Reed challenges.

My smile widens. "An alpha coming for his mate. And trust me—you are not prepared for what that means."

# TWENTY-SIX

## RYKER

The third night falls with an unnatural stillness, as if the forest itself holds its breath in anticipation of what comes next.

Our forces assemble in the darkness—Ghost River wolves, Mountain Striders, my own Shadowmist fighters—strategically positioned around the compound's perimeter. Every wolf knows their role, their target, their extraction point.

Elias approaches where I stand overlooking the compound, now visibly on alert with increased patrols and guards stationed at every entrance.

"They know something's coming," he observes quietly. "But not what or from where."

"Good." I survey the defenses one final time. "Are the diversions in place?"

He nods. "Eastern ridge and southern approach. On your signal."

I feel the weight of the coming violence settle into my bones. Blood will flow tonight. Some of it may be ours. But Thaddeus's forces will suffer far worse.

"Begin," I command.

The eastern diversion ignites first—literally. Fires erupt at multiple points along the ridge, creating the impression of a sizeable force approaching with torches. Alarms sound immediately, warriors rushing to defensive positions as the southern diversion activates—howls echoing through the valley, suggesting another large group closing in from that direction.

I watch as Thaddeus's forces divide, responding predictably to threats that don't exist while leaving vulnerabilities we've carefully identified over the past two days.

"Second phase," I order into the communications device our tech wolves rigged for the operation.

On my command, a smaller but real attack launches against the western perimeter—just enough force to engage their remaining exterior guards while creating a corridor through which I can enter.

I shift, my massive black form coalescing in the darkness. Unlike traditional assaults where I would lead from the front, this mission requires a different approach. My elite team— five of our deadliest fighters—forms around me as we move silently toward our entry point, a service tunnel our scouts identified.

The guards stationed there never see us coming. One moment they stand vigilant, the next they lie dead, their throats torn out before they can raise the alarm. We drag their bodies inside the tunnel, obscuring evidence of our entry.

The passageway narrows as we descend, forcing us to proceed in single file. The air grows thicker, heavy with the mineral scent of underground spaces and the distinctive musk of wolf-kind. Through our pack bond, I maintain silent communication with my team—directing, adjusting, coordinating without words that might alert our enemies.

We encounter the first serious resistance at a junction where the service tunnel connects to the main complex. Six guards, better armed and more alert than those outside, patrol the intersection. Silver-tipped spears gleam under harsh lights, a visible warning that they're prepared.

I signal my team to hold position while I assess. The silver weapons present a problem—even a glancing blow could weaken us significantly, compromising our mission before we've truly begun.

I shift back to human form, my decision made. "Hold here," I instruct softly. "I'll clear the junction. If I fall, complete the mission."

Before they can object, I move forward alone, staying within shadows that cling to the tunnel walls. The guards are disciplined but comfortable in their routine, attention focused outward toward the sounds of distant fighting rather than the darkness behind them.

Their mistake.

I take the first guard silently, my hand clamping over his mouth while my other arm snaps his neck with a single violent twist. I lower his body noiselessly, claiming his silver spear before moving to the next target.

The second guard dies as quietly as the first. The third notices something amiss, turning just as I reach him—enough time for his eyes to widen in recognition before my stolen spear pierces his throat, preventing a warning cry.

The remaining three panic as their companion falls. They respond with commendable speed, silver weapons raised as they form a defensive triangle.

"The shadow wolf," one hisses, recognition flaring in his eyes.

I don't waste breath on words. These wolves stand between me and my mate. Their lives are forfeit.

I launch forward, using the first guard's body as a shield

against their initial thrust. Silver-tipped spears pierce the corpse as I drive forward, breaking their formation. In close quarters, their long weapons become unwieldy while my stolen spear finds vulnerable flesh.

The fourth guard falls, his chest punctured. The fifth manages to score a shallow cut along my arm with his silver blade. Pain flares, sharper than normal injury, but I push through it, driving my weapon up under his ribcage. The sixth breaks, turning to flee, but dies with my spear through his back before he can take three steps.

Six bodies lie at my feet, the junction secured. I signal my team forward as I bind the silver wound quickly. It burns, but not enough to significantly impair me. Not yet.

"Inner compound ahead," I tell them as they join me. "Expect heavier resistance."

We move deeper into the complex, following the route our intelligence suggested where Kitara is most likely held. The diversions outside continue to draw attention away from our infiltration, but we encounter increasingly organized resistance as we penetrate further.

At a heavily reinforced doorway, we face our first major obstacle—a squad of eight elite guards bearing the Grand Alpha's insignia. These aren't ordinary wolves but specialized fighters, their movements synchronized and disciplined as they attempt to intercept us.

"Alpha," one of my team murmurs, "silver dust in the air. They've prepared this choke point."

I can smell it now—the metallic tang that warns of danger to our kind. They've created a defensive position where wolf strength will be compromised, forcing us to fight at reduced capacity.

"Alternate route?" I ask, though I already know the answer.

"None. This is the only way to the inner sanctum."

I nod, decision made. "I'll breach. You follow and secure."

Before they can object, I shift, my massive form filling the corridor. The silver in the air immediately begins to affect me —a burning sensation in my lungs, a heaviness in my limbs that would weaken a normal wolf substantially.

But I am not normal. I am Ryker Ashmere, alpha of the Shadowmist Pack, and my mate lies beyond these wolves. There is no force in existence that will prevent me from reaching her.

I charge.

The elite guards brace for impact, silver weapons forming a wall of lethal points. In open ground, I might have maneuvered around them, used superior mobility to my advantage. In this narrow corridor, with silver dulling my reflexes, I have only one option—through them.

The collision is brutal. Silver spears pierce my shoulder and flank as I crash into their line, but momentum carries me forward, massive jaws closing around the throat of the center guard. Blood sprays as I tear through flesh, using the dying wolf as a battering ram to disrupt their formation.

Pain flares where silver touches me, but rage and determination push it aside. I tear through a second guard, then a third, my team following in my wake to engage those I pass.

A silver blade slices along my back, burning like frost and fire combined. I snarl, twisting to rip the weapon from my attacker's hands before tearing his arm from his body. He falls screaming as I continue my advance.

The doorway is breached, the guards eliminated, though not without cost. Silver burns mar my hide, and one of my team lies dead, two others wounded. A harsh price, but one I expected to pay.

Grief will come later.

Beyond the doorway lies a circular chamber with multiple

exits—a hub connecting different sections of the inner compound. I shift back to human form, conserving strength while my regeneration addresses the silver wounds as best it can.

"Secure the chamber," I order the remaining wolves. "Hold this position. No one follows us, no one escapes to warn the others."

My wounded fighters nod grimly, taking defensive positions while I scent the air, seeking any trace of Kitara. The silver dust has weakened my senses, but there's a small scent, barely detectable, pulling me toward one particular corridor.

I follow that pull, moving with greater caution now. The inner sanctum will be more heavily defended, the wolves guarding it more dangerous than those we've encountered thus far. And somewhere ahead waits the true prize—not just Kitara, but the opportunity to fulfill the prophecy that has shaped both our fates.

Thaddeus.

The corridor descends deeper into the mountain, ancient stone giving way to newer construction. The air grows colder, charged with something that raises the hair on my arms despite my shifted form—old magic, the kind wolf-kind rarely acknowledges but instinctively fears.

A set of massive double doors blocks the passage, inscribed with runes that seem to shift and move when viewed directly. Two guards stand before them. These are no ordinary wolves. Their scent carries the distinctive markers of those who've undergone blood ritual enhancement, their eyes gleaming with unnatural intensity in the dim light.

They see me approach, but neither raises alarm. Instead, they step forward in perfect unison, bodies beginning to shift but maintaining bipedal form—a half-transformation that reveals the extent of their unnatural enhancement. Claws extend from human hands, jaws elongate without completing the change to muzzle, muscles bulge beneath skin that remains hairless.

"The shadow wolf comes," one intones, voice distorted by partially shifted vocal cords.

"You will go no further," the other adds. "The seer is being prepared. The ceremony approaches."

Cold fury washes through me at their words.

"Step aside," I order, my voice eerily calm despite the rage building within, "or die where you stand."

Their response is to extend wickedly curved claws that gleam with silver inlay—weapons that are part of them, impossible to disarm or drop.

"We are the Chosen," the first declares. "Blood-bound to the Grand Alpha himself. Your strength means nothing here."

I don't waste breath arguing. These aren't ordinary guards to be intimidated or reasoned with. They're fanatics.

I shift again, ignoring the silver wounds that slow the transformation. Their eyes widen slightly—they expected the silver to have weakened me more substantially, to have prevented another shift so soon. Their miscalculation will cost them everything.

They attack together, moving with unnerving synchronicity. Silver-laced claws slice through the air where I stood a heartbeat before, missing as I launch upward, using the corridor's height to my advantage. My jaws close on the first guard's shoulder, teeth piercing enhanced muscle and tendon to crush bone beneath.

He screams—a sound no natural wolf would make—as I use his body as leverage to avoid his partner's attack. Silver claws rake the air inches from my flank as I tear the first guard's throat out with a savage twist.

The second guard is faster, more cautious after seeing his partner fall. He circles, those unnatural eyes calculating as he assesses my wounds, my stance, my advantages and vulnerabilities.

"You bleed, shadow wolf," he observes, indicating the silver injuries that continue to burn across my hide. "Soon you'll weaken. Then you'll die. All as the Grand Alpha has foreseen."

I snarl in response, my patience exhausted. This creature's life means nothing.

We clash again, my greater mass against his enhanced speed. His claws find purchase, opening new wounds across my shoulder and back, silver burning into flesh with each strike. But he's fighting for duty, for a master who values him only as a tool. I'm fighting for my mate, for the bond that defines my existence.

It's no contest.

My jaws close around his throat despite the silver claws tearing at my sides. Blood fills my mouth as I crush his windpipe, maintaining my grip until his body finally stops its struggle.

I drop him, blood dripping from wounds that heal too slowly thanks to the silver contamination. I shift back to human form, approaching the doors with caution. The runes carved into them seem to pulse as I near, resonating with a magic that makes my skin crawl.

*Kitara,* my wolf growls. He too can smell her on the other side.

Her familiar sweet scent is tinged with sweat, blood and fear. They're hurting her. Preparing her for whatever ceremony they've planned

I place my hands against the ancient wood, feeling the magic push back against my touch. It burns, not like silver but deeper, seeking to repel something fundamental in my blood.

But Thaddeus made one critical miscalculation. The wards were created to repel shadow blood, but they don't account for a claiming bond that connects that blood to another. Through Kitara, I have an anchor. Just as I'm a tether for her when she scries, so too is she a tether for me.

I lean into the doors, and the wards flare, magic crackling

visibly along inscribed lines as they resist. I push harder, dropping my shoulder to heave against it. A crack appears— small at first, then widening as the protective magic fractures. With a sound like breaking glass, the wards shatter and the massive doors swing open to reveal the chamber beyond.

Torches line the walls, casting dancing shadows across rune-inscribed floors. At the center of the circular room stands a raised dais where silver chains bind a familiar form to an altar of black stone.

*Kitara.*

Her eyes find mine across the distance, relief swimming in their depths.

"Ryker." My name has never sounded so sweet.

Between us stand a dozen wolves—guards and what appear to be ritual practitioners in ceremonial robes. At their center, a woman with steel-gray hair holds what looks like a silver dagger.

"The shadow wolf breaches the Sacred Chamber," she announces, sounding more surprised than alarmed. "The bond must be even stronger than we calculated."

I step forward, naked and blood-covered but radiating enough lethal intent to make several guards step back instinctively.

"Release my mate," I order, my voice carrying the full weight of alpha command, "or what follows will become legend for its brutality."

The woman—clearly the leader of whatever ritual they've been preparing—studies. "The bond manifests physical effects even through silver suppression. Remarkable. We really must document this before severing it."

"You know not what you meddle with," I warn her, taking another step forward. The guards tense but don't attack, clearly waiting for their command.

"On the contrary," she replies, "I understand precisely what I'm dealing with. A claiming bond of exceptional strength, maintained across silver suppression, between an alpha with shadow blood and a seer who cannot shift. The scientific implications alone—"

"Ryker!" Kitara yells, struggling on the dais. "Lithia! They took her—"

The woman signals, and a guard strikes Kitara across the face, silencing her. The blow makes rage explode through me, vision narrowing to a crimson tunnel focused entirely on those who dare harm my mate.

"Touch her again," I growl, "and I will ensure your death lasts days."

My growl—or perhaps the blood dripping from my silver wounds onto the ancient stone—finally penetrates the woman's scientific detachment. Fear flickers in her eyes for the first time.

"Guards," she orders, backing toward Kitara with the ritual dagger still in hand, "kill the shadow wolf."

They attack as one, silver weapons gleaming in torchlight. But these aren't the enhanced monsters that guarded the doorway—these are ordinary wolves, skilled but unprepared for the fury they face.

I shift again, ignoring the burning agony of transformation with silver still in my system. My massive form fills the ceremonial space, claws scrabbling for purchase on smooth stone as I launch toward the first line of guards.

They try to form a defensive wall between me and the altar, but their formation breaks under the sheer momentum of my charge. Bodies fly, silver weapons clatter against stone, screams echo as I tear through flesh and bone with single-minded purpose.

A spear pierces my flank, silver burning into muscle. I snarl, turning to rip the wielder's head from his shoulders before continuing forward. Another guard manages to bite my foreleg, but the wound only feeds my rage.

I fight with cold, calculated savagery—not the mindless

berserker fury they clearly expected but the practiced lethality of a predator who has survived decades of warfare. Each movement is economical, each kill efficient. I don't waste energy on displays of dominance or unnecessary violence—I simply eliminate obstacles between me and my mate.

Kitara is my only thought.

Their leader changes tact as I approach.

"Stay back," she warns, pressing the ritual dagger to Kitara's throat. "I'll kill her right now if you come closer. She'll be lost to you forever."

I pause, blood dripping from my jaws, bodies of fallen guards littering the floor around me. The threat is real.

But Kitara meets my gaze across the distance, and I see no fear in her eyes—only fierce determination and absolute trust.

*Do it,* she mouths silently.

In the heartbeat between one moment and the next, I understand. She's creating an opening, drawing the woman's attention to the dagger at her throat rather than my approach. It's a risk—a terrible one—but Kitara believes in me. In us.

I shift my weight slightly, muscles tensing in preparation. The woman misinterprets the movement as hesitation, a momentary victory that makes her smile.

"That's right," she says, confidence returning. "You understand what's at stake. Now back away or—"

Kitara bites her, her teeth sinking deep into the woman's arm.

The woman screams, whirling toward Kitara. I strike—jaws closing around her throat. Bones shatter beneath my teeth as I wrench, ripping her throat clean out. The woman's body falls to lie at my feet, her dagger clattering uselessly to the ground. The wound will kill her, but not before she suffers for her crimes.

The few remaining guards break, running for the exit in blind panic as I tear through Kitara's silver chains with claws and teeth, ignoring the burning pain as the metal touches my flesh. When the last restraint falls away, I shift back to human form, gathering her into my arms with desperate gentleness.

"Kitara," I breathe against her hair, her name a prayer and praise all at once.

Her arms wind around my neck, weak but determined, her body sagging into mine as the silver's suppression fades and her strength begins to return. I feel her through the bond again—blazing back into me like the sun cresting the horizon after endless night.

"I knew you'd come," she whispers, voice fierce despite its tremble. "Even when I couldn't feel you—I *knew*."

I crush her closer. Her presence floods my senses, her scent, her heartbeat, the way her breath stutters just before she speaks. Through our rejoined bond, I feel it all—relief, fury, exhaustion... and love. Gods, the love. It hits like lightning in a dry forest, consuming and unstoppable.

"I love you," I say, my voice hoarse and ragged and truer than anything I've ever spoken. "I love you, Kitara. I've loved you since the moment I first saw you."

I kiss her forehead. Her cheeks. Her nose. I kiss every part of her face like I'm putting pieces back together. Like I'm branding myself into her skin.

She tilts her face up to mine, her eyes blazing despite the exhaustion, and cups my jaw. "I love you too," she says, steady and sure. "I don't know when it started, but it's yours. All of me."

The wolf in me howls, and I nearly give in to the urge to fuck her right here, right now. On a throne of blood and violence.

But her safety comes first, and we aren't free of this place of horror just yet.

"Lithia," she says aloud, pulling back to meet my gaze. "They separated us. Thaddeus has her somewhere else—I think they want to use her as additional leverage."

"We know. Dane is searching for her," I assure her. "He'll find her."

She slumps, clinging to me. "Thank the gods."

Behind us, Dr. Reed makes a wet, gurgling sound—still alive despite her torn throat, but drowning in her own blood. Good.

I gather my mate in my arms, holding her close as I turn toward the exit.

Elias stands in the doorway with one of the guards, a knife pressed to the guard's throat.

*This isn't over.*

"Thaddeus?" I demand.

The guard squirms. "I don't—"

Elias nicks his skin, a warning of what is to come.

"The northern complex."

I nod once. "Elias?"

"I'm on it."

He disposes of the guard and moves to leave just as I hear the faint sound of metal striking stone. I move to cover Kitara but I'm too late.

Kitara gasps, her hand flying to her neck. "Ryker!"

I crouch, frantically pulling her hands from her neck. A silver syringe is embedded in her throat, its contents already emptying into her bloodstream. I spin in time to see the dying woman's arm fall limply to the stone floor, her final act of vengeance complete.

"No!" I roar, but it's too late.

Kitara stares at me with growing horror, one hand clutching the injection site. "What did she—" Her eyes go wide with terror. "Ryker, I can't—"

She bucks, writhing in pain. A howl escapes her—terrible and devastating, unlike anything I've ever heard before. Then her body goes limp in my arms.

"Kitara!" I press my hands to her face, but her eyes stare

sightlessly at the ceiling. No breath. No heartbeat. No response.

Our claiming bond falls silent.

*She's gone.*

I throw my head back and release a sound of pure anguish.

My mate is gone.

# TWENTY-SEVEN

Darkness.

Death isn't the cold, empty void I expected. This darkness pulses with warmth. The silence is filled with memory, with the whisper of countless voices that came before.

I'm floating, weightless, in a space between spaces. And I'm not alone.

"Child." The voice comes from everywhere and nowhere, familiar yet strange. "You carry our gift well."

I turn—or think I turn, movement means nothing here—and see her. An elderly woman with silver hair that seems to hold starlight. Her eyes shift between colors like an aurora. She wears robes that appear to be cut from the night sky itself.

"Cheyenne." I know her name instantly.

"Welcome, Kitara." She approaches with a smile both sad and proud. "I wish we were meeting under better circumstances."

"Am I dead?" The question comes without fear, only curiosity.

"Not dead. But not alive, either. You stand at the

threshold, dear one. The silver poison burns through your gift, severing the pathways that make you what you are." Her expression grows grave. "Soon, there will be nothing left but silence."

Pain flickers through me—physical, but deeper still. It is the agony of losing part of my soul.

"Why?"

Cheyenne extends her hand and I take it, gasping as power flows between us, racing up my arm like lightning.

"You follow in my footsteps, walking the path between what is and what could be." She drops my hand. "That is my final gift to you."

She turns but I catch her cloak, halting her. "I don't understand. Why am I broken? Why can't I shift? Why am I here?"

She glances over her shoulder, her gaze locking with mine. "You were never broken, child. You were crafted. Shaped by forces older than the packs themselves. And when the moment comes—when all seems lost—remember this, love is the strongest magic of all."

"I don't—"

"You will." She begins to fade, her form dissolving like mist through my fingers. "Soon."

The vision fractures, reality bleeding through the cracks.

"Until we meet again, dear one."

And then—

Silence.

# CHAPTER
# TWENTY-EIGHT

## RYKER

My howl echoes off the stone walls until my throat goes raw, the sound of absolute devastation.

Elias crashes into the chamber, takes one look at Kitara's lifeless form in my arms, and leaps into action.

"Get a healer here, NOW!" he roars to someone behind him. "And bring the emergency kit!"

I can't speak. Can't think. Can only hold her cooling body and feel the gaping void in my head, my heart, my soul. The silence in my mind is more devastating than any physical wound.

"Alpha." Elias kneels beside me, his voice gentle but urgent. "Let me check her pulse."

I snarl, pulling her closer. No one touches her. No one—

"Ryker." His use of my name rather than my title cuts through the haze of grief. "If there's any chance to save her, we need to act now."

Reluctantly, I allow him to press fingers to her throat. He's still for a long moment, then his eyes widen.

"There's something. Faint, but..." He looks up at me with desperate hope. "She's not gone. Not completely."

Elena, our lead healer, bursts into the chamber with her medical kit, taking in the scene. She drops beside us, opening her bag to pull items free.

"Silver poisoning?" she asks, examining the injection site.

"Yes," I rasp, my voice barely human.

Her expression darkens, but she immediately begins working—checking Kitara's vitals.

"Her voice," I whisper. "It's gone silent."

My wolf claws at my chest, frantic, howling for the mate we can no longer feel.

"That doesn't mean she's dead," Elena says firmly, though I catch the worry in her eyes. She pulls her stethoscope from her ears. "Her pulse is weak, but she's fighting."

*Fighting.* The word gives me hope to cling onto.

"What can I do?" I demand.

"Keep talking to her. The mate bond might be silent, but love..." Elena's hands never stop moving as she works. "Love transcends magic, Alpha. If anything can reach her now, it's that."

I bury my face in her neck, pressing my lips to her mark. "Come back to me, little seer," I whisper. "Don't you fucking dare leave me."

And then I feel it.

Not a sound, but a *shift*—in the world, in the air, in *me*. My control slips.

Power floods my veins. My claws punch through my fingertips. Bones groan beneath my skin as my wolf surges forward, frantic and enraged. The shift is coming whether I want it or not. Without her grounding me, the bond spirals and I can't stop it.

I throw my head back and roar, the sound ripping through the den like a storm.

"Ryker!" Elias reaches for me, but I bare my teeth. Too late. I'm going feral.

My beast rises, snarling, shaking with the need to tear something apart. It smells her blood, her fading magic, and wants to make the world burn. My vision darkens at the edges.

Kitara.

But just before the shift takes me completely—

She breathes.

A single, gasping inhale, ragged and wet, like a soul dragged back through fire.

My heart stops. The bond flares—flickering, faint but there.

"Kitara?" I whisper, brushing my knuckles across her cheek. Her fingers twitch. Her lashes flutter. Then her eyes crack open, and I nearly collapse with relief.

They're unfocused but open.

"Alpha, move," Elena orders, gently bumping me out of the way. She mixed a putrid smelling poultice, thick as tar. I know the smell well—it's a salve infused with nightshade, ash, wolfsbane, and a concoction of other herbs all designed to draw the silver from the skin. She holds up a knife but I take it from her.

"No, I'll do it." I make tiny slice in my mate's skin. Elena follows the glide of my knife with her fingers, gently applying the thick salve. Kitara stares unseeing at the ceiling, her breathing shallow but steady.

It takes but a minute for the salve to begin its work, drawing the silver from Kitara's blood. It boils beneath her skin, bubbling to the surface like poison pushed through a sieve. It beads like mercury before it's brushed away by Elena with careful, gloved hands.

I hold Kitara's head in my lap, running my fingers through her hair as I watch the silver flow.

Slowly, painfully, my mate begins to stir. Her breathing slows and deepens. Her body stiffens, then relaxes as she blinks, her gaze snapping into focus.

"Ryker."

Relief assaults me. Her voice is weak, thready. But it's *her*.

"I'm here," I breathe, crushing a kiss to her temple, to her cheek, to the shell of her ear. I don't even care that I'm shaking. "You're safe, Kitara. You came back to me."

Her fingers curl against my chest as if she needs to feel me beneath her skin.

"I heard you," she whispers, hoarse. "I got lost… and then I heard your voice."

Elena exhales sharply. "She's stabilizing. Her vitals are climbing." She turns away to dispose of the silver-soaked cloths, giving us space.

I cradle Kitara closer, pressing my forehead to hers. "You scared the shit out of me," I murmur, my throat raw. "You almost died."

She blinks slowly, her brows knitting. "You were going to shift."

"I was *already* shifting," I admit, voice tight. "I couldn't feel you. It was like... my soul just—" I stop, swallowing hard. "You're the only thing that keeps me sane."

A tear slips from the corner of her eye, trailing down her temple. "I didn't want to leave you."

"You didn't." I take her hand, pressing it flat against my heart. "You'll *never* leave me."

For a beat, we breathe together. Her fingers are still trembling but she's here.

Alive.

*Mine.*

Elena returns, her tone all business again. "She needs to rest. The silver traces will linger in her system for a few days —maybe longer. You'll need to watch for flare-ups, memory gaps, seizures—"

"Let's discuss this at home," I cut in, already lifting Kitara into my arms. "Come."

Kitara tucks her face into my neck, resting heavily against

me. Her lack of protest and the silence that still rings through our bonds stirs my wolf's concern, but I reassure him that she'll be fine.

She has to be.

# TWENTY-NINE

Ryker carries me from the depths of Thaddeus's compound. The fresh air feels wonderful after days in that silver-lined cell, the rising sun painting the sky in colors so vivid they almost hurt my eyes.

*I'm alive.*

I should be dead. By all rights, that injection should have killed me. But I'm here. Breathing. My heart beating steadily against Ryker's chest as he carries me to safety.

Gratitude floods through me—not just for my life, but for the male who refused to let me go.

"Thank you," I whisper against his neck, the words barely audible.

His arms tighten around me.

"Always," he murmurs back, pressing a kiss to my temple.

Our escape is not the chaotic flight I expected but a measured withdrawal. The carefully planned assault has left Thaddeus's forces in disarray—communication disrupted, command structure fractured, defenders scattered or eliminated. What resistance we encounter is disorganized and easily dispatched by the escort that meets us at the compound's outer perimeter.

"Lithia?" I ask as Vex approaches, his expression grim.

"Still missing," he confirms.

The news is a hit.

"And Thaddeus?" Ryker asks, his voice roughened by the night's violence.

Vex's expression darkens. "No sign of him. The northern complex was empty when our forces breached it."

Ryker sets me gently on my feet, keeping one arm around my waist for support as his gaze sweeps the compound below.

I close my eyes, reaching for my gift.

Nothing.

I try again.

*Silence.*

"I can't see," I whisper.

Ryker's head turns sharply. "What?"

"The visions. They're gone."

"You just need to recover," he says. "The silver took more from you than you realize."

I shake my head, frantically grasping for any trace of our bond.

Nothing—all remains silent.

I shake my head, panic rising sharp and acidic. "No. No, Ryker—there's *nothing.* I can't hear you. I can't *feel* you."

The wind cuts through the woods below, whistling through broken stone and blood-soaked earth. Somewhere in the distance, a wolf howls.

I'm empty.

Tears sting my eyes as a hollow ache blooms. My gift—*the thing I was hated for, prized for, used for*—is silent. I don't know who I am without it.

"I don't know how to be… me without it," I whisper, curling into myself. "Now I truly am broken."

Ryker doesn't hesitate. He pulls me into his arms, wrapping his warmth around me like a shield against the cold. "You are not your gift, Kitara," he murmurs, fierce and low. "You are so much more."

But his words are a kindness I can't touch right now.

Because this isn't just about magic. It's about identity. About being seen—for the first time—and now ripped back into invisibility.

"I was never enough with it," I choke out, my voice unraveling. "Not for my parents. Not for the pack. Not for anyone. It was the only reason they kept me. The only reason I wasn't cast out or put down or left behind. If I wasn't enough with it, then I'm certainly less without it."

The words pour out of me like blood from an open wound. "All my life, I've been told I was wrong. A failure. Too human. Too different. But at least I *saw*." My breath hitches. "Now there's nothing. I don't know who I am without them whispering through my bones."

I press my fists to my chest, as if I could reach inside and pull the silence out with my bare hands. "It's like someone ripped out a part of me and left a void. And I—I don't know if I'll ever feel whole again."

My tears come harder now. Not silent ones, but the kind that hitch in my throat and drag from my lungs like grief made flesh.

"I'm scared," I finally confess. "Gods, I'm so fucking scared."

For a long beat, Ryker doesn't speak. He just lets me sob into the hollow of his throat, lets me fall apart in his arms.

Only when my body starts to tremble from exhaustion does he speak again, voice low and fierce.

"Then be scared," he says. "But don't believe for one second that you're less. They broke you to control you. I will help you put the pieces back in any shape you choose—even if we have to start from ash." He leans in, pressing his forehead to mine. "I nearly lost you, Kitara. I understand that you're hurting and a piece of you has been ripped away. It may come back in time, it may not. But I will remind you, every damn day, that the best part of you isn't your sight. It's your fire. It's your heart. It's the way you never stop fighting—even when the whole world tells you to surrender."

I close my eyes, letting his words anchor me.

Even without my visions... I'm still here. Still tethered to him. Still breathing.

Still *me*—even if I have to learn what that means all over again.

I close my eyes, letting his words anchor me.

"I love you," he says quietly, the words settling into the silence between us like a promise. "Not the seer. Not the gift. You, Kitara. Just you." His thumb brushes away another tear I didn't realize had fallen.

"I love you too," I whisper.

He holds me while I grieve, offering comfort. Finally, I nod, and he lifts me, taking me away from this cursed place.

We eventually withdraw to a plateau overlooking the compound—high ground that offers strategic advantage while remaining visible enough to serve as an obvious challenge. As allies tend to the wounded and position defensive forces, Ryker secures a sheltered area for us.

"Rest," Ryker urges, brushing a strand of hair from my face. "I'll wake you when it's time."

I want to argue, but my body betrays me. My eyes close despite my best efforts, and I slip into healing sleep with Ryker's presence a protective shield around me.

When I wake, the sun has climbed higher, its warmth soaking into my skin and chasing away the last ghost-sensations of the silver's cold burn. Ryker sits beside me, his massive frame between me and any potential threat, his attention divided between the compound below and something held in his hands.

"You've been busy," I observe, recognizing the shadow silver dagger he'd given me, somehow recovered during the chaos of our escape.

He glances up, relief evident in his expression as he sees me awake and alert. "How do you feel?"

"Stronger." I sit up, taking stock of my body. The fatigue remains but has receded. "Better. What's happened?"

"Scouts report movement in the valley. A contingent approaching from the east—not large but still a threat."

"Thaddeus?"

Ryker nods. "Along with Zella, and his personal guard. They'll reach the plateau within the hour."

"He could have fled. Regrouped. Why come directly to us when his position is weakened?"

"Because this was never about military advantage or political calculation." Ryker hands me the shadow silver dagger, watching as my fingers close around its hilt. "This is about destiny, and the future of wolf-kind itself. He believes confronting me is necessary—not just to maintain his authority but to preserve his vision of what our people should be."

The explanation rings true, fitting with everything I've learned of the Grand Alpha. He doesn't see himself as a tyrant clinging to power but as a guardian protecting necessary order—making any sacrifice worthwhile, any cruelty justified, for the greater good.

Elias approaches, inclining his head respectfully to both of us before delivering his report. "Our forces are positioned as directed, Alpha. Ghost River wolves to the northeast, Mountain Striders to the west. Our own fighters in defensive formation around the plateau itself."

"Good." Ryker rises, his massive frame silhouetted against

the morning sky. "When Thaddeus arrives, our people are to maintain position. Do not engage unless I fall. This ends today."

The order carries absolute authority, acknowledged by Elias with grim understanding. This final confrontation will not be decided by armies or strategy but by a direct challenge.

*Do not engage unless I fall.*

He says it so calmly. So certainly. As if it's just another tactical command, not the line between life and death.

Ryker has no intention of dragging anyone else into this. This is his burden, his reckoning. Alpha against alpha. Son against father.

And gods, it hurts.

Not because I doubt him. Not for a second. I've seen what he can do—his strength, his cunning, the brutal grace with which he leads. But that doesn't soften the knot forming in my gut. It doesn't quiet the ache of knowing he's deliberately stepping into the fire, willing to burn so no one else has to.

It doesn't lessen the knowledge that I can't see the outcome of his decision.

My fists curl at my sides. I want to scream. To beg him not to go. To demand another way.

But there isn't one.

This is how it has to be.

I lift my eyes to him, silhouetted against the dawn, every inch the alpha he was born to be. I want to run to him. I want to fight beside him. I want to tear Thaddeus apart for making this necessary.

Love, fury, and despair tangle in a desperate writhing knot in my chest, but I stand my ground—his mate, his equal—and anchor myself in the storm.

Ryker isn't alone.

Not while I breathe.

"And if his guard interferes?" Elias asks.

"They won't." Ryker's certainty is absolute. "Thaddeus believes he can win."

As Elias withdraws to relay the orders, I stand beside my mate, studying his profile. The silver wounds from last night's fight have mostly healed, but I can see how the contamination lingers, slowing his recovery and diminishing his full strength. He's far from peak condition for the coming confrontation.

"You're worried," he observes, not looking at me but clearly sensing my concern.

"You've been weakened by silver. He'll be coming at full strength."

His smile is slight but genuine. "Have more faith in your mate, little wolf."

"It's not lack of faith," I correct, turning to face him fully. "You've fought through silver contamination, sustained multiple injuries, expended enormous energy breaking through magical wards. Thaddeus comes fresh, rested, with generations of power behind him."

Ryker finally turns to me, his mismatched eyes holding mine with unwavering confidence. "And yet I have something he doesn't."

"What's that?"

His hand cups my face, thumb brushing my cheekbone with gentle reverence. "Belief that what we have is worth fighting for. Worth dying for, if necessary."

The simple truth of it silences further argument. He knows exactly what he faces, understands the disadvantages and accepts them without reservation or doubt.

Before I can respond, an alert calls from our perimeter. They've arrived.

We move to the plateau's edge, standing together as the small contingent emerges from the forest below. Thaddeus leads, his white hair gleaming in sunlight, power rolling before him like heat off desert stone. Zella follows a step behind, her expression coldly professional as her gaze sweeps the plateau.

The dozen guards fan out behind them but maintain distance—close enough to protect but far enough to indicate this is not yet combat but parley.

"Ryker Ashmere," Thaddeus calls, his voice carrying effortlessly up the slope. "I see you've recovered your pet. How touching."

"Thaddeus Solomon," Ryker returns, matching the formality. "I see you've brought your spy. Did she prove worth the investment?"

Zella's expression tightens, but she remains silent as Thaddeus laughs.

"More than worth it. Five years of intelligence on everything to do with your pack." His gaze shifts to me. "And most valuable of all, confirmation that your seer is worth the fight."

I feel Ryker tense. I half expect him to reveal that I'm now sightless, but he keeps that to himself. He tilts his head toward the cleared field. "Let's not delay this any further. Shall we?"

The invitation hangs in the air between them—direct, unambiguous, impossible to misconstrue or evade.

"Very well." Thaddeus turns to his contingent, issuing commands with the easy authority of one accustomed to unquestioning obedience. "Maintain position. This matter will be settled as tradition demands—alpha to alpha."

The guards acknowledge with various gestures of respect and submission, falling back to form a loose perimeter at the forest edge. Only Zella remains close, her position symbolically significant—right hand to the Grand Alpha, visible evidence of where her loyalty lies.

The traitor.

Thaddeus begins climbing the slope toward us, his movements unhurried. Despite his age—which must span centuries by wolf reckoning—nothing in his physique suggests weakness or diminishment. He moves with the contained power of a predator who has never known a true challenge, secure in strength proven through countless victories.

Ryker turns to me, his expression softening briefly. "Wait at the perimeter with Elias."

"No." My response is immediate and absolute. "I'll stay with you."

"Kitara—"

"I'm not fragile," I interrupt, meeting his gaze steadily. "And I'm not just your mate but Alpha Female of the Shadowmist Pack. Whatever comes, we face it together."

I watch as his frustration gives way to pride, respect, and beneath it all, a deep-rooted certainty that we belong side by side.

"Together then," he agrees as Thaddeus crests the rise, coming to stand thirty paces from us at the plateau's center.

Up close, the resemblance between father and son becomes more evident—not just in physical stature but in the quality of presence each commands. They are not identical— Ryker's frame is leaner, more defined by combat and survival, whereas Thaddeus carries more solid mass—but the underlying similarities are unmistakable.

"You've caused considerable damage to my compound," Thaddeus observes, his tone almost conversational. "Killed many wolves under my protection. Created disorder where there should be harmony."

"You kidnapped my mate," Ryker counters evenly. "Torture my second, and planned to sever a claiming bond sanctified by wolf law."

Thaddeus sighs, the sound genuinely weary. "Always so dramatic. So certain of your righteousness." His silver gaze shifts to me. "Has he told you who he truly is, little seer? What blood runs in his veins?"

I feel Ryker stiffen beside me. So Thaddeus does know Ryker is his son.

"He's told me everything," I reply, meeting that ancient gaze without flinching. "Including who you are."

"Ah." Something flickers in Thaddeus's expression—not surprise but perhaps disappointment that this particular weapon has been denied him. "Then you understand why this confrontation was inevitable from the moment he claimed you."

"Because you fear prophecy," I state simply. "You've spent centuries trying to outrun what seers have foreseen—that your reign ends at the hands of your son."

Thaddeus laughs, the sound holding no humor. "Prophecies can be broken. I fear nothing but the chaos that follows when natural order is disrupted." He focuses on Ryker once more. "Your mother's blood made you unstable, prone to emotion rather than reason, to rebellion rather than duty."

"My mother's blood made me whole," Ryker corrects. "Capable of seeing beyond rigid tradition to what our kind could become if freed from restrictions that no longer serve any purpose but maintaining *your* control."

The air between them crackles with tension—not just the anticipation of physical conflict but the collision of fundamentally opposed worldviews. On one side stands Thaddeus, representing a rigid hierarchy that sorts wolves into categories of value based on ancestry and adherence to tradition. On the other, Ryker embodies possibility—a future where difference becomes strength rather than stigma, where choice supersedes compulsion.

"You truly believe you can improve on systems that have preserved our kind for centuries?" Thaddeus asks, genuine curiosity evident beneath the contempt. "That your ragtag collection of outcasts and misfits represent progress?"

"I believe the strongest pack is built on loyalty freely given rather than submission enforced through fear," Ryker replies. "I believe our time has come."

The statement sits between them—simple, direct, impossible to misinterpret. Thaddeus studies Ryker for a long moment.

"You're weakened," he observes clinically. "The silver in your system hasn't fully cleared. Your wounds from last night aren't yet healed." His smile holds no warmth. "Did you think I wouldn't notice? That I'd fail to recognize the advantage timing presents me?"

"I counted on you noticing," Ryker replies, his voice steady. "Just as I counted on your pride demanding you face me despite knowing what prophecy foretells."

Thaddeus rolls his massive shoulders, power gathering visibly around him.

"Then let's conclude this unfortunate chapter," he declares, his voice carrying absolute finality. "Challenge accepted."

The transformation begins—bone and muscle flow like liquid, fur erupts along restructuring limbs, Thaddeus's face elongates into a muzzle filled with teeth designed for tearing flesh. Where the Grand Alpha stood moments before now towers a massive wolf—white fur gleaming in sunlight, silver eyes holding the cold calculation of a predator who has never known defeat.

Ryker shifts in response—his transformation slightly slower due to silver contamination but no less impressive. Black fur ripples across expanding muscle, scars visible as silver lines where hair refuses to grow. His mismatched eyes —one gold, one blood-red—hold absolute focus as he completes the change, his massive form nearly matching Thaddeus's in size.

They circle slowly, mutually understanding that only one will leave this plateau alive. I step back, giving them space. I can see Ryker's absolute concentration as he seeks weaknesses in an opponent renowned for having none.

Thaddeus strikes first, targeting Ryker's silver-wounded shoulder with precise aim. Teeth snap, missing by millimeters as Ryker twists away, using momentum to conserve strength.

They separate, reassess, circle again. The next exchange comes faster—Thaddeus driving forward with devastating power. Ryker meets the charge but redirects rather than absorbing, using his opponent's greater mass against him. Blood sprays as teeth find flesh, though in the blur of motion it's impossible to tell who struck first or paid the highest price.

The fight unfolds with brutal intensity—no wasted movement, no theatrical displays. This is violence stripped to its essence, alpha against alpha for territory and a future.

Thaddeus fights with vicious precision, each attack targeting a weakness.

Ryker counters, fiercely unpredictable and devastatingly accurate. He doesn't try to match Thaddeus directly—that's a battle he can't win in his current state—but creates openings where none should exist, transforming defensive movements into surprising attacks.

Blood darkens their fur as the confrontation continues—black and white stained crimson under the warm sun. I can feel Ryker's pain, his increasing struggle as silver contamination combines with fresh wounds to slow his responses.

*Wait. I can feel?*

My heart stutters.

Yes, there's a faint feeling, like an echo or the distant buzz of a bee. I close my eyes, focusing on the feeling—hardly daring to hope—and reach for my gift.

It disappears, dancing out of my grasp.

I open my eyes, watching as the wolves crash into each other, blood and fur flying.

*Come on, Kitara. You can do this.*

I close my eyes once more, and imagine the bond between Ryker and I as a golden thread, gossamer-thin but sturdy. I reach for it, winding it around my fist, until it pulls tight.

There's a gruesome thud as the alphas trade blows, a particularly vicious exchange that leaves them momentarily separated, and breathing heavily. Thaddeus's white coat now bears streaks of red, evidence that Ryker's attacks have found targets despite the Grand Alpha's superior condition. But the damage is unequal—Ryker's black fur is matted with blood from reopened wounds and fresh injuries, his breathing labored, his stance revealing the toll of sustained combat.

The thread tugs and through it I feel a whisper of Ryker's exhaustion.

*It's working!*

"Yield," Thaddeus growls, the word distorted by shifted vocal cords but comprehensible. "End this farce."

Ryker's answering snarl holds no surrender.

They clash again, the impact audible across the plateau. This time, I feel the impact through our connection, feel Ryker's desperate determination to keep fighting despite his injuries.

*I'm here, Ryker. I feel you.*

Whether he knows it or not, his fighting grows more violent. Teeth find purchase, muscle tears, blood sprays across stone as they roll in desperate struggle.

The thread pulses, and a voice whispers to me gently.

*Pull.*

I yank, and suddenly I can hear him as clearly as I can hear my own thoughts.

*Pull*, the voice whispers again.

I do, and a dozen of other connections slam into me, spreading out like threads on a spider's web. It is a pack bond —usually reserved for only alphas. Through it, I sense the feelings and thoughts of the pack as they will their alpha to victory.

*We're with you,* I send to Ryker. *All of us.*

His snarl answers, and I hear his reply in my head.

*Mate.*

Thaddeus circles, measured confidence in every step. He's bleeding from multiple wounds, but none critical, none slowing his approach. He's winning, and both know it.

"It was always going to end this way," Thaddeus says, voice carrying despite his shifted form. "Prophecy or not, natural order prevails. The stronger leads. The weaker follows."

Through our bond, I feel Ryker's fading strength, his desperate search for reserves already depleted. He stands his ground despite crippling injury, undiminished even as his body fails him. In that moment, I understand with perfect clarity—he will die here rather than yield, sacrificing everything for the future he believes in.

*No!*

My vision snaps back with the force of a thunderclap. One moment I see only blood and stone—the next, the future unfurls before me like a map inked in fire. I see Thaddeus's next move before he makes it—his weight shift, the way his back paw digs into earth, the sharp twitch of his shoulder before the lunge.

He's going for Ryker's throat.

*Pack,* I cry silently. *Lend me your strength.*

The threads flare—dozens, then hundreds—blazing gold and silver, twining around me in a net of shared will. I feel them answer my call with grief, fury, devotion. Love. They send it all.

I reach through our bond to my mate, no longer a passenger to his experience but an active participant. Where silver poison lingers in his system, I push it back. Where wounds drain his strength, I shore up his faltering reserves.

I don't know how I'm doing this—if it's the bond itself or some undiscovered facet of my gift—but I feel him respond, renewal flowing through our connection like spring water through parched earth.

Thaddeus charges again, expecting weakness, anticipating the kill that will end the challenge in one decisive moment. Instead, Ryker twists with unexpected speed to evade the primary attack while countering with a brutal force that catches even the Grand Alpha by surprise.

We're one as we face him, Ryker using my vision to anticipate every move.

Ryker's teeth find the vulnerable flesh where neck meets shoulder, sinking deep into Thaddeus's muscle. He snarls, twisting to dislodge the attack, but Ryker holds firm, driving deeper despite the Grand Alpha's desperate effort to break free.

Blood gushes as arteries tear, Thaddeus's struggles growing frantic. His massive form thrashes, claws raking Ryker's already wounded body, opening new gashes that add to the growing pool of crimson beneath them.

Through the bond, I taste the blood, feel the effort it takes to hold the Grand Alpha down.

*Keep going.*

Ryker doesn't release—not when claws tear his flank, not when teeth find his foreleg, not when Thaddeus's full weight crashes against him in increasingly desperate attempts to escape the killing bite.

Thaddeus's struggles gradually weaken, his movements becoming uncoordinated as blood loss takes its toll. In a final, desperate effort, he shifts back to human form—the transformation tearing flesh further against Ryker's locked jaws but potentially creating space to escape.

The maneuver fails. As Thaddeus completes the change, Ryker adjusts his grip, maintaining the lethal bite that continues to drain life with each heartbeat. The Grand

Alpha's hands rise, fingernails lengthening to claws that rake desperately at his attacker's face, missing Ryker's eyes by millimeters.

"You don't... understand," Thaddeus gasps, blood bubbling from the catastrophic wound. "Without me... chaos... pack against pack..." His silver eyes find mine over Ryker's massive form. "The seer... she sees... tell him..."

But whatever final manipulation or revelation he intended dies unspoken as strength leaves him completely. His hands fall limply to his sides, his head lolls back, silver eyes staring sightlessly at the morning sky.

The Grand Alpha is dead.

For a long moment, absolute silence holds the plateau. Ryker maintains his grip until certain no deception remains, then releases the body, letting it fall to bloodied stone with unceremonious finality. He staggers back, wounds from the brutal confrontation finally taking their toll.

He shifts back to human form—the transformation clearly agonizing in his damaged state but necessary for what comes next. Blood covers his skin, some his, some his father's, the distinction meaningless in the aftermath.

His gaze finds mine across the distance, exhaustion and grim satisfaction warring in his expression. One step toward me, then another, his determination to reach my side overriding injuries that would fell any ordinary wolf.

I'm distantly aware of Thaddeus's wolves, including Zella, running into the forest, fleeing from the crime. But none of that matters to me. Only Ryker.

I move, hurrying across the battlefield just as Ryker takes another step. But his legs give out, his massive form collapsing.

"No—no, no, Ryker—" I gasp, catching him as he falls. My knees buckle under his weight as I lower us both to the ground. "Stay with me. Please."

"It's done," he whispers, voice raw from transformed vocal cords and extreme exertion. "The prophecy... fulfilled."

"Yes," I confirm, moving to support him as his strength finally falters. "It's done. You did it, Ryker. You've changed everything."

He manages a small, pained smile before consciousness leaves him completely.

My hands shake violently as I press trembling fingers to his throat, seeking his pulse—needing it.

Nothing.

Then—

*There.*

Faint. Fluttering. But present.

A sob tears from my lips, relief and terror colliding so violently I nearly choke. I feel light-headed, dizzy, my stomach swirling with nausea. I realize I've been holding my breath and suck in a ragged gasp, air catching in my throat as I try to steady myself.

"Elias!" I scream, my voice hoarse and broken. "Elena! Healers! Now!"

I press my hands to Ryker's chest, palms flat over his heart. The bond between us sparks like fire in my veins. I pour into it—every ounce of will, of strength, of love— desperate to keep him tethered.

"Live," I whisper, pressing my forehead to his, ignoring the blood and grime. "Live, my Alpha. My mate. My love." My voice cracks, breaking entirely on the last word. "This isn't how our story ends. Not yet. Not like this."

His heartbeat flickers beneath my hands—uneven, fragile, but still fighting.

And through our bond, I feel it—that wild, primal essence that makes him who he is. The wolf. The protector. The fighter.

He's not gone.

Not yet.

Around us, the world rushes into motion. Healers press salves to his wounds and administer remedies to flush the silver from his blood. Elias barks orders, forming a shield wall around us as Ryker lies vulnerable.

But I don't move.

I stay anchored to him, hands on his chest, willing him to live.

"Fight," I whisper. "Please."

# THIRTY

## RYKER

Darkness.

Not the comforting shadows of my territory but absolute absence. There's no light, no sound, no sensation beyond floating disconnection. I drift without anchor, without reference point, without certainty that I continue to exist in any meaningful sense.

Am I dead? Is this the void that follows when a wolf's final breath fades into silence?

I search for panic but find only distant curiosity. If this is death, it lacks the peace promised by the old tales. No reunion with fallen pack mates, no ancient forests to run beneath eternal moonlight. Just... nothing.

Then, a faint but unmistakable tug. A reminder that I remain tethered to something beyond this emptiness.

*Kitara.*

Her name forms without sound, a thought rather than a word, but it carries weight that pulls me toward the unknown.

The tether strengthens, pulsing with a familiar rhythm— our bond, reaching across whatever separates us. Through it flows not just connection but memory, identity, purpose. I am Ryker Ashmere, Alpha of the Shadowmist Pack. I faced Thaddeus in combat. I fulfilled the prophecy.

I am not finished.

Sensation returns gradually—first as distant awareness of my body, then as localized pain so intense it would buckle a lesser wolf. Every system protests, every cell screams with the damage sustained in combat with Thaddeus. Silver contamination lingers, slowing natural healing and complicating recovery.

But beneath physical distress, the bond pulses stronger with each moment—Kitara's presence flowing into me, her determination supporting mine, her strength supplementing depleted reserves.

*Live.* Her voice reaches me, distant but clear. *Fight.*

The command focuses scattered awareness, providing direction where none existed. I've never surrendered a fight in my life—not to silver, not to superior numbers, not to seemingly impossible odds.

I won't start now.

Consciousness returns with painful abruptness—light piercing closed eyelids, sound crashing against sensitive ears, every nerve ending simultaneously reporting damage. My body feels broken beyond repair, held together only by stubborn refusal to acknowledge defeat.

I force my eyes open despite protest from screaming muscles. Light resolves gradually into recognizable surroundings—not the plateau where I fell but our den's healing chamber. The air carries familiar scents—healing herbs, pack presence, home.

And strongest of all, Kitara.

She sits beside me, exhaustion evident in every line of her face, the dark circles beneath her eyes suggesting she hasn't slept in days. Her hand rests on mine. Through our bond, I feel her pouring strength into me with single-minded purpose, refusing to acknowledge the possibility of failure.

"Stubborn," I manage, the word emerging as a barely audible rasp from a throat damaged by battle and transformation.

Her head snaps up, eyes locking onto mine, and in that single moment—

Hope blooms.

It spills across her features like sunlight breaking through a storm. And then, tears. Unstoppable, silent, and real. Her lips tremble as her breath catches, eyes filling until the tears spill over, trailing down her cheeks unchecked.

"Ryker?" she whispers, the word breaking on a sob.

"Still here," I manage, though each syllable feels like dragging sound through broken glass. "Thanks to you."

She doesn't speak. Can't. Her throat works around the words, but nothing comes out, just more tears, falling faster now. Her hands tremble as they reach for mine, clutching me like she's afraid I'll disappear if she lets go.

The sight of her like this—so fierce and brave for everyone else, now undone by relief—it shatters me.

This is what pulls me back fully. Not the prophecy. Not the victory.

*Her.*

"Don't cry," I rasp, thumb weakly brushing away a tear that's already been replaced. "You'll make me start."

That earns a watery laugh, broken and beautiful, and gods, it's the sweetest sound I've ever heard.

"You've been unconscious for days. The healers weren't certain..." She stops, unable or unwilling to voice the possibility that had clearly haunted her. "But I knew you'd come back."

I try to sit up, immediately recognizing my mistake as pain flares. Kitara's hand presses gently but firmly against my chest, preventing further attempts.

"Don't," she warns, concern evident in her voice. "You sustained catastrophic injuries. Silver poisoning. Internal damage that's still healing. The fact you're conscious at all is miracle enough for now."

Memory returns in fragments—the plateau, Thaddeus's challenge, the brutal combat that followed. "I killed him."

"Yes," she confirms, understanding without elaboration which "him" I reference. "The prophecy is fulfilled. Thaddeus is dead."

The confirmation should bring satisfaction, perhaps even triumph. Instead, I feel only tired. "You guided me."

She flushes. "The pack helped. You were right. My visions weren't gone, just dimmed by the silver."

I nod, wincing when the movement causes the world to tilt. "And after?"

"Chaos, as he predicted," Kitara admits. "The power structure collapsed as news spread. Some allied alphas declared independence. Others fight for Thaddeus's position, believing they should assume the mantle of Grand Alpha."

I absorb this information, finding it unsurprising if somewhat disappointing. "And our pack?"

Here her expression softens, pride evident beneath continuing concern. "Standing strong. Our allies from Ghost River and Mountain Strider Packs maintained protection while you recovered. Our borders are secure. Our people safe."

"Lithia?"

Her face drops. "Still missing. But we continue to search."

"And you?" I ask, studying her with growing concern as my initial disorientation fades. I sense not just her exhaustion but her near-depletion, as if she's expended everything while I hovered between life and death.

"I'm fine," she answers automatically, the claim so obviously false it would be laughable under different circumstances.

"Liar." I manage to raise my hand despite protesting muscles, cupping her cheek with a gentle touch that belies my harsh assessment. "You've been keeping me alive. Pushing yourself beyond safe limits."

She doesn't deny the accusation, her expression revealing both determination and vulnerability that makes my chest ache in ways unrelated to physical injury. "I couldn't lose you."

"You haven't," I assure her, thumb stroking her cheekbone. "You won't."

The moment stretches between us, fragile and profound.

A commotion outside the healing chamber interrupts our connection—voices raised in what sounds like argument rather than threat, familiar tones suggesting pack disagreement rather than external danger.

"What now?" I ask, frustration evident despite physical weakness.

Kitara sighs, reluctance clear in her expression. "Alphas from twelve packs have gathered outside our territory. They're demanding council. They want to decide what happens now that Thaddeus no longer rules."

"And they expect my participation? In this state?" The absurdity would be amusing if it weren't so irritating.

"Some expect the wolf who killed Thaddeus to claim the position of Grand Alpha," she clarifies, watching my reaction carefully. "Or at minimum, to participate in the selection of his successor."

Understanding dawns with cold clarity. Of course they would assume that—wolf tradition has always dictated that the victor in an alpha challenge inherits not just the position but all associated authority and territory. By killing Thaddeus in formal combat witnessed by multiple packs, I've inadvertently positioned myself as potential successor to everything I oppose.

"I didn't fight to replace him," I state flatly, voice strengthening with renewed purpose. "I fought him to end a system that crushes difference under the guise of tradition."

Kitara nods, unsurprised by my response. "I've told them as much. Some understand. Others..." She shrugs, the gesture eloquently conveying wolf-kind's resistance to radical change. "They want someone in charge. Someone to maintain order in territories accustomed to centralized authority."

I consider this, recognizing both problem and opportunity presented. What follows Thaddeus's fall matters as much as the fall itself—perhaps more. If another tyrant simply takes his place, nothing truly changes for our kind.

"Help me sit up." I ignore the protest evident in Kitara's expression. "If they want to speak with the wolf who killed Thaddeus, let them speak with both of us."

She starts to object but stops. With careful support, she helps me into a seated position—the movement starting fresh waves of pain.

"Elias," I call, knowing my security chief likely hovers nearby despite not being immediately visible. "Enter."

The door opens instantly, confirming my assumption. "Alpha. It's good to see you conscious."

"Report," I order, needing more information before addressing whatever council has gathered outside our territory.

"Twelve alphas with small contingents have assembled at our southern border," he confirms, validating Kitara's earlier statement. "They're maintaining respectful distance, but their presence creates tension among the packs. Some view it as opportunity for new alliances. Others fear potential hostility if negotiations go poorly."

"Their stated purpose?"

"Officially, to address succession following the Grand Alpha's death." Elias's expression suggests skepticism.

"Unofficially, to assess whether you intend to claim Grand Alpha status and whether they should resist or support such a claim."

I nod. "And our position?"

"Secure for now. Ghost River and Mountain Strider packs maintain alliance, providing a buffer against potential aggression. Our own forces have recovered from the assault on Thaddeus's compound, though morale would improve significantly with visible evidence of your recovery."

The subtle suggestion doesn't escape me—my people need to see their Alpha alive and functioning, even if far from full strength. "Arrange council," I decide. "Not here—neutral ground. Two days from now."

Elias nods, accepting the instruction without question despite the obvious concern he shares with Kitara regarding my physical state. "Location?"

"The Moon Circle where seasonal councils were traditionally held before Thaddeus consolidated power in his compound." The choice is deliberate—invoking older traditions that predate the rigid hierarchy. "No more than three representatives per pack. Enforced neutrality. All weapons visible."

"It will be arranged."

As he withdraws to implement instructions, Kitara's hand finds mine. "Are you certain about this? You're nowhere near recovered."

"Wolves respect strength," I remind her, no need to elaborate on the obvious to one who understands pack dynamics as intimately as she does.

"An appearance of strength when you're still recovering could be dangerous," Kitara says, her fingers tightening around mine. "If they sense weakness..."

"They'll sense determination," I correct her gently. "And they'll see us together—Alpha and Alpha Female, united in purpose." I bring her hand to my lips, pressing a kiss against her knuckles. "This is how change begins, little wolf. Not just by ending what was, but by showing what can be."

Her expression softens, worry giving way to pride despite lingering concern. "Then we face them together."

"Always," I promise.

THE NEXT TWO days pass in careful preparation—physical recovery accelerated by pack healers' expertise and Kitara's continual support through our bond. By the morning of the council, I can stand without assistance and walk short distances, though full strength remains a distant prospect.

The Moon Circle is an ancient gathering place—a perfect ring of standing stones weathered by centuries of exposure—positioned where territorial boundaries once met before Thaddeus consolidated power under centralized rule.

As our contingent approaches, I see other packs have already assembled—representatives maintaining careful distance from each other, traditional rivals watching with barely concealed hostility despite the neutrality this space supposedly enforces.

Kitara walks beside me, her presence both practical support and symbolic statement. Behind us follow Elias and two senior wolves selected for both combat skill and diplomatic temperament—the minimum escort protocol demands while providing necessary security.

Conversation ceases as we enter the circle, all eyes turning to assess the wolf who killed Thaddeus. I feel their scrutiny—measuring my injuries, calculating my current strength against potential threat or opportunity, evaluating whether I represent continuity or disruption to established order.

Yuren of Moonclaw approaches first, his silver-tipped hair

gleaming in the morning light. His bearing suggests neither submission nor challenge.

It seems the Moonclaw Pack had become tired of Xavier's machinations, with Yuren now serving as Alpha. I didn't ask what happened to Xavier, but based on the fresh scars on Yuren's skin, one could guess.

"Alpha Ashmere," he greets formally, careful to use pack title rather than presumptive Grand Alpha designation. "You honor us with your presence, particularly given your... recent exertions."

The delicate phrasing draws scattered laughter from assembled alphas—acknowledgment of the brutal combat that ended Thaddeus's reign without directly referencing patricide that technically occurred, though few present know that particular truth.

"The honor is mutual," I return with equal formality, refusing to show weakness despite the effort required to maintain an upright position. "Though I question whether honor motivates this gathering or merely practical concern about what follows Thaddeus's fall."

Direct address cuts through diplomatic pretense, drawing murmurs of appreciation from several alphas who prefer blunt conversation to political maneuvering. Yuren's expression tightens briefly before smoothing into practiced neutrality.

"Both, perhaps," he acknowledges with diplomatic skill that's made Moonclaw influential beyond their territorial holdings. "Thaddeus maintained certain structures that provided stability, whatever one might think of his methods. In his absence, questions naturally arise about how those structures continue—or whether they should."

"They shouldn't," I state simply, no embellishment necessary for such fundamental position. "The centralized authority Thaddeus built served his personal power rather than wolf-kind's collective welfare. It crushed difference rather than celebrating the strength our diversity brings. It enforced submission rather than encouraging alliance between equals."

Silence greets this declaration—not rejection but consideration, assessment of implications that radiate beyond simple power transfer.

Selena of Red River steps forward, her distinctive copper hair marking her as clearly as her direct gaze. "Bold words, shadow wolf. But what alternative do you propose? Territorial disputes were common before centralized authority. Pack wars decimated our numbers. The fae courts exploited our divisions to nearly destroy us entirely during the Blood Wars."

Valid concerns. I incline my head, acknowledging the legitimate question behind the challenge.

"I propose a council rather than dominance. Representatives from each territory meeting regularly to address common concerns, resolve disputes before they escalate to violence, coordinate response to external threats. Not ruled by a Grand Alpha imposing will from above but governed by consensus among equals."

The concept isn't entirely new—wolf history contains examples of successful council governance before ambitious alphas consolidated power through combat prowess rather than leadership skill. But suggesting a return to such systems represents a fundamental shift from generations accustomed to centralized authority.

"And who would lead such a council?" demands Arturo of Blackclaw Pack, his tone skeptical, bordering on dismissive. "Without final authority, debates become endless. Without hierarchy, strength means nothing."

"Rotating leadership," Kitara suggests before I can respond. "Each territory providing council head for a limited term, ensuring all perspectives receive equal consideration while preventing any single pack from dominating proceedings."

Her proposal draws surprised consideration—not just for content but for source, the Alpha Female speaking as equal partner rather than a subordinate mate. Through our bond, I feel her momentary uncertainty followed by renewed confidence as several alphas nod thoughtful agreement.

"An interesting proposal," Yuren acknowledges, his gaze shifting between us. "But practical questions remain. Thaddeus controlled significant shared resources—training facilities, healing compounds, communication networks. Who administers these under council governance?"

"Those who built them," I state firmly. "Many so-called shared resources were constructed through labor Thaddeus extracted from subordinate packs, then controlled to maintain dependency. Each facility returns to those who created it, with access negotiated through council rather than dictated by central authority."

The declaration causes visible stir among assembled representatives—some expressing alarm at potential loss of resources their territories have come to rely upon, others calculating advantages regained if facilities originally built within their lands return to their direct control.

"And Thaddeus's personal territory?" Selena asks, the question carrying significant implications beneath its simple surface. "The compound itself contains generations of accumulated knowledge, wealth, resources. Who claims these spoils?"

Traditional wolf law provides clear answer—the victor in alpha challenge inherits not just position but all associated holdings. By killing Thaddeus in formal combat witnessed by multiple packs, I have strongest claim to everything he controlled.

"No one claims them," I state, the declaration drawing audible gasps from several representatives. "Knowledge will be shared among all packs through council oversight. Wealth distributed proportionally based on contributions extracted from each territory during Thaddeus's reign. Resources allocated according to need."

"You would surrender your right of conquest?" Arturo demands. "After defeating the Grand Alpha in direct combat?"

"I didn't fight him to replace him," I repeat the words spoken earlier to Kitara, letting them carry across the gathering with quiet intensity. "I fought him to end the system. Taking his place would perpetuate exactly what we oppose—power maintained through fear rather than earned through respect."

Silence follows this declaration—profound consideration rather than rejection, assessment of possibility that challenges generations of assumed truth about how wolf-kind must organize itself to survive.

"Bold vision," Yuren finally concedes. "But visions require practical implementation to manifest. How do you propose transitioning from centralized authority to council governance without creating a dangerous power vacuum in the interim?"

I incline my head, acknowledging the valid point before responding.

"Immediate establishment of a provisional council including representatives from each territory," I propose, the solution developed during recovery days with input from Kitara and senior wolves. "Initial three-month term focused solely on establishing permanent structure, operating procedures, resource allocation. No substantive decisions regarding territorial boundaries or inter-pack disputes until permanent council convenes under agreed governance."

The approach balances pragmatic necessity against philosophical ideal—maintaining sufficient structure to prevent chaos while creating space for new systems to develop organically rather than through an imposed framework.

"And your role in this provisional council?" Selena asks.

I glance at Kitara, the moment of silent communication speaking volumes to those observant enough to recognize true partnership. "Equal representation of Shadowmist territory, nothing more," I reply simply. "Though we offer our den as a neutral meeting ground until permanent facilities can be established elsewhere, if council agrees."

The offer carries both practical value and symbolic significance—extending hospitality that demonstrates commitment to collaboration. Several alphas nod appreciation of the gesture, traditional rivals included among them.

For the next several hours, discussions continue—practical concerns are addressed, potential obstacles identified, alternative structures proposed and evaluated. Throughout, Kitara remains beside me, contributing insights that reflect both her unique perspective as seer and her growing understanding of pack dynamics beyond Silvercrest's rigid hierarchy.

When the sun begins its westward descent, marking the conclusion of formal council, consensus emerges—not complete agreement on all points but sufficient common ground to move forward with provisional structure while permanent governance develops. Representatives depart with commitment to reconvene in seven days with selected council members from each territory.

As final contingents withdraw from the Moon Circle, leaving only our small group in the ancient gathering place, Kitara's hand finds mine—silent support as the accumulated strain of extended appearance begins to manifest in trembling muscles and renewed pain from still-healing wounds.

"You should be resting," she observes.

"Soon," I promise, unwilling to show vulnerability until

the last rival pack disappears from view. "It went better than expected."

"They're pragmatic enough to recognize that attempting to merely replace Thaddeus with another Grand Alpha would trigger territory-wide conflict none could win decisively."

Kitara's assessment demonstrates a growing political acumen. She is growing into her role as the Alpha Female.

"Exactly."

We begin our return journey as shadows lengthen across ancient stones, our small contingent moving at a pace accommodating my still-limited endurance. Through forests that once marked boundaries between territories governed by fear, we walk toward a future built on a different foundation.

The path ahead remains uncertain—but certainty was never the objective. Only possibility. Opportunity for wolf-kind to evolve beyond rigid structures that served select alphas while crushing difference under the guise of necessary tradition.

As our den comes into view, I feel a bone-deep satisfaction that transcends physical pain and lingering silver contamination. Not triumph over a fallen enemy but quiet pride in the foundation being laid for what comes next.

Kitara's arm slides around my waist.

"You did it," she says softly.

"No, we did it," I correct gently. "What comes next depends not just on us but on all wolves willing to imagine a different future than they've known."

"We'll build it together," she declares with quiet certainty.

As we cross the threshold into our den—welcomed by a pack that's risked everything for our future—I find myself grinning.

The future awaits, unwritten but full of promise. And for the first time in generations, those who walk different paths may find themselves not outcasts to be feared or controlled, but valued members of community stronger because of differences rather than despite them.

It is enough. For now, it is more than enough.

I take Kitara's hand, pressing a kiss to her knuckles.

"I'm feeling very weak, mate." I lean against her. "You may need to give me a sponge bath tonight."

She laughs, the sound light and free.

"As you wish, Alpha."

# CHAPTER
# THIRTY-ONE
## THREE MONTHS LATER

The northern winds have shifted, bringing the first crisp hints of winter to Shadowmist territory. While the forest outside begins its hibernation, inside our den, a different kind of change is unfolding.

I stand before the mirror in our bathing chamber, studying my reflection with a mixture of wonder and apprehension. My hands trace the gentle swell of my belly—still small, but undeniably there.

"What are you thinking?" Ryker asks, leaning against the doorway. His wounds from the final battle with Thaddeus have healed, though several new scars mark his powerful frame.

"That I never imagined this would be my future," I answer honestly, meeting his mismatched eyes in the mirror. "Alpha Female. Council member. And now…" I trace my fingers over my stomach. "Mother."

He crosses the room, coming to stand behind me. His large hands cover mine on my belly, his touch gentle.

"Regrets?" he asks, his breath warm against my neck.

"Not one," I reply, leaning back into his solid warmth. "Though I'm still terrified."

Through our bond, I feel his understanding—deeper now than ever before. In the months since the battle, our connection has continued to strengthen, so much so that I often don't know where one of us ends and the other begins.

"The healer says everything is progressing perfectly," he reminds me, pressing a gentle kiss to my temple. "And Elena has delivered dozens of pups without complication."

I sigh, turning in his arms. "It's not the birth that frightens me. It's what comes after." I lay my palm against his chest, feeling his strong heartbeat beneath my fingers. "What if our pup can't shift either? What if they—"

"Stop," he interrupts, capturing my hand and bringing it to his lips. "Nothing about you is broken, Kitara. Haven't we proven that a thousand times over?" His eyes—one gold, one crimson—hold mine with fierce intensity. "Whether our pup shifts, sees, or possesses entirely different gifts we haven't imagined yet—they will be perfect. Because they are ours."

The absolute certainty in his voice soothes the anxiety that has periodically surfaced throughout my pregnancy.

My wolf stirs within me, equally reassuring. *Our pup will be strong*, she insists. *She is an alpha.*

"Besides," Ryker continues with a small smile, "the world our pup will grow into is already changing. The council system is taking root. Territories are beginning to cooperate rather than compete. Even those who initially resisted are starting to see the benefits."

He's right, of course. The provisional council established after Thaddeus's fall has evolved from idea into reality—a rotating body of representatives from each territory, meeting monthly to address common concerns. Just last week, I sat in a council session where a newcomer from a distant eastern territory was welcomed with respect rather than suspicion. A small victory, but significant.

"Come," Ryker says, taking my hand. "The pack has a surprise for you."

He leads me through our private chambers into the main living area. There, set before the stone hearth, sits a cradle carved from oak. Intricate patterns trace its curved edges—wolves running beneath a crescent moon, stars scattered among them like watchful eyes. The craftsmanship is exquisite, each detail rendered with loving precision.

"Heath made it," Ryker explains, watching my reaction closely. "With help from some of the younger wolves. The entire pack contributed in some way—the cushioning is stuffed with down collected by the pups, the blankets woven by the elders."

I approach the cradle slowly, tears blurring my vision as I trace the carvings with my fingertips. The gesture represents something I once thought impossible—acceptance by a pack.

"It's beautiful," I whisper, emotion tightening my throat.

Ryker slides his arm around my waist. "They wanted to show their support and their loyalty to you."

Three months ago, such a demonstration would have seemed unlikely. The events surrounding Thaddeus's fall changed everything. My actions during the crisis—particularly using our bond to help Ryker survive his wounds—earned me the respect of our pack.

A knock at our door interrupts the moment. Ryker tenses slightly—an instinctive protection response he hasn't fully shed despite the relative peace of recent months.

The fact I'm pregnant hasn't helped either. If anything, he's become even more protective. Just last week he forbade me from participating in the pups' schooling in case I got knocked over by accident.

He learnt rather quickly where he could shove *that* idea.

"Enter," he calls, his body shifting subtly to place himself between me and the doorway.

Elias appears, his expression difficult to discern. "Forgive the interruption, Alpha, Alpha Female. The border patrol has returned with news."

"What news?" Ryker asks, immediately alert.

Elias's eyes flick to me briefly. "They found something at the northeastern boundary. Or rather... someone." He hesitates, uncharacteristic for our stoic security chief. "Two someones, actually."

My heart leaps. "Lithia?"

A small smile breaks through Elias's composed facade. "Yes. Alive, though not unharmed. And she's not alone." Something in his tone catches my attention. "She's with a rogue wolf. Male. Says he helped her escape."

Ryker stiffens, his hand finding mine and squeezing tight. Through our bond, I feel a storm of emotions—relief about Lithia, rage at whatever was done to his second, and wary suspicion about this unknown male.

"Where are they now?" he demands.

"The healers have them both. Elena says Lithia's injuries are significant but not life-threatening. The male is in better condition. She's conscious and asking for you both." Elias clears his throat. "Levi is already there."

This last detail brings Ryker's head up sharply. "Levi? I didn't summon him."

"No, Alpha," Elias confirms with a slight twitch of his lips. "He was... already in the healing chambers when they arrived. He hasn't left Lithia's side since."

Ryker's brow furrows at this unexpected information. But I'm unsurprised. Levi's determination to track Lithia down since her disappearance went well beyond the normal dedication of a pack mate for another.

"Thank you, Elias," I say, already moving toward the door. "We'll go immediately."

As we hurry through the winding corridors of the den, wolves step aside respectfully, their expressions revealing they've already heard the news. Lithia's kidnapping had left a wound in the pack that couldn't fully heal until her return.

The timing seems almost prophetic—one chapter closing as another begins.

"She survived," I murmur, partially to myself. "All this time... and with help."

Ryker's face is tight with controlled emotion. "Lithia is one of the strongest wolf I know," he says, voice rough. "If anyone could survive what they planned for her, it would be her. But a rogue..." He shakes his head, clearly concerned about this unknown variable.

We reach the healing chambers, where the scent of medicinal herbs hangs heavy in the air. Elena, our lead healer, meets us at the entrance, her expression somber but not grave.

"She's stable," she informs us quietly. "Dehydrated, malnourished, with evidence of silver restraints used long-term. Several poorly healed fractures that we'll need to re-break and set properly. But her mind is clear, and her wolf intact."

"And the male with her?" Ryker asks, his voice tight.

"Calls himself Kier. No pack markings, but strong. He has silver burns too, though not as severe. Says he was held in the cell next to hers." Elena's professional demeanor slips slightly. "I warn you, there's... an unusual dynamic between them and Levi. You'll see."

Curious now, we follow Elena into the healing chambers. The room is warm and dimly lit, the air filled with the scent of healing salves and the unmistakable metallic tang of silver residue. Lithia lies on a pallet near the hearth, her once-powerful frame diminished by captivity. Her silver-blonde hair has been shorn close to her scalp, and new scars mark her already scarred face.

But her eyes—those striking silver eyes—are clear and focused as we enter. On one side of her sits Levi, his posture protective, fingers intertwined with hers in a gesture of intimacy. On her other side stands a wolf I don't recognize. He's tall and lean, with unusual dark-copper hair and eyes the color of burnished gold. His stance is alert but not threatening, and there's something in the way he positions himself, equally protective of Lithia, yet with an awareness of Levi that speaks of concerns far more complex than simple rivalry.

Lithia attempts to rise, a gesture of respect ingrained through years of pack hierarchy.

"Don't," I say quickly, moving to her side and gently pressing her back down. "You need to rest."

Lithia's gaze meets mine, surprise flickering across her features before she nods slightly. "Alpha Female," she acknowledges, her voice hoarse but steady. Then her eyes shift to Ryker. "Alpha. It's good to see you survived."

A muscle ticks in Ryker's jaw as he kneels beside her, his gaze flicking briefly to Levi's hand holding hers, then to the rogue wolf standing vigil on her other side. "What happened?" he asks, the question encompassing everything— her capture, her treatment, her escape, and clearly, these unexpected connections.

Lithia closes her eyes briefly, gathering strength or perhaps ordering her thoughts. "They separated us immediately after the ambush," she begins. "I was taken southeast to Moonclaw territory, then north. They kept me in silver to prevent shifting—and to ensure I couldn't be tracked through pack bonds."

Her fingers tighten around Levi's, a gesture I'm certain Ryker doesn't miss. "They wanted information. About our defenses, our allies, your plans." A grim smile touches her lips. "I wasn't particularly cooperative."

I can read between those simple words to the torture they must imply. My wolf snarls within me, protective of the wolf who protected us despite her initial reservations.

"But Yuren has been alpha since the fight," I say, glancing at Ryker.

"Rogues of the Moonclaw," the male wolf speaks for the first time, his voice carrying the slight accent of the western territories. "I suspect they'll be back with more numbers in the future."

"Kier was in the cell beside mine," Lithia says, glancing at the copper-haired wolf. "Another of Thaddeus's prisoners. We kept each other sane. Talked through the walls when the guards weren't around. Then Thaddeus fell," Lithia continues. "I felt it—we all did. The power shift resonated through all territories. The guards were distracted, arguing about what it meant for them. Zella came for a bit, stirring up leadership trouble. It was then that Kier managed to break free. He could have run..." Her voice softens. "Instead, he came back for me."

The look that passes between them speaks of a bond forged in darkness—not quite like what Ryker and I share, but significant nonetheless. Levi's jaw tightens almost imperceptibly, but he doesn't release her hand.

"You escaped while wounded and in silver?" I ask, unable to hide my admiration.

Her silver eyes meet mine. "I made a promise to my Alpha and his mate. Death wouldn't release me from that oath." She shifts slightly, wincing. "But that's not what's important. What matters is what I learned while in captivity."

Ryker leans forward, though I notice his gaze keeps returning to the unusual triangle formed by Lithia, Levi, and the rogue wolf. "What did you learn?"

"The betrayal goes deeper than Zella. There's a faction—wolves from multiple territories who believed in Thaddeus's vision of control and hierarchy. They're organizing, planning to disrupt the council system before it can fully establish."

My hand moves instinctively to my belly, the protective gesture not lost on Lithia. Her gaze softens momentarily.

"The facility where they held us housed at least three

seers," Kier adds, his golden eyes serious. "All kept separate, all heavily guarded."

Alarm flashes through me, mixing with protective instinct. My hand presses more firmly against the small swell that houses our pup—potentially another seer in the making. "Other seers?"

Kier nods. "Not wolf though. One is a bear, another human. I'm not sure about the third."

Ryker's expression hardens. "Names? Locations?"

"Some," Lithia confirms. "Enough to begin hunting them." She attempts to shift position and grimaces. Both Levi and Kier move simultaneously to help her, their hands overlapping before they exchange a look I can't quite decipher.

"But that can wait until I've recovered enough to lead the hunt myself," she finishes.

The determination in her voice brings a small smile to my lips despite the seriousness of her news. This is the Lithia I remember—fierce, loyal, unstoppable.

"Rest first," I tell her gently. "Heal. We'll discuss the details when you're stronger."

She looks ready to protest, then relents with a small nod.

Ryker rests a hand briefly on her shoulder—a rare gesture of physical affection from our alpha. "Kitara is right. Rest now. That's an order."

A ghost of a smile touches Lithia's lips. "Yes, Alpha."

As we leave the healing chambers, I find myself leaning more heavily against Ryker, the events of the day catching up to me. He adjusts immediately, his arm sliding around my waist to support me.

"You should rest too," he murmurs, concern evident in his voice. "The pup demands much of your strength."

I shake my head. "We need to discuss what Lithia told us. If there's truly an organized resistance forming—"

"Tomorrow," he interrupts gently. "We'll gather the senior wolves tomorrow and begin planning. Tonight, you rest."

Through our bond, I feel his absolute stubbornness—his mate and unborn pup first, all else second.

As we walk back to our chambers, I find myself reflecting on how much has changed—and how much remains uncertain. The old world collapsed with Thaddeus, but the new one is still taking shape, vulnerable to those who fear change.

Back in our chambers, the cradle waits by the hearth—a symbol of the future we're building. Ryker guides me to our bed, his touch gentle as he helps me settle against the furs.

"Sleep," he urges, pressing a kiss to my forehead.

"Stay with me?" I ask, needing to be held.

He smiles—one of those rare, unguarded expressions that transform his fierce features. "Always."

He stretches out beside me, holding me close, one hand coming to rest protectively over our growing pup. I feel the bond between us pulse with love, determination, and the fierce promise to protect what we've built together. Whatever threat gathers in the darkness, it will find us ready.

My wolf settles contentedly, certain in a way only she can be.

*We are pack*, she whispers. *We are family. We are unstoppable.*

For once, I find myself in complete agreement with her.

*Yes*, I think, as sleep begins to claim me. *Yes, we are.*

Thank you so much for reading Kitara and Ryker's story!
I hope you fell in love with the Shadowmist Pack.
This is my first time writing shifters, but it certainly won't be
my last!
Get ready for more Shadowmist!

Want more sexy shifters and bonus content?
Be sure to check out my website
EvieMitchell.com

# ABOUT E.V. MITCHELL

**E.V. Mitchell** is the darker, wilder side of bestselling romance author **Evie Mitchell**, venturing into the realms of romantasy, paranormal romance, and monster romance.

Known for writing body-positive romance with heart-pounding spice, E.V. Mitchell blends monsters, myths, and magic with scorching hot heroes and heroines who embrace their darkness.

Find the rest of her books at EvieMitchell.com.

You can catch up with Evie on all socials at @EvieMitchellAuthor or @EVMitchellAuthor

Visit Evie's website for her current booklist
www.EvieMitchell.com